THE
13TH VAMPIRE

ALICE HEMMING

Manor Lodge School
Rectory Lane
Shenley, Herts
WD7 9BG
01707 642424

Other books by Alice Hemming:

The *Dark Unicorns* series:

The Midnight Unicorn

The Darkest Unicorn

The Cursed Unicorn

The Blazing Unicorn

The Frozen Unicorn

THE 13TH VAMPIRE

ALICE HEMMING

■SCHOLASTIC

Published in the UK by Scholastic, 2023
1 London Bridge, London, SE1 9BG
Scholastic Ireland, 89E Lagan Road, Dublin Industrial Estate,
Glasnevin, Dublin, D11 HP5F

SCHOLASTIC and associated logos are trademarks and/or
registered trademarks of Scholastic Inc.

Text copyright © Alice Hemming, 2022
Cover illustration © Kayt Bochenski, 2023

The right of Alice Hemming to be identified as the author of this work
has been asserted by her under the Copyright, Designs and Patents Act 1988.

ISBN 978 0702 32361 4

A CIP catalogue record for this book
is available from the British Library.

All rights reserved.
This book is sold subject to the condition that it shall not, by way of trade or otherwise, be lent, hired out or otherwise circulated in any form of binding or cover other than that in which it is published. No part of this publication may be reproduced, stored in a retrieval system, or transmitted in any form or by any other means (electronic, mechanical, photocopying, recording or otherwise) without prior written permission of Scholastic Limited.

Printed by C&C in China
Paper made from wood grown in sustainable forests
and other controlled sources.

1 3 5 7 9 10 8 6 4 2

This is a work of fiction. Names, characters, places, incidents
and dialogues are products of the author's imagination or are used
fictitiously. Any resemblance to actual people, living or dead,
events or locales is entirely coincidental.

www.scholastic.co.uk

To Ruth

PROLOGUE

CASTLE BEZNA, HIGH UP IN THE FALNIC MOUNTAINS

ONE HUNDRED AND EIGHTY-FIVE YEARS AGO

She awoke to the sound of splintering wood. Shouting, banging, glass breaking. Something was wrong. The sounds were distant — two floors below — but they filled her with dread. The townspeople had finally come. After years of persecution, they'd learned to fight back. The preyed upon had become the predators. They'd come in full force, not from one town or village, but all together, as she knew they would.

Their cries grew closer.

"Come out, fiends!"

"Enough is enough!"

"You can't hide any longer!"

Doors slammed.

"There is no escape!"

She knew what to expect. Doors ripped from their hinges. Boards prised away from windows. They would push back the drapes to let sunlight seep into every dark corner. Up in the attic, where she liked to sleep, there were no windows or doors. Her sister was somewhere on the floor below, which the trespassers had yet to reach. Yet.

She must find Griselda and bring her to safety. The attic spanned the entire south wing of the castle. As she flew through its dark spaces, she counted the beams, trying to guess which part of the castle she'd reached.

The voices grew closer as the townspeople spread through the castle hunting them down, room by room, feet thumping up the stairs. Ever closer to her sister.

"We know your names!"

It was true. For years, the townspeople had seen monstrous faces at their windows and in their nightmares. They'd done their research and knew who they were looking for. The townspeople called to them one by one. They called out to the Dorins: I, II and III. To Adriana, Novak and Niklaus. To Edwin and Selig. To Aalis, Ottilie and Ehren. To her sister, Griselda.

She hated hearing Griselda's name on their lips. They made it sound like a curse.

Where was *Griselda?*

She reached the spot in the attic which she thought lay above her sister's chamber and found a place where the boards didn't quite meet. She could peek through and see what was happening below. At first, the light was startlingly bright. So bright it hurt her eyeballs. But she forced herself to look. She brought her cape in front of her face so her eyes were covered. In this way, looking through the weave of the fabric and then the gap in the boards, she was able to bear the brightness.

It was not her sister's room. It was Ottilie's. Ottilie must have slunk into a corner or a wardrobe to try to hide, but they'd found her. They grabbed her arms and dragged her across the floor. She couldn't see Ottilie's face and for that she was grateful. But she saw the faces of her hunters: faces contorted with fear and anger as they crowded around, the points of their sharpened wooden stakes thrust forward like daggers.

They said Ottilie's name as though she was a monster.

"Ottilie – now you will pay."

Of course, Ottilie *was* a monster to them. They would never know how she loved to sing and dance, twirling and spinning, her long skirts fanning about her in a circle.

She felt she should do something to help, but what? If she called out, she would only alert the hunters to her presence. They would show no mercy – she was sure of that. The only person she could protect was herself. And, she hoped, her sister.

When Ottilie screamed, the sound penetrated the floor of the attic, shooting right up to her core. She stopped watching and rolled on to her back, covering her ears rather than her eyes. But there was no respite from the screams. Ten more echoed around the castle. From the ballroom. From the grounds – someone fleeing to the safety of the crypt, perhaps, but in vain. Then one last chilling scream from what must be the room next door. A bitter taste rose from her throat and she clamped her hand over her mouth. Griselda. They'd found Griselda.

Her beloved sister.

Taken from her by the hunters.

Along with the others.

All twelve of them.

As the thirteenth, she knew it would be her turn next.

She wanted to cry and scream, but she forced herself to stay quiet. She knew she must make herself small, like a bat. It was what she did best. They all had their talents. Some were best at seeking out prey, others at flying long distances. She could fly a little but she was best at hiding. Hiding and disguises. She wrapped her arms tightly around herself and thought herself small, until she looked like any average bat, sleeping in the attic. She stayed as still as she could, curled up, unable to prevent the occasional shiver. What if the townspeople didn't find her – what then? Would they burn the whole place down and tear it to the ground?

The voices below grew quieter – no longer angry, but also not celebratory. Perhaps relieved. The satisfaction of a job complete. Didn't they know the job wasn't complete? They hadn't found *her*.

How had they missed her?

It was only then that she realized she hadn't heard her own name. Not even once. Could it be that the townspeople didn't know their enemy quite as well as they thought? Could it be that, in all those years, they'd only ever counted twelve?

The voices gradually ebbed away and the footsteps receded.

She waited and waited for her name.

She waited to hear floorboards creak in the room below. Her ears strained, searching the silence.

Maybe there would be no warning. Maybe they'd burst into the attic all at once, bringing their merciless daylight with them.

But there was nothing.

Had the townspeople gone for good? Were they back home proclaiming they'd rid the castle of the scourge for ever? Or was the silence a trick? Perhaps they were still down there, waiting for her to come out of hiding. Waiting to ambush her with their sharpened stakes and their faces full of hate.

She shuddered. She couldn't bring herself to leave her hiding place.

Hours passed and darkness fell. It was only then, as the soft, safe cloak of night wrapped itself around her, that she truly believed the townspeople had gone.

Back in human form, she crossed the attic, creaked open the hatch and emerged like a small creature coming out of hibernation. She dropped to the floor of the room below and gazed around. There was no Ottilie, of course. No greeting from anyone. Moonlight gave the room a gentle glow and a strong breeze blew through the open window. Dusty footprints covered the floor. The thick rug had been rucked up and pushed to the side. She straightened it. Slammed the window shut. Pulled the curtains across.

She wouldn't go into the adjoining room – Griselda's – for fear of what she might find. But she explored the rest of the castle, swooping into every room and desperately searching for another survivor.

She checked the stairs, the kitchen, the servants' quarters and the library. Even the grounds. But she found no one. The castle had never been so quiet. The silence was even worse than the chilling screams of the daytime slaughter. The silence meant she was alone.

Her instinct was to close all the open doors and to board up the uncovered windows in preparation for the bright daytime. But that would arouse suspicion.

She knew what she must do.

She'd let the townspeople think their job was done.

She'd find a safe place where she could lie low.

And she'd wait until the time was right to return.

.

IN THE TOWN OF VALESTI

FIFTY YEARS LATER

CHAPTER ONE
THE LAUNDRY COUSINS

The town of Valesti was known for its crooked and colourful houses, its fields of sunflowers and its fluffy plum dumplings. It lay at the foot of the Falnic Mountains, a cluster of pointed spires and tiled roofs. Beyond, the deep oranges and browns of the tree-covered mountains contrasted with the cloudless morning sky.

Walking towards the town from the outskirts were two girls, arm-in-arm, stepping in time. They were separated by only six months in age but nearly a head in height. As they walked, the taller one sang in a fairly tuneful voice:

> *"We're Dol and Vivi, the laundry cousins.*
> *Bring us your corsets, cos we've washed dozens!"*

Her cousin, Dol, laughed. "Make up another, Vivi. I love your songs."

Vivi grinned. "Plenty more where that came from!

> *"Bring your knickers, big and small.*
> *We don't care – we've washed them all."*

They both collapsed into giggles, then Vivi stopped and unlinked her arm, turning to look at Dol. "Tell you what, let's not go into the laundry today. I'll make up songs all day long!"

Dol's laughter dried up and her eyes widened. "What do you mean, don't go in?"

"Just what I say. Let's run away for the day. Let's go to the mountains and forage for food. We could catch fish from the streams with our bare hands and eat the wild berries from the hedgerows."

Dol shook her head. "But I don't want to go into the mountains. People tell scary stories about them."

Vivi sighed. "Very well, we'll stay down in the valley and forage there. We'll run through the sunflower fields and get fat on the seeds like little mice."

"But what would Ma say? She'd be in a proper temper if we didn't show up to work. I can't think what she'd do."

Vivi had been living with her aunt and cousins for just under a year, since the death of her parents, and she'd seen plenty of flashes of that temper from Aunt Ina. "I'll think of something to tell her. Maybe I'll say we were struck down with a fainting sickness caused by unwashed bloomers. Or that we forgot our way to work this morning, or that one of your scary mountain monsters carried us off to its lair."

Dol continued to shake her head with emphasis. "She'd never believe us and we'd both get in trouble."

Vivi gazed out at the autumn colours in the mountains. "Well, you don't have to come if you don't want to. I'll go by myself."

"Oh, please don't, Vivi. It will be dreadfully dull at the laundry without you. We can still have fun together, can't we? You can make up some more songs while we work. The others will like that, too."

Vivi took Dol's arm again. "Very well. But I'm still having a picnic. Would you like a plum, Dol?"

"Where would we find a plum?" They walked some more steps, rediscovering their earlier rhythm.

"Up there." Vivi pointed over the garden wall of one of the big houses, to a tree laden with purple fruit.

"They belong to Mister Vrdoljak. He won't be happy if we steal his fruit."

"But it's an overhanging branch. Any fruit on this side of the wall is our property."

Dol squinted up at the fruit uncertainly. "Are you sure?"

"Oh, I don't know! It doesn't matter what the rules are because Mister Vrdoljak isn't going to see us. Come on, give me a leg up."

Dol cupped her hands together and Vivi stepped into the makeshift stirrup, one hand on Dol's shoulder. It gave her the lift she needed to reach the branches.

The plums smelled delicious. She twisted one off the branch and put it in her pocket, followed by another and another. They were soft and ripe and barely needed any tugging.

"I can't hold you much longer," called Dol in a strained voice. She was strong from her work at the laundry but had a tiny frame and Vivi was too heavy for her.

"Just one more," said Vivi, reaching to the branch above, but Dol cried, "I'm going to drop you!" and did just that, her hands wrenching apart. Vivi, plum in hand, tumbled down and fell on her side, her pocket full of fruit protecting her hip from a nasty bump.

"It's fine, nothing's too bruised!" said Vivi, examining the fruit rather than herself.

Dol offered her hand to Vivi. Her eyes darted about as if she expected the plum police to appear from behind the wall. "Come on, let's not be late," she said, pulling Vivi to her feet.

Vivi bit into the plum that she was still holding and the red juice dribbled down her chin. They set off again in the direction of the laundry, walking around the house. She patted her pocket. "Want one?"

"No!" said Dol, dropping her voice to a whisper. "Mister Vrdoljak is sitting right there on his steps."

Vivi waved brazenly to the owner of the fruit, who narrowed his eyes suspiciously. Vivi continued with the song.

> *"Petticoats, bustles, we don't care;*
> *We'll even wash your underweaaar!"*

Vivi's voice rose a few notches in volume for the last line and the man stood up from the steps and stared at them. Dol giggled. "Shhhhh! Mister Vrdoljak will hear you."

"Well, we've washed his underwear plenty of times so he should appreciate the lyrics."

Mister Vrdoljak shouted out – his voice following them down the street, "Hey, you two! Where did you get those plums?"

"Foraging rights!" called Vivi, then tugged on Dol's arm. Together, they ran giggling through the narrow alleyways, the soles of their boots slapping on the cobblestones.

Near the centre of town, the cousins reached a squat red-brick building with a sign:

INA STROUD'S SEND-OUT LAUNDRY
Local Laundresses, Hygienic and Speedy Service

Still giggling, they pushed open the door and immediately shrugged off their coats. There may have been a nip in the air outside, but inside the atmosphere was permanently hot and steamy. The smell was unique: laundry soap, sweat and ammonia.

"Afternoon!" called Lilith from over in the corner, although it was only eight o'clock in the morning. Her usual joke. Lilith arrived at half-past five most days. With large, capable hands she pressed the linens and tablecloths, ready for morning delivery to the hospital and hotel. She had two missing teeth and was always ready with a smile and a cheery word. "How are you girls today?"

"Well, I wanted to go for a picnic in the mountains, but Dol insisted on coming into work. We brought some snacks with us instead." Vivi threw one of the bruised plums to Lilith, who caught it with a gap-toothed smile.

She turned it over in her hands. "Well, thank you, my dear. This looks like one of Mister Vrdoljak's best plums to me. I hope I'm not eating stolen goods!"

"Ask no questions and you shall hear no lies," replied Vivi, and Lilith bit into the plum, happily waggling her eyebrows.

Vivi took her place at the ironing board next to Lilith. She pushed back her hair, which hung lankly, having lost any bounce due to the steam. She tied it up and wiped her hands on the front of her dress. It was the same thin cotton dress all the laundresses wore so they weren't overwhelmed by the heat. Still, she knew she'd be soaked through with perspiration within a few minutes. She gazed at the towering mountain of ironing for a moment, then reluctantly heaped the first double bedsheet on to the board.

Dol was already over at the dolly tub, attacking the clothes in the soapy water for all she was worth. The industrial-sized metal tub almost reached her waist and it took strength to push and rotate the wooden plunger. Her knack with the dolly tub was partly the reason that people called her Dol, along with the fact that Dorothea was a mouthful to say. Vivi's own given name was Viviana, and people rarely called her that, either. It sometimes made her wonder why their parents bothered to give them such long names in the first place.

There were already several irons heating up in the tailor's stove and Vivi selected one. She took it back to her board and dragged it over the sheet, making sure she didn't hold it in one place for too long and scorch the fabric. She'd done *that* enough times. Lilith winked at her. Lilith had been ironing sheets for so many years, she had it perfected. Her pile of crisply folded rectangles stood tall and proud. Vivi had a long way to go.

Therese and Ivette arrived, chatting animatedly as usual. A welcome cool breeze blew in through the door with them and they both got to work immediately. Therese heated more water in the giant copper on the laundry stove and Ivette took up her usual position by the mangle. Vivi liked Therese, who was the oldest there. Vivi thought she resembled a kindly grandmother, not that Vivi had known either of her own grandmothers. She wasn't as keen on Ivette, who was just a little younger than Therese. Ivette rarely had a good word to say about anyone.

"In a hurry today, are you, Vivi?" asked Therese with a chuckle as Vivi slowly dragged her iron back and forth.

Vivi smiled sadly. "Have you seen the size of that pile of sheets? I could work at it like a machine and I'd still never get through it."

"I'll do some of them later," called Dol, plunging the dolly stick.

"Don't you go helping her, Dol, you've got your own work to do," said Ivette.

Dol's cheeks reddened. "I don't mind. My work won't take me all day."

"That's because you work hard, unlike your idle cousin over here."

"Charming," said Vivi sarcastically. She didn't care what Ivette or the others thought about her. If Dol wanted to help, then that was up to her, wasn't it?

The door opened again, letting in another fresh blast of cool air. Vivi often begged her aunt to leave the door open, especially in the hotter months, but she wouldn't allow it. Aunt Ina didn't want ash and dirt blowing in from outside and marking the clean laundry.

The visitor was another of Vivi's many cousins, heaving a huge bag of laundry from the hotel, as he did every day. He could have fitted into the bag himself.

Vivi waved at him. "Hello, Eddie, how are you keeping?"

He dumped the bag of washing on the floor, put his hands on his hips and narrowed his eyes at Vivi. "I am not Eddie. I'm Ralph."

Vivi grinned and began folding her sheet into a small rectangle, pressing it with every fold. It still didn't look as neat as Lilith's. "How do you expect me to tell the difference between you and your brothers? There are so many of you and you're all small and freckled." This was an ongoing joke between them, based on the fact that she had mixed up her younger cousins when she first arrived in Valesti.

"Eddie's seven," said Ralph, "and I'm eight. Sven and Ollie are only four. You should be able to tell us apart by now."

Dol stopped her plunging and collected the bag from her brother. "Don't mind Vivi – she's only teasing." She ruffled his already scruffy hair, then pointed to some rolled up papers sticking out of his breast pocket. "What have you got there?"

Forgetting the teasing, Ralph puffed out his chest. "Notices," he said, with an air of importance.

"Notices about what?"

Ralph wiped his nose on his sleeve. "Dunno. A coach driver was sticking 'em up in the town square and asked if I could help. I said I knew folk down the laundry and up at the hotel. I said I knew half the town. I got a coin for my trouble."

The women laughed indulgently as Dol took one of the papers, unrolled it and peered at it.

Vivi put her iron back on the stove and skipped over to join her. "What's it say, Dol?"

Dol was clever. She could read and write better than anyone Vivi knew. Although she'd left school at Ralph's age, she'd learned more in that time than most people would learn in ten years. She did every crossword puzzle in the newspaper and read books, too. Great big books full of words – mysteries that she always figured out before the end. Vivi could just about read and write, but it was a struggle and she tripped up on the longer words. Dol was always trying to help her improve.

"Read it with me, Vivi. You know most of these words, I'm sure of it."

Vivi shook her head impatiently. "No, you're so much quicker than me. Come on, read it for us! This lot all want to hear it as well, don't you?"

The laundresses stopped their work for a moment, nodding and laughing. It wasn't every day that notices were handed out around the town, and they were all eager to hear what it said.

CHAPTER TWO

AN IMPORTANT NOTICE

Dol put on her reading glasses. They weren't really *her* glasses. She'd inherited them from their grandfather, which explained why they looked so large on her head and kept slipping down her nose. Vivi looked over Dol's shoulder as she read the heading of the notice aloud.

HER LADYSHIP THE COUNTESS MAROZNY OF CASTLE BEZNA ANNOUNCES A GREAT OPPORTUNITY

"Pah!" cried Ivette, going back to her mangle. "We all know what Countess Marozny has to say – it'll be the same notice she sent out last year and the year before that. She never gives up!"

Vivi threw her a stony look. The previous year's notice must have been sent before she came to Valesti. "I wasn't here last year or the year before that, so I want to know what it says."

"Me too!" said Ralph. "I never heard any notice before. Go on, read it, Dol!"

Dol continued in her best reading voice.

Announcing a great opportunity for one genteel young woman of sixteen to eighteen years of age from a good family.

Her Ladyship the Countess Marozny seeks a lady's companion to provide conversation, companionship and refined entertainment.

Applicants should be trustworthy, honest and willing to learn. Knowledge of foreign languages, drawing, dancing and/or music preferable. The successful applicant will be selected after an interview with her ladyship. A year's education and lodging at Castle Bezna will be provided.

If you would like to be considered, please meet the coach at five o'clock on Friday evening in the market square.

Vivi's jaw dropped open, and she whisked the notice out of Dol's hands. This was surely big news. Wasn't it? A job opportunity with a *countess* at a *castle*? Someone rich enough to print out official advertisements for a job. But the other laundresses appeared unmoved.

Ivette smiled smugly, turning the handle of the mangle. "Just as I thought, the same message she sends every year."

Lilith *mmm-hmmed* in agreement. "You would think she'd get the message by now. No girl from Valesti is ever going to take her up on that offer."

Vivi couldn't understand what they were talking about. "Why not? A year's lodging in a *castle*? Wouldn't that be better than living down here? Wouldn't it be better than ironing and scalding and rinsing all day?"

"Not when you know the history of Castle Bezna," said Ivette.

Lilith wrapped an unironed sheet around her like a cape,

reached one arm over her face, then swept it away with an evil grin. "Castle Bezna – also known as Vampire Towers!" She added a sinister laugh for effect.

"Everyone knows to stay away from Castle Bezna," said Therese, swirling the newly mangled batch of clothes in the copper.

"That place is cursed," agreed Ivette. "You can go up there, but you might never return!"

Ralph's eyes widened. Dol handed him the bag of fresh washing Lilith had just pressed. "You, time to head up to the hotel with this little lot."

"Awww, I wanna stay and hear about the vampires!"

"It's not vampires you should worry about – it's Ma if we're late with these linens. Go on, off with you – Vivi will tell you some scary stories at bedtime."

Reluctantly, and with some effort, Ralph picked up the bag. "Be seein' you," he said and tottered out the door, the bag balanced on his back.

With young ears out of the way, the women continued telling their tales.

Dol was back at the dolly tub, emptying out the latest load. "I told you bad things happen in the mountains, Vivi."

Vivi laughed, perching on the counter near the doorway and

studying the notice. "I know, but vampires? People really believe this?"

Dol nodded. "It's not just stories. You remember it, don't you, Therese?"

Therese stopped swirling for a moment and cast her eyes up to the ceiling. "Oh yes, I remember it all from when I was a child. Castle Bezna used to be a beautiful place, like something out of a fairy tale. Owned by the Marozny family – all rich aristocrats, going back generations. They kept themselves to themselves—"

"Until they all died!" interrupted Ivette triumphantly.

Vivi gaped. "The whole family?"

Lilith nodded. She had moved on to ironing shirts, and turned one over on the ironing board. "It was thought that they died of some mysterious wasting disease—"

Ivette snorted. "Not so mysterious as it turns out!"

Lilith ignored her and continued. "After they died, the castle remained empty for a couple of years, while the authorities looked for the rightful heir to the Marozny fortune. There was apparently one living relative, but they couldn't track 'em down."

"Meanwhile, the others moved in," said Therese. "Just a few to begin with. Three generations, all called Dorin, as I remember. Pure evil. They treated the castle as their own."

Vivi was completely transfixed by the story now. She listened intently, swinging her legs under the counter. "Where did they come from?"

"No one ever knew," said Therese.

"And were they ... vampires?" she asked in an excited whisper.

All three of the older laundresses nodded together. Dol grimaced and continued working away, not even appearing to be listening any more.

"Yes, vampires," said Lilith. "In the beginning no one realized. Until livestock was killed and people from the villages and towns were found dead in the streets, bite marks on their necks. Then people began to call the castle Vampire Towers."

"As the vampires realized their power, they became brazen. They stopped hiding away and stalked the towns and villages," said Therese. "In one of the villages, twin girls were taken from their beds and never seen again."

Lilith shook her head at the horror of it all. "One poor man lost his whole family to those monsters. He was nearly destroyed by the grief."

"Ten people were killed in Valesti alone. There's a monument to them in the square. It calls it the 'bloodsucking plague'," said Dol, quietly joining in.

"No one could go out after dark. People hung garlic on their doors and windows," added Ivette. "A few people tried to get them to leave, but they all met with sorry ends. And all that time, at Vampire Towers, the number of vampires grew."

Vivi leaned back on her arms. "Their number grew? But how? Where did they come from?"

Ivette pushed some more clothes into the mangle and turned the handle furiously. "Nobody's certain, but those in the know say some local folk weren't only killed – they were turned into vampires themselves."

Therese shrugged. "Eventually, there were twelve vampires up there, living like royalty and preying on the poor folk in the towns and villages all around. The people lived in fear every day, until they decided enough was enough. They found out everything they could about their enemy. Then they gathered together a huge band of hunters from every town and village in these parts. One day they stormed the castle and killed them all."

"All twelve of them. A nasty business," added Lilith.

Vivi couldn't believe it. "I've lived in this town for nearly a year and no one's ever mentioned vampires."

Therese sniffed as she mixed up some starch. "It's an ugly period of history. No one likes to think of their nearest and dearest putting stakes through hearts and chopping off heads. They all did what had to be done to rid themselves of those monsters – my father and uncle included." Her voice cracked a little as she spoke, and Vivi realized that she still felt emotional about the subject.

"They should have razed Castle Bezna to the ground," said Ivette.

That was exactly what Vivi had been thinking. "Why didn't they?"

"They would have done, but not long after the twelve vampires were killed, the young countess arrived – the last surviving member of the Marozny family and the rightful heir. She inherited the castle and the entire Marozny fortune." Therese shook her head slowly. "She was only about my age – just a young woman."

"Where had she been all that time?"

"Nobody knows. There are all sorts of rumours as to where she came from," said Ivette, the flattened clothes appearing from between the rollers of the mangle as she talked.

"From not far away, I heard," said Lilith. "She'd been living up in the mountains all alone. People thought she might marry once she moved to the castle, but she never did, and in fifty years she never has been able to persuade anyone to join her there."

"There were those two girls years ago – do you remember?" asked Ivette.

The details all seemed to be coming back to Therese now. "Ah yes – Dorïce Engel and Margareta something."

"Lang-Mayer," said Ivette. "Lived at the big house on the edge of town. Her family still do. Think they're better than the rest of us." She sniffed.

"Yes. Well, neither of them lasted the year. Apparently, both girls found opportunities elsewhere. One married a rich man, didn't she? And the other went travelling around the world."

Ivette pursed her lips. "That's what was *said*, but the truth is no one saw or heard from either of those girls ever again. Not their friends or families – no one. People stopped replying to the countess's notices after that."

Vivi frowned. "But what do people think happened?"

Therese gave Ivette a warning look. "Nothing."

Vivi looked at Dol, whose eyes were downcast. "Oh, come on, tell me. It's not fair if you all know and I don't."

Ivette glanced at Therese, who threw up her hands. "Very well, tell her…"

"Tell me *what*?" asked Vivi.

"This is all rumour, mind," said Ivette, eyes darting to check with Therese, "but *some* folk think there was a vampire up in those mountains that was never found. A *thirteenth* vampire. And that it still hides in the forest somewhere, waiting for the right time to strike."

"But people like to talk," said Lilith, "and this isn't based on any fact. There have been no more vampire attacks – no more bodies found."

"Just the missing girls…" said Ivette.

"… and healthy livestock killed off in the mountains," added Therese.

Lilith clucked her tongue. "Two flighty girls wanting to get away from Valesti and a few dead sheep in fifty years. Don't mean there's a vampire on the loose."

Dol shuddered. "Maybe, but you wouldn't catch me up at that old place. Once Vampire Towers always Vampire Towers."

"And you're not the only one, Dol." Ivette nodded at Therese. "In the years after Dorïce and Margareta disappeared, just a handful of girls from Valesti replied to the countess's notice. None of them made it to Castle Bezna – they all turned back halfway, frightened on the journey. For the past few years, no one has dared go. Mark my words, that coach will travel back up to Castle Bezna just as empty as it is now."

CHAPTER THREE

AUNT INA

The women's chatter died down as they concentrated once again on their jobs, but Vivi continued to stare at the notice, even though she wasn't able to read it as well as Dol. Just holding it made her fingers tingle and her heart race. This was an opportunity – *a great opportunity*! If she went to live in a castle then she could stop worrying about upsetting her aunt, who she was sure would one day tire of her and throw her in the workhouse.

Vivi wandered over to Dol and spoke in a low voice, out of earshot of the others. She pointed at the notice. "I could do this."

Dol dropped the dolly stick for a moment. "You wouldn't!"

"Why wouldn't I?"

"After everything you just heard!"

"About vampires?"

Dol nodded fervently.

"It doesn't bother me. If it happened all those years ago, then it's ancient history now. Twelve vampires, dead and gone, and a lonely countess with more money than she knows what to do with – what's so scary about that?"

Dol's eyes were wide. "What about the *thirteenth vampire*?"

Vivi laughed loudly. "There is no *thirteenth vampire*! You heard Lilith, didn't you? There were *twelve* vampires and they were all finished off by the hunters."

Dol resumed plunging, then stopped again and pushed back her hair. "I know, but still ... the castle is all on its own up there in the middle of that dark forest ... and there are all those rumours about another vampire on the loose."

"Countess Marozny lives there, doesn't she? She's not been killed off by vampires yet."

"Well, no, but the countess sounds like an odd woman. She never goes anywhere, you know…"

"Yes, but if she's the same age as Therese then she's seventy or eighty, at least. No family and living all alone in an enormous castle. And, unlike Therese, she doesn't have to work. She just sits in her castle all day counting her money! She'll be looking for someone to leave her fortune to. Why shouldn't that someone be me?"

Dol laughed nervously. "You are joking, aren't you, Vivi? I can't always tell. You wouldn't really go up to Vampire Towers … would you?"

"I would. Imagine. I go up there, the countess leaves her castle to me and I live the life of a princess."

"But the countess would never choose you. You're not the right age, for one thing. It says in the notice she wants a companion between the ages of sixteen and eighteen."

"Well, I'm nearly fourteen—"

"You're not fourteen for three months!"

"That's what I said, *nearly* fourteen. Which means I'm fifteen next year, which is practically the age she asked for. Besides, I'm tall. No one would ever know."

"It says 'genteel'. That you should know French and music! She wants someone to provide 'refined entertainment'!"

"But I *do* know music. And dancing. You love my *refined* entertainment!"

Vivi thrust the notice into the pocket of her dress. She climbed on to the counter by the door as if it were a stage, and sang in her best music hall voice:

"Twelve dead vampires don't scare me
Like working in this laund-uh-ry!"

Dol let out a panicked cry and flapped her hands at Vivi. "Come down from there! We've got work to do and Ma said she'd be stopping by this morning. She'll have something to say if she catches you up there."

But Ivette, Therese and Lilith all clapped their hands in time to the beat. Liking nothing more than an audience, Vivi continued her song.

"Castle Bezna might be scary
But dirty linens make me wary!"

The laundresses laughed along. Vivi picked up a pressing cloth from the counter, twirled it around and kicked up her feet to one side and then the other. Her hair escaped from its ponytail and fell loose around her shoulders.

> *"Keep your scrubbing stains and sploshing.*
> *Keep your lines of dripping washing!*
>
> *"No more ironing sheets for hours;*
> *It's fun and games at Vampire Tow-errrrrrs…"*

Vivi looked up at the ceiling for the last note, making it last as long as she could. Then she stood with her arms wide, expecting thunderous applause.

But there was just the hiss of the stove, the sound of vigorous plunging and an otherwise worrying silence. When she looked around the room, everyone else was focused intently on their work. And Aunt Ina was standing in the middle of the room, arms folded across her chest.

"Good morning, Viviana," she said, stonily.

"Good morning, Aunt Ina," replied Vivi, climbing down from the counter.

Aunt Ina was Vivi's ma's younger sister. She looked a lot like her sister although she lacked her sense of humour. She shared the same features as Dol and the boys, though she tried to hide her freckles with rice powder. Vivi didn't look like her ma or her aunt. She had her father's height and shared his large mouth and wide eyes, too.

Aunt Ina kept her arms folded and tapped her foot on the floor. Apparently, she expected Vivi to explain herself.

"I was just taking a short break," mumbled Vivi.

"I see. You were asked to iron bedsheets today."

"Yes, Aunt Ina," said Vivi, even though it was a statement rather than a question.

"And you have been working so hard you required a break."

Another statement, to which Vivi didn't have an answer. "I … erm…"

"No doubt, when I inspect the shelves, I will be most impressed by your output."

Vivi followed nervously as her aunt strode over to her ironing board. Dol gave her a sympathetic look, while Ivette smiled expectantly.

"This is your shelf, correct, next to Lilith?" Aunt Ina put her hand on the shelf with one ironed sheet on it.

"Yes, Aunt Ina." Vivi studied a knot of wood in the floor.

"Is that really all you've managed to get through today?"

Vivi chose not to mention that it was actually quite neatly folded. That she was improving. Instead, she shrugged. "I don't think ironing bedsheets is one of my strengths."

"I wholeheartedly agree, Viviana." Her aunt pursed her lips and Ivette sniggered, hastily disguising it as a cough. "Unfortunately, your strengths don't include scrubbing or starching or plunging. Neither do they include pressing collars and cuffs."

"No, Aunt Ina."

"I am fast running out of work to put your way. I'm beginning to think you inherited more from your layabout father than his height."

Ouch. Vivi felt the eyes of the other laundresses on her as she continued to study the floor.

Her aunt tutted. "This is a laundry and it is a business. My business. May I suggest you identify your strength and identify it quickly? Otherwise, you'll be doing the fetching and carrying instead of Ralph. Do I make myself clear?"

"Yes, Aunt Ina," said Vivi, resuming the ironing with as much enthusiasm as she could muster. "I'll try."

She would try. What was her alternative? She didn't want to be demoted to a runner like one of the little ones. Or worse, for her aunt to give up on her altogether. Without Aunt Ina, she had no one left.

This was the first time her aunt had actually said outright that Vivi was like her father, although Vivi was sure she'd thought it plenty of times. Her father, who should have looked after Vivi when her ma was ill, had spent all their money at the local tavern and ended up falling into the docks and drowning weeks before her death. Maybe Vivi *was* like her father. Idle. Good-for-nothing.

Aunt Ina moved along to inspect everyone else's work and responded positively to what she saw. Dol received a particularly warm smile. Of course.

As soon as Aunt Ina had gone, Ivette began to laugh. "Any more tunes for us, Vivi?"

"No," said Vivi, with a scowl.

"Leave the poor girl alone," said Lilith, patting her gently on the arm.

After that, Vivi tried to put her head down, stop her chatter and iron the sheets. She managed three – all fairly well-folded – in about the time she'd ironed the first.

She kept working like that for most of the day, but she didn't quite manage to catch up. At four o'clock, Therese and Ivette went home (Lilith had left at lunchtime), and Dol came over to help her finish her ironing load. Dol would never leave Vivi by herself.

When they had finished, Vivi stood upright, arching her

back, trying to ease the muscles that had tightened into knots. Dol beamed at her. "See, Vivi, you can get so much done when you try."

Vivi bent her head down to the ironing board, feeling the heat on her forehead, and moaned. She looked up to see Dol's smile had collapsed into an expression of concern.

"I can't," said Vivi.

"You can! Look – a whole pile of sheets in no time. You've even folded them beautifully."

"No, I mean I can't live this life. Doing this every day ... for ever. Standing on my feet all day in this heat, washing other people's dirty things."

"But you worked before. In the market back in Ingusport."

"I know, but that was *my* life. This is your life and your ma's, but not mine. This is what my ma ran away from when she was just a bit older than me. She would have never wanted me back here. If I stay, then either I will explode from the frustration of it all, or Aunt Ina will end up having to throw me out. I must get away."

"But where would you go?"

"I told you," said Vivi, smoothing out the notice from the countess on the ironing board. "I'm going to reply to this advertisement. I'm going to find the coach and go to the castle."

Dol stretched out her fingers to ease the stiffness. "Ma will never let you go."

Vivi stuck out her bottom lip. "I won't tell her."

"The coach driver will never take you."

"Why not?"

"Like I said before, you're not from a 'good family'. It asks for that as clear as day in the notice. Countess Marozny will be looking for one of the girls from the big houses. She'll never take you on."

"I *am* from a good family," said Vivi, jutting out her chin. "One of the best."

"You know what it means."

"Oh, I know what it means, all right. She doesn't really mean a *good* family at all. She means a well-to-do family – a family with money – but I don't think that's fair. I'm just as good as any of the girls who send their frocks here. She'll see that when she meets me."

"She won't, Vivi! She'll take one look at you and she'll know you're not like her. She's a countess! She wants a genteel girl with the right manners and the right clothes."

"Ah, but that bit's easy to fix. I can be as genteel as the next girl. Watch me."

At the back of the laundry was a rack of clothes that people hadn't yet collected. Each item had a ticket pinned to it. Vivi disappeared amongst the frocks.

"What are you doing, Vivi?"

Vivi emerged holding a flouncy evening gown in front of her. It was a pale salmon pink with a frilled floor-length skirt and a pleated bodice. She swished it from side to side. "If I was wearing *this*, the old countess wouldn't question my family history."

Dol giggled nervously. "But you can't wear that – it's not yours."

"Nothing to stop me borrowing it, though. This dress has been left here, forgotten, for weeks. Its owner won't remember it until the next summer ball comes around, by which time they'll be getting a new dress made anyway. Surely someone like that can afford to share?"

Vivi slipped the dress over the top of her own simple frock, wriggled it around and stuck her arms through the sleeves. The full skirt drowned her and the bodice gaped.

"It's too big," said Dol, in between giggles.

"Ah, but if I do this…" Vivi stood on tiptoes, so she was no longer treading on the hem. "And this…" She cinched in the dress at the back with her left hand. "I can look as la-di-da as the rest of them. Why, hellooo, I'm Countess Viviana!"

Dol's smile wavered. "You're not really going to go, are you, Vivi?"

With her free hand, Vivi attempted to twist up her long, loose hair. She held it on top of her head in a rough approximation of a wealthy woman's hairstyle. "Why *wouldn't* I go? It's not like I'm needed here."

"You are needed!"

Vivi released her messy updo and it fell loose again.

"You know that's not true. The laundry was running very well before I arrived. I do half as much work as everyone else and what I do manage is never up to scratch."

Dol said nothing.

"If Ivette was here, she'd agree with me!" Vivi laughed but Dol didn't join in. She lowered her gaze.

"I need you," said Dol, quietly. "All these years I never had a sister, then you came along and my life changed. I can't just go back to how it was before."

"You don't need me! You'll carry on happily enough. You'll have the whole of your bed back, for one thing."

"I don't want it back. I'll be far too cold."

Vivi smiled at her with affection. "You'll be fine, Dol. You don't need me or anyone else. Besides, I'll be back again in a year. Or sooner, depending on how long the countess lasts out!"

Dol took the printed notice from the ironing board and stared at it forlornly. "It says to meet the coach on Friday. That's tomorrow. That can't possibly be enough time to prepare."

Vivi laughed. "Prepare! It's not like I have anything much to pack, is it? I'll be ready to go in no time."

CHAPTER FOUR

GOODBYE

The next day, the girls left work together. Instead of going home, or via the bakery to buy cheap end-of-the-day pastries, they walked down the narrow streets towards the town square.

Despite Dol's protests, Vivi had changed into the flouncy dress the minute the other women had left the laundry. She'd spent most of the previous evening working by candlelight to adjust it, but she wasn't the best seamstress, and it was still too big – it kept slipping off her shoulders as she walked. Gooseflesh covered her arms. She'd refused to wear her coat as it looked all wrong with the dress.

She'd stuffed her work dress and coat into her old carpet bag, plus a hairbrush, handkerchiefs and a photograph of herself as a baby with her parents. Her father – standing tall in his Sunday suit – looked much sterner in the picture than he had in real life. Ma, holding baby Vivi in her arms, was smiling.

Along with these few possessions, Vivi had thrown in some old pillowcases to pad out the bag and make it look as though she owned more than she really did. One of the leather straps had broken, so the bag didn't close properly, but the gap didn't show if Vivi held it tightly against her body. For now, Dol had insisted on taking one strap, and Vivi held the other, the bag bouncing between them.

As they approached the end of the lane, where it opened out into the town square, Dol pointed across to the other side. "Look, there's the coach waiting. I can't see a queue of girls – Ivette was right."

It was a small black coach, with two dark horses. Vivi's heart flipped at the sight of it. Her life was about to change.

"Just me, then – the perfect candidate!" She smiled at Dol and took the strap of her bag from her cousin, hiking both straps on to her shoulder. "I'll leave you here."

Dol looked across the square, sadly. "Can't I come to the coach with you?"

"No. It's best I do this next part on my own." Vivi most definitely didn't want Dol to come with her. If her plan was going to work, Vivi had to create a certain impression. She was worried Dol might give the game away before Vivi had even boarded the coach. Unlike Vivi, Dol was no good at pretending. Besides, she might cry, and that would be embarrassing for everyone. Even at this moment, her cousin was twisting a handkerchief in her hands, eyes welling up.

"What am I going to tell Ma?"

Vivi put the bag down for a moment. "About what?"

"About where you've gone, of course!" Dol's eyes were wide. She was so sweet, thought Vivi. She actually thought her mother would care if Vivi disappeared. In actual fact, Aunt Ina would likely be relieved to have less disruption at the laundry *and* one less mouth to feed. Vivi didn't hold it against her aunt. Anyone would feel the same in her position and Vivi was her niece, after all, not her daughter. "I'm sure she'll understand."

"She won't! She'll be distraught when she discovers where you've gone and if she finds out I knew and didn't stop you…"

Vivi smiled. "Why don't you make something up? Tell Aunt Ina you have no idea where I went."

Dol's hand flew to her chest. "I couldn't do that!"

"I bet you could. Telling tall tales is an art form. Or a craft, like spinning wool. The secret is to start with a sliver of truth and then twist it. Say I stole a dress from the laundry and ran off to be a vampire!"

"It's not funny, Vivi. If you worked a little harder and stopped telling tall tales, then Ma wouldn't come down on you so hard. You have to start being honest. With yourself and everyone else. Open up to people who love you – let them in. I know you never expected to end up here with us, but it doesn't mean you can't have a good life."

It was a long speech for Dol and she stopped abruptly and looked down at her feet.

"I haven't ended up anywhere yet, Dol, that's the point. I'm still looking for where I belong."

"I know you still miss your parents, Vivi. I know you'd do anything to get away from the laundry, but do you really have to go to Vampire Towers to do that?"

"Not this again." Vivi sighed with frustration. "Come on, Dol, that's all silly tales told by silly people who like a silly story. You're far too clever to believe things like that. I'm off on a marvellous adventure. Can't you be happy for me?"

The sun was low in the sky and the evening chill was already in the air. Vivi shivered.

"Here, take my mantle." Dol removed her cloak and wrapped it around Vivi's shoulders. It was made of thick, dark grey wool and wasn't quite such a ridiculous pairing with the dress as Vivi's coat had been.

Vivi tried to shrug it off. "I can't take this – it's your best one. Aunt Ina would be furious. I'm not cold."

"Don't be silly – I can see your gooseflesh. Take it. Really." Dol might have been shy and sweet-natured, but she could be stubborn when she wanted to be.

"Thank you," relented Vivi. "But take my coat." She unpacked it from her bag and handed it over.

Dol put the coat on and the girls looked at each other for a moment in silence. Then Dol spoke. "You know, if she's as old as we think, the countess might be in frail health. You wouldn't want to look after an invalid, Vivi, you said as much—"

"Are you still trying to put me off going? The countess isn't asking for a nursemaid. She wants a companion – didn't she say? She'll have other people to look after her."

"What if the coachman won't take you there?"

"He will." Vivi would make sure of it.

Dol wrinkled her brow. "Will you be gone for very long?"

"The notice said a year, didn't it?"

"A year is a long, long time." The tears started to spill from Dol's eyes and she dabbed at them with her hanky. Vivi tried to distract her with humour.

"The countess might only last six weeks, by which time her favourite companion – me – will be living in the castle like a queen. Baths full of rose petals. Roast peacock every night for my dinner. I'll send a coach for you then. A golden coach, pulled by unicorns."

That extracted a small laugh from Dol, finally. She looked up at Vivi with watery eyes. "Will you write to me?"

"Oh, Dol, you know me and writing. I'm not very good at it and it takes me so long—"

"Will you try? As soon as you get there? Let me know you're safe?"

Vivi sighed. That puppy dog expression. "Yes, I'll write."

Looking much happier, Dol threw her arms around Vivi and gave her a farewell hug. As Vivi strode off, Dol stood waving, looking small and forlorn in the too-big coat. Vivi waved once but then she turned and didn't look back. Dol needed to head home, not stand around watching her.

Vivi crossed the town square with purpose. The expanse of

cobblestones was almost empty of people, but a great flock of pigeons had taken advantage of the peace: strutting, cooing and pecking at the ground. As Vivi walked towards them they scattered, flying away to perch on nearby rooftops.

She passed the tall stone monument at the centre of the square. She'd seen it countless times, but this time she stopped to take a proper look. There was the inscription to the victims of the vampires carved into the stone. She couldn't read many of the words, but she picked out 'bloodsucking' and 'plague', which she remembered Dol using.

Below the inscription, running around the monument, was a list of those who died. Vivi didn't have time to read the names; she had somewhere more important to be. It was interesting, though, to think all this had really happened. It wasn't just stories.

She looked over at the coach, which had seen better days: its wheels were chipped and one of the kerosene carriage lamps looked in danger of falling off. The pair of glossy horses were saddled up and ready to go. The coachman, in his uniform of full-length box coat and long boots, was pacing alongside it with his head down.

"Good evening!" Vivi shouted, trying out her newfound plummy voice as she walked towards the coach.

The driver, who wore tinted eyeglasses under his top hat,

looked over in her direction. Vivi thought he saw her, but then he looked away and began climbing into the raised driver's seat. Was he leaving already? Surely not. Five o'clock, the notice had said. Vivi checked the tall clock in the square. It was only a quarter to.

"Excuse me!" she called out, waving at him. "Wait a moment!" But he continued to look straight ahead and pulled on the reins. The horses slowly moved forward, the coach trundling shakily over the cobbles.

"No!" screeched Vivi, forgetting her fake voice. "Not without me!"

The coach was heading towards the clock tower, but Vivi knew that to get to the castle, the driver would have to turn the coach around. The only route out to the mountains – and presumably to Castle Bezna – was over the river.

Vivi hitched up the straps of her bag with one hand, bunched up her long dress with the other, and began running towards the bridge. Luckily, she could run fast. She kept glancing back over her shoulder and, sure enough, the coach did turn around, circling the town square and heading in her direction.

She reached the bridge first, panting with exhaustion. She stood right in the middle of the road, threw her bag down on the ground and waved both arms above her head.

The driver had no choice but to stop.

"Whoa," he called to the horses, who obeyed, clattering hooves slowing to a halt just steps away from Vivi. "What do you think you're doing?" he shouted, "Trying to get yourself killed?"

"I was calling! Didn't you hear me calling? It's not five o'clock yet!"

As the driver climbed down and secured the horses, Vivi pushed back her sweaty hair and tried to gather herself, her racing heartbeat slowing a little. She realized that this coachman was actually a coach*woman*: short and wide-hipped with jaw-length hair, swept to one side under the black hat. She analysed Vivi with eyebrows raised above her round glasses. "How can I help you?"

Vivi raised her chin and gazed back confidently, though she was still getting her breath back. "I am here in response to the notice sent by Her Ladyship the Countess Marozny. I wish to journey to the castle this evening to meet the countess." She adopted the tone of the rich women who delivered their gowns to the laundry. The sort of tone that told you they wanted something done quickly and didn't expect an argument. The sort of tone that the previous owner of Vivi's dress would have used.

The coach driver's smile widened as she looked Vivi up and down, taking in the frilled dress, the well-worn mantle and the scruffy carpet bag. "Oh, that's what you wish, is it? Well, I'm not sure you're quite what the countess will be expecting."

Vivi felt the heat rise in her cheeks in anger. She straightened her back and met the coach driver's gaze. "I have to say you're not quite what I was expecting, either," she said, imperiously.

For a moment, the coach driver looked like she wasn't quite sure how to take this, then she guffawed. "That has been said before. But I'm afraid I really can't take you. You're not quite the right … fit."

"I can't see a queue of other girls waiting to get on the coach, can you?" Vivi pointed back to the square to illustrate her point.

The driver lifted her glasses and wiped her eyes with a handkerchief. "You're a right one, you are. And you're correct – you're the only one. The first one in years."

"So are you going to take me there? It's the least you could do after you nearly drove off without me."

The driver frowned. "How old are you?"

"Sixteen," replied Vivi, without a moment's pause.

"And do you have a name?"

"I am Miss Viviana…" Vivi searched around for a suitable-sounding surname. A name of someone from a 'good' family. A more genteel name than her real family name – Peste – or her aunt's name, Stroud. "Miss Viviana De…" She glimpsed the pattern of roses on her carpet bag. "DeRose. Miss Viviana DeRose." Perfect. She liked the way it sounded, plus her middle name was Rosa, so it was almost true.

"Oh, that's your name, is it? Well, Miss DeRose, I'm Janette Arvesson. Everyone calls me Jarv for short and you may, too."

"Well, Jarv, will you please take me to the castle as I've requested?"

Jarv pushed her glasses up her nose. "I suppose so. I'm just the driver, after all. The countess can decide what to do with you when you get there." She opened the door, raised her hat and beckoned Vivi inside with an exaggerated flourish of the hand, as she might do for royalty.

Vivi climbed inside but Jarv didn't close the door. She leaned in and said, "Now, if you change your mind on the journey, let me know, and we'll turn right back around again – no harm done."

"Why the – why *on Earth* would I change my mind?"

Jarv paused, as if she was considering her words carefully. "The castle is in rather a bleak and lonely location."

"I know it's bleak and lonely." Vivi rolled her eyes. "I'm not setting off for somewhere known as Vampire Towers expecting a summer picnic, am I?"

The coachwoman chuckled. "It's just, most of the other girls – the few that replied to the notice over the years – they never made it through the forest, let alone as far as the castle."

Vivi let this information sink in. "Well, I'm not like other girls."

Jarv chuckled again. "I can see that, Miss DeRose." She reached into the coach and passed her an old parasol someone must have left behind. "Still, if you *do* change your mind en route, knock on the roof with this and I'll be down in a jiffy."

If the coachwoman thought Vivi would be knocking on the roof, then she was wrong. Vivi wasn't afraid of anything. That was a side effect of losing both her parents at such a young age: the worst had already happened. Jarv swung the door shut and Vivi placed her bag by her feet. She examined the parasol: folds of black silk edged with lace. The sort of item someone from a 'good' family might own.

They lurched to a start. As they crossed the bridge out of town, Vivi wriggled in her seat to try to get a good view of the ducks and geese in the river below. Dol still loved to feed the ducks, even at the age of thirteen. Vivi didn't mind accompanying her and they'd spent many hours on that bridge and down at the water's edge, surrounded by greedy honking waterfowl.

Within minutes, they'd left the town behind and were out in

the famous sunflower fields. The summer glory days had passed and the great heads of the sunflowers hung forward, petals crisping at the edges, almost ready for the harvest. But even now that the sunshine yellows had muted to browns, the fields were still a beautiful sight. Row upon row of flowers stood like soldiers waiting for orders.

Vivi marvelled that these fields were just a few miles from the centre of Valesti and yet she'd seen them only once or twice. There was never any time for strolling through the countryside when you worked tirelessly as a laundress. It added to her anticipation of the adventure ahead. She wondered about the girls who'd changed their minds on the way to the castle. Why would they have been brave enough to leave their home and town, only to change their minds halfway?

The coach rocked wildly and Vivi clutched the window's edge to prevent herself from being thrown forward. She didn't know whether to blame the road or the driver. Possibly both were at fault. But surely travel sickness and a bruised behind couldn't have been enough to send the countess's potential protégées running for home. Vivi guessed it wouldn't be long until she discovered what had put them off.

CHAPTER FIVE

THE JOURNEY

The journey continued. Vivi listened to the sound of the coach wheels turning on the uneven ground and the odd cry from Jarv commanding the horses. They passed through Valesti's outlying farmland, into the dense forest. Then all she could see was trees. Beautiful trees, taller than the tallest townhouses, their autumn foliage bright in the evening sun. She stared at them for a time, wondering if she might spot animals or birds hidden in the depths, but all she saw was a repeat pattern of trunks and leaves.

In the forest, it was cooler and she wrapped her mantle tighter. The road became bumpier and steeper, which made it an effort to lean forward in her seat. Instead, Vivi sat back, wondering how much of the journey remained. She wasn't used to being on her own like this. She was always with someone, whether it was with her rowdy rabble of cousins in her aunt's house, or at the laundry with the usual team. She wasn't completely sure about being on her own. It allowed unwelcome thoughts to creep in.

As far as she could remember, Vivi had only ever travelled in a coach once before, after her ma's death. Her aunt, who was a stranger to her at the time, had come to Vivi's hometown of Ingusport for the funeral and had taken her home with her. Vivi would have preferred to stay put, to try and work at the fish market on her own, but she had no choice: she was still a child and her aunt was the only relative the authorities could trace. People always told her how lucky she'd been to have someone to take her in and provide her with food and a roof over her head. She could have ended up in the workhouse like so many others.

That journey to Valesti was almost a year ago. Aunt Ina hadn't stopped talking: sharing childhood memories of Vivi's ma, tales of cousins whose names she didn't recognize and places she didn't know. When Aunt Ina wasn't talking, she was offering food: cheese pastries, rice-stuffed cabbage rolls and fluffy plum dumplings.

But Vivi hadn't been able to reply, or to eat a thing. She'd barely heard a word of what her aunt had said. Despite Ma's long illness, her death had still come as a shock. All Vivi could think about was how she'd never see her ma or her town again, how she'd never be happy anywhere else. After a while, she'd fallen asleep, hoping she'd wake up and discover the previous weeks had been nothing but a bad dream.

By the time they'd reached Valesti, her aunt had given up on the conversation and the food. She'd no doubt decided Vivi was a sullen, uncommunicative sort. She probably wished she'd left her behind to take her chances on her own, Vivi had thought.

But now, in the coach travelling towards Castle Bezna, everything was different. Vivi wasn't tired and wouldn't sleep even if she was. She was too excited about what might lie ahead.

Vivi took another look at the parasol Jarv had handed her. It had a polished wood handle, a black silk canopy with deep lace edging and a pointed silver tip. She began to open it up inside the carriage. Dol would have told her that it would bring bad luck, but Vivi never paid much attention to superstitions. A person could be unlucky or not, no matter if they walked under a ladder or passed a black cat, or whatever else you weren't supposed to do. Anyway, there wasn't enough space to fully open it. Vivi noted a couple of holes and a broken rib, but it was otherwise in good condition.

She folded it back up and glanced out of the window again. They were heading steeply uphill, so steeply that the horses had slowed right down. They were now at the forest's edge, with a view of the tree-covered mountain out of one window and the sheer drop down into the valley out of the other. Somewhere down there was Valesti – the sunflower fields, the laundry, Dol and her aunt and all the cousins – but she couldn't see any of it.

The sky had darkened rapidly; evening was upon them. The moon was up already, shining and full. She was glad of it, as it meant they were unlikely to be plunged into total darkness.

Suddenly, the eerie quiet of the mountains was disturbed by a high-pitched tweeting sound like loud birdsong, coming from the valley. Strange, because she hadn't been aware of any birds at all during the first part of their journey. She leaned further forward, but was thrown backwards as the coach came to a sudden halt.

One of the horses whinnied and she called out to Jarv, "Is everything well?"

If Jarv replied, her words were drowned out by the sound – more like squeaking than tweeting, Vivi thought now. Then, a sudden black cloud rose from the valley: a mass of beating wings. Bats! She recognized their shape and the erratic manner of their flight. She and Dol often saw them on their early morning walks to the laundry, but never like this: a whole swarm, flitting and flapping. As the bats came nearer, Vivi could hear the beating sound of their wings and their loud cries. They were heading directly for the coach.

The horses snorted and stamped their hooves. Vivi hoped they wouldn't bolt off the side of the mountain, taking her and Jarv with them. But the bats were just as much of a danger: they'd topple the coach if they hit it all at once.

Vivi closed her eyes for a moment, a feeling of dread passing through her, and, as she opened them, the bats flew up and over the vehicle, just missing them. There was a loud thump on the side of the coach, where a straggler had perhaps misjudged its way. Then the cloud passed, and the squeaking and flapping disappeared into the forest.

The horses calmed and there was a rap on the roof of the coach. Jarv's voice floated down to her.

"You all right down there?"

"Yes!" she cried. "Why wouldn't I be?" She tried to appear calm, although her voice cracked as she spoke. She wasn't sure

Jarv had heard, but then they were off again, trundling along the mountain road as if nothing had happened.

It took a while for her heartbeat to return to normal, but that was due to excitement, she assured herself, not fear. She smiled to herself. Bats? Was that what had scared off the other girls? A girl that feared a bat or two didn't deserve to live in a castle. What she'd seen was a phenomenon – part of her adventure. It would be something to put in her first letter home to Dol.

She felt a bit bad when she thought about her cousin and the sadness on her face when she'd said goodbye. But Vivi knew this separation was what they needed. It didn't do anyone good to rely on people – Vivi knew that from experience. When her ma had been ill in bed, despite her struggle to talk, she'd shared some important advice.

"I never had anything in this life, and I wanted so much more for you, Vivi. Promise me you'll lead a better life. A bigger life."

"I promise, Ma."

"You'll have to be strong. There won't be anyone to help you so you have to help yourself. Find that strength inside, Vivi."

They weren't exactly her ma's last words but they were the last ones Vivi remembered. Dol could do with hearing those words. Vivi would share them in the letter, too.

No sooner had the coach started moving again, than the rain began. Strange, because down in the valley it had looked like such a clear night. No doubt the mountains had their own weather system.

The wind and rain hammered the coach, which rocked unsteadily from side to side. It was still moving forward, but only just. Vivi's stomach lurched and her head swam. She'd never been on board a boat before, but she guessed sailing on rough seas would feel similar. In the dark and the rain, the tree trunks stopped looking like individual entities and merged into a large mass.

The raindrops grew heavier until it sounded as though the coach was being pelted with gravel. Hailstones bounced against the glass.

The coach stopped again. Vivi wiped the steam off the window and peered out, trying to ascertain exactly where they were, but all she could see was the distant trees.

A sudden wrench on the coach door that Vivi was leaning on made her jump back. But it was just Jarv.

"Excuse me, Miss DeRose," said the coachwoman, climbing

into the carriage. An icy wind followed her, even though she closed the door swiftly. Her nose was red, her long coat looked dark and heavy with rain, and the brim of her top hat had collected a layer of hailstones. She sat on the seat next to Vivi, who shuffled over as far to the other side as she could to avoid getting wet herself.

Jarv removed her hat, opened the door again, and tipped the hailstones out. She closed the door and put the hat on the seat between them, then removed her eyeglasses and set them in the brim. She looked different without them: her dark hair curled softly on her cheek and her blue eyes had faint lines at the corners. Vivi wondered why the coachwoman wore the glasses: perhaps to protect her eyes from flying debris as she was driving. Jarv removed her gloves next and rubbed her hands together, blowing on them. Puddles began to collect under her boots on the shiny wooden floor.

"Why have we stopped?" asked Vivi.

The coachwoman smiled. "Only a fool would take a carriage up these roads in a hailstorm. The higher we go, the narrower they get. The horses know the route but I can't see a thing."

Vivi peeked out at the stony track. "So what are we going to do?"

"Sit it out. It's all we can do. The hailstones can get big around here so I've led the horses to shelter under the trees out of harm's way. I'm going to rest in here with you. Get as comfortable as you can – it may be some time 'til we get going again."

Vivi lost track of how long they were sitting in the coach. Jarv, who was obviously used to napping inside the vehicle, leaned her head back against the hard seat and stretched her legs out straight. Within moments, she was asleep, her breath a heavy almost-snore, head rolling from one side to the other as they were buffeted by the wind.

Vivi couldn't sleep. She was unsettled by the movement of the coach and the sound of the relentless hail. In her limited experience, hailstorms were usually over more quickly than this. The white spheres were the size of marbles now, and Vivi was worried they'd crack the glass of the windows. There was so much that could go wrong out here. The horses could get frightened and run away. They'd be truly stranded then. Or a hail-loving highwayman might take advantage of their situation. She glanced at the pillowcase-stuffed bag at her feet. A highwayman would be sorely disappointed if that was his only haul.

After what felt like hours, the hailstorm was over and the howling wind dropped. It was still raining, but the coach was no longer lurching as if it were under attack. Jarv woke up, stretching and smiling as if she'd been dozing on a feather bed. "Doesn't look like we'll be here for the whole night after all."

Vivi raised her eyebrows. She hadn't realized that had been a possibility. "It's still raining."

Jarv snorted. "I don't let a few raindrops put me off, Miss DeRose. Wouldn't last long in this job if I did." She put her gloves back on, grimacing as she slid her hands in: they must have been still quite wet. "Now's a good moment to let me know if you want to carry on up to the castle, or turn around and head back to the town. There's no shame in it, you know, if you've changed your mind."

Vivi sighed. "I'm not scared of bats, or narrow roads. I'm not scared of forests, castles or old ladies. And I'm certainly not scared of a little rain."

"Fair enough, I'll get going again. To Castle Bezna!" said the coachwoman, replacing her hat with a grin. She hopped out, and Vivi didn't catch what she said as she closed the door, but it sounded like "rather you than me".

The next part of the journey passed quickly. As soon as she had the carriage to herself, and the rocking momentum of the journey began again, Vivi felt her eyelids grow heavy. At one point she thought she saw another bat diving towards the coach, but then sheet lightning flashed and it was gone. They drove back into the thick forest and darkness enveloped them. Her whirling mind calmed and she relaxed for the first time since the journey had begun.

She must have fallen asleep because it was something of a shock when the carriage jolted to a stop and Jarv's voice floated down to her from outside. "We've arrived, Miss DeRose!"

Vivi rubbed her hands over her face and circled her shoulders to wake herself. She stared out of the window, but all she could make out was trees, then Jarv, standing in front of the door. Jarv was completely soaked through, although she still looked cheerful enough. She opened the door and announced, "Castle Bezna."

Vivi shivered in the chill of the night, every part of her body objecting to the idea of leaving the carriage for the cold, dark and wet. She couldn't see a castle – she could see nothing apart from the rain, churning up the dirt of the road. She stepped out of the carriage carefully, hitching up the hem of her dress and taking care not to step deep into a puddle. She took the parasol with her, but Jarv noticed straight away. "That's not yours."

"I thought it might belong to the countess. I can return it to her," said Vivi, always ready with a good reason.

"The countess? No, it doesn't belong to her. She hasn't sat in this carriage for ten years or more."

"Ten years? But I thought you lived here – that you were her driver?"

"Her driver? No – she never travels far enough to need one. I do errands for her – delivering letters, food and the like, but I wouldn't want to work for someone full time. I have my own work to do and I wouldn't have it any other way."

"Where do you live?"

Jarv pointed down the slope. "About five miles in that direction."

"In the village of Bezna?"

"No, the village is behind the castle and through the forest. I'm just off the mountain path, neither here nor there, but I'm her closest neighbour." Jarv smiled. "Anyway, you can keep the parasol. You may have more need of it than I do."

"Thank you." Vivi opened it up before Jarv changed her mind, and the coachwoman tipped her hat and climbed back up to her seat. "You need to head that way."

Jarv was pointing up the slope.

Vivi followed the line of her hand and gasped. They were much nearer the castle than she'd realized.

In the dim light, she'd thought the dark silhouettes looming over them were mountain peaks or trees. Now she saw some of those shapes were the towers of Castle Bezna. The Vampire Towers. The full moon shone hazily through the rain, picking out details on its spiked turrets. Ornate twisted balustrades and screaming gargoyle faces glowed eerily. Vivi wasn't close enough to see the faces in detail, but it was quite possible to imagine they belonged to vampires.

She shivered.

Near to where they were parked, a twisting flight of stone steps led up to an arched doorway. She couldn't see any lights. Was anyone home?

She looked back at Jarv.

"It's up those steps, miss. I'll leave my headlamps on until you've found the path."

"What? Are you leaving me here by myself?"

"I am indeed. It's past my bedtime." Jarv smiled again. "I thought you weren't afraid of anything."

Vivi looked up again at the pointed spires and the twisted trees. She swallowed. "I'm not."

Trying not to tread in too many puddles, Vivi made her way to the steps. If Jarv had believed Vivi was a real lady, would she have abandoned her to find her own way to the front door? Vivi doubted it. She wished she *were* a real lady. Not only would she have a reliable escort, but maybe she'd have some clue about how to walk in a long dress in the rain.

Her hands were full – the bag in one and the parasol in the other – so she was unable to hold her hem off the wet ground. She tried to drape it over her bag-carrying arm, but that still left the other half of the hem trailing on the ground. In the end, she gave up.

The parasol, meant for sunny days, wasn't providing much shelter. Rain dripped continuously through its holes, one in front of her right shoulder and the other behind her left ear. Still, it was better than nothing.

The coach's broken headlamp threw its beam off into the forest, but the other lamp pointed straight. Jarv stayed put until Vivi had located the steps and climbed the first few.

Then Jarv urged the horses forward. Vivi watched as she drove off into the night, the beams from the headlights cutting wildly through the darkness.

Vivi was alone now.

The bottom few inches of her dress were sodden and dirty and Vivi could feel raindrops creeping into the neck. Halfway up the stone stairs, she stepped on to the hem and the fabric ripped.

No wonder the countess was never seen out in public if she had to manage all these steps every time she returned home. Vivi forced herself to keep climbing, getting closer to a warm, dry shelter with every step.

Near the top, she reached an unlatched wrought iron gate that swung back and forth, creaking. A flash of lightning lit up the sky and a strange, winged creature eyed her from the gatepost. Vivi jumped but quickly realized it was just a stone sculpture, one of a pair. She tried not to pay them any attention, ignoring their bulging eyes and talons glistening in the rain. She passed through the gate, securing the latch behind her.

After a few more steps, she reached the dark porch, which provided some respite from the rain. The great wooden door to the castle stood in front of her. It was arched and covered in iron studs. Vivi allowed herself a moment to regain her breath, then she tugged at the thick bell pull. From inside the castle came a deep clanging.

Icy rainwater continued to trickle down the back of her dress from her wet hair.

Seconds passed.

No one came to the door.

It was late. Vivi wasn't sure of the time, but she guessed it could already be the early hours of the next day.

She couldn't spend the night here in this porch.

Jarv had said she was the nearest neighbour. Where did she say she lived again? Five miles away? If there was no answer at the door, then Vivi would have to trudge all that way and seek shelter. Why couldn't Jarv have waited a few more minutes?

Just as Vivi was beginning to resign herself to the idea of a five-mile walk in the dark, the door swung open.

CHAPTER SIX
COUNTESS MAROZNY

In the doorway stood a tall woman in a black high-collared dress, with hair pulled back in a tight bun. Her pale, powdered face was brightly lit by a candle in a chamberstick, and the shape of the black dress was lost in the shadows. This gave the unnerving impression of a floating head. Vivi was standing on the top step, but the floor of the hall was yet another step up, which meant the severe-looking figure in the doorway loomed over her. The woman wrinkled her nose as she peered down at Vivi, looking from the dripping parasol to the soiled hem of her dress and back up to her face.

This woman did not look like a maid or a butler. In fact, she gave the distinct impression she owned the place.

Vivi found her voice. "Countess Marozny?" she asked, pronouncing each syllable clearly in her well-to-do voice.

"Yes," came the reply, sounding more like a question than an answer.

"My name is Miss Viviana DeRose."

The countess peered at her closely as if assessing something. "Alive!" she pronounced, triumphantly.

Vivi glanced up nervously. "I'm not sure I understand…"

"Your name – Viviana – means 'alive'."

"Oh," replied Vivi.

"And your full name is Miss Viviana De … Rose?" the countess repeated her name incredulously. Vivi nodded.

"I see. And why exactly, Miss DeRose, are you standing on my doorstep at this hour?"

"I am here because of your notice … the request.,. Your coach driver brought me here, but we were delayed due to the inclement weather."

The countess opened her eyes very wide. "My notice? Of

course! Why, you must forgive my surprise, but I've sent that same notice down to the local towns for a decade or more. For the past few years there has been little response." There was a pause and the countess smiled a small smile. "Now, I see, I have my response at last, even if it's not quite what I expected. Please, come in and dry yourself."

Vivi stepped up into the hallway and the countess closed the door behind her. A small part of Vivi wondered what she was walking into, although it was mainly a relief to leave the rain outside. They stood in a narrow hallway with carved wooden panels on each wall.

The countess's candle provided a pool of yellowy light, illuminating a coat rack, an umbrella stand and the black-and-white floor tiles on to which Vivi was dripping.

In the shadows stood a tall wooden clock in a case, with a delicately carved pattern that made Vivi think of spider webs. Vivi glanced at the clock face but couldn't make out the time in the dim light.

"Here, let me take your things while you dry off. I regret there are no staff available at this late hour."

Vivi nodded knowledgeably, as if she knew all about the availability of staff. She wondered why the countess was not tucked up in bed herself, but thought it was probably impertinent to ask. She placed her bag on the floor, shoved the tattered parasol in the umbrella stand and removed her sodden mantle. She felt ridiculous, knowing that the dress was inappropriate for the weather and occasion, let alone four inches too big around the waist and three inches too long.

As she was hanging Dol's mantle on the rack, the countess reached for Vivi's bag. "I will put this in your room for you to unpack later."

"No! I mean, I can't let you take that – it's heavy!" Vivi snatched it back. The bag fell open, and its contents dropped to the floor in a heap. It didn't take close examination to see her possessions were mainly pillowcases.

The countess blinked. "Not so heavy after all," she said, mildly.

"I ... my maid must've packed the wrong bag," said Vivi, bending to scoop up the items and stuff them back.

"No matter. Jarv will call back in the morning. We'll send her for the right bags."

"No!" Vivi couldn't bear the thought of the driver returning to Valesti to pick up her threadbare old frocks.

The countess met her gaze, her eyes holding an unspoken question.

"There is no need. This dress will suit me well." Vivi lifted her chin.

The countess paused for a moment, fingertips together as if giving the matter some thought. "Very well. Follow me. We will find you a light supper."

She turned and made her way down the corridor, the light from her candle casting long shadows on the stone walls. She moved surprisingly quickly despite a hobble in her walk, boot-heels clacking on the floor tiles. Vivi followed along behind, aware she was trailing dirt and trickles of rainwater. Although it was dry inside the castle, there was no warmth, and Vivi shivered and rubbed her hands together. They passed a staircase, then the countess stopped abruptly in front of two facing wooden doors. She opened the one on their right. "The dining room," she announced, leading the way in.

Vivi had never set foot in a dining room in her life and wasn't sure what to expect. When she stepped inside, she nearly gasped at the splendour. More polished wooden panels, a great fireplace with a painting of people and horses hanging above it. The room was dominated by a long table covered with a bright white cloth. It was big enough to seat all her cousins and more but was only set at one end, for one person. Light shone from a chandelier overhead and, on the table, tapered white candles flickered in crystal candlesticks. If the strong smell of smoked fish was anything to go by, then kippers were on the menu. Vivi's mouth watered.

The countess pulled out the seat at the head of the table. In this brighter light, Vivi could see the countess's hair was grey, but appeared almost black against the whiteness of her skin. It was hard to believe that she was the same age as Therese. Despite her fine dress and make-up, she had a frailer appearance. Vivi was sure she'd never last a day in the laundry.

"Please take a seat," said the countess.

"But surely this place is set for you. You weren't expecting me!"

The countess waved her protests away and Vivi sat, as instructed, in front of the shining silverware, bag at her feet. She hoped her clothes wouldn't leave damp patches on the floor or elegant furniture.

Her host took a place to Vivi's left. She removed the lid of the large silver dish – kippers, as Vivi had thought – and transferred a small plump fish on to a plate. She placed the plate in front of her guest, then poured tea from an ornate teapot into a delicate porcelain cup. She added milk and two cubes of sugar, then stirred and pushed the cup towards Vivi. Although there were spare cups, she poured no tea for herself and made no move to take any food. She smoothed out the stark white tablecloth in front of her where a plate should have been.

Vivi took a grateful sip of tea, enjoying the warmth of the steam coming from the cup almost as much as the sweet liquid itself. "Will you not be dining?" she asked her host.

The countess blinked. "I don't seem to have much of an appetite."

Having eaten very little all day, Vivi found it difficult to relate to that statement, but she let it pass without comment. Vivi looked at the array of cutlery in front of her and selected the fish knife. She knew what a fish knife was, and they'd even owned some at home. Her father had once brought home a whole canteen of cutlery, though he never did say where he'd found it.

Vivi slid her knife in above the fishtail and eased out the backbone and all the fine bones attached, depositing them on the side of the plate. The countess scrutinized Vivi as she navigated the tricky food. If it was some kind of etiquette test, then Vivi would pass. She'd grown up in a port town and could gut, skin and fillet any fish you could name, let alone debone it at the dinner table.

She took forkfuls of the smoked flesh and chewed each one, savouring the flavour and interspersing each mouthful with a sip of sweet tea. Delicious. The most delicious thing she'd eaten in a long time, but she didn't want the countess to think she was unused to fine food.

"Thank you, erm, Countess."

"You may call me 'my lady'."

"Ah, I see." Vivi swallowed. "Thank you, my lady."

"And I shall call you Miss DeRose, which is your family name, correct?"

Vivi nodded.

The countess leaned slightly towards Vivi, hands folded neatly on the table. "Tell me about your family."

Vivi had of course been waiting for this question and had some answers prepared. She took a deep breath. "My parents are both dead." (True.)

She took a forkful of kipper, chewed, and swallowed.

"I come from Ingusport, a port town. On the coast, obviously." (True.)

Forkful, chew, swallow.

"My father, Matthew DeRose, was captain of a sailing vessel and drowned at sea." (Lie, lie, true. Her father, Matthew Peste, did drown at sea, but after falling in the docks on his way home from The Ship tavern.)

The countess kept her direct gaze on Vivi as she sipped her tea.

"My mother kept house. I was educated at home. She died ... that is, she passed away of tuberculosis." (Lie, true, true. Ma and Vivi both worked at the fish market, earning enough to support themselves and her idle, layabout father. Her ma taught Vivi what she could whenever they could find the time.)

Forkful, chew, swallow.

"After their deaths, I was left without fortune and was sent to live with my mother's sister in Valesti." (True.)

"And why, may I ask, Miss DeRose, did you respond to my notice?"

"My aunt has many children and has found it difficult to support me. I hoped this opportunity might benefit all concerned." (True enough.)

The countess proffered a basket of bread rolls and Vivi took one. Her instinct was to rip it open, smear it across her plate to soak up all those buttery juices, and stuff the whole thing in her mouth. Instead, she broke off tiny pieces at a time, spread each one with butter and nibbled at it as a lady might.

A crystal decanter stood on the table. The countess unstoppered it. "Wine?"

Vivi's mouth was too full of bread to reply, so she shook her head.

"Of course, you are still a child," said the countess, absently, as she poured herself a glass and placed it on the table in front of her. "How old are you exactly?"

Vivi swallowed the bread. "Sixteen," she lied.

"Sixteen. Really?"

It sounded like a rhetorical question, so Vivi didn't reply.

As the countess moved the decanter back to its original position, a dribble of dark red wine dripped on to the tablecloth, like blood from a cut. The small spots slowly spread into purply-red blotches and Vivi had to stop herself from dabbing at them with a napkin. Perhaps she had learned something in the laundry after all. Dried wine stains were particularly difficult to remove – only chloride of lime would shift them.

The spots didn't seem to bother the countess, who barely glanced at them. She traced the diamond-shaped patterns in her glass with a fingernail, then brought the glass to her lips and took a small sip. "I like you, Miss DeRose. You have an interesting way about you and I suspect that, as your forename suggests, you might bring some life to this old place."

Vivi wondered if that meant she'd passed the interview. She was trying to formulate a polite way of asking (along with requesting another kipper), when the clock chimed – two deep, clanging sounds. Two o'clock, then – much later than she was usually up. She tried and failed to stifle a yawn.

The countess stood, pushed back her chair and lit her chamberstick from one of the candles on the table. "You're tired, Miss DeRose. I shall lead you to your room."

Vivi didn't protest. She pushed back her own chair, grabbed her bag and followed the countess out of the dining room. They walked back along the corridor towards the front door, the countess's footsteps echoing. Instead of going through to the entrance hall, they turned right, and headed up the staircase. The staircase was wide and splendid but the steps were steep. The countess climbed with some difficulty, slowing down as she did so.

"I'm afraid..." she said, wheezing with the exertion, "your bedchamber is some distance away, in the north tower. You, however, are young and sprightly. No doubt you'll manage these steps with ease."

Vivi smiled. If she were on her own, she would bound up the steps two at a time, but she kept patiently behind the countess.

On the first floor, they entered another cavernous room of a similar size to the dining room.

"The gallery," explained the countess, with a vague gesture towards the walls, as if it were normal to own a room for pictures and nothing else. The gallery was unlit, so Vivi couldn't see very well other than to notice that the paintings seemed to be portraits.

Before Vivi could examine them further, the countess picked up her pace again. They walked through a room containing a spinning wheel and tapestry frame, towards a door on the facing wall.

That door led to an unadorned stone corridor, with a much lower ceiling than the grand rooms Vivi was becoming used to. The countess stopped and unlocked a wooden door. "This will be your bedchamber."

Countess Marozny entered first, the glow of her candle revealing the room. It was small and basic. It was also round, which was peculiar. A single bed was pushed against one wall, leaving a curved gap on one side, into which a spindly wooden nightstand had been squashed. On that same wall, high up near the ceiling, was a small curtain-covered window, which was currently being hammered with rain. A single armoire and marble-topped washstand stood opposite. A threadbare rug provided some softness on the stone floor and a folded blanket rested on top of a squat three-legged stool. Perhaps the room had once belonged to a servant. Still, for the past year, Vivi hadn't even had a bed to herself, so having her own room was the height of luxury.

The countess lit a candle on the nightstand. "I'll leave you to unpack now," she said with a wry smile, perhaps thinking of the meagre contents of Vivi's bag. "The housekeeper, Madam Varney, will bring you breakfast in the morning."

"Thank you," said Vivi, although her eyelids were so heavy she'd stopped paying attention.

The countess turned in the doorway. "The key to this room is in the lock. I suggest you keep your door locked at night and put the key somewhere safe, Miss DeRose."

The countess gave no reason and Vivi didn't ask. As soon as her host had left, she obediently turned the large brass key in its lock and put the key on her nightstand. She'd never heard of a place where you had to lock yourself in at night, but then she'd never lived in a place with locks on the doors. She shivered, trying to forget that her new home was known as 'Vampire Towers'. She had to get that idea out of her head. The vampires had been gone for years, and the castle was just a scary-looking place. A scary-looking place where she had her *own bedchamber.*

She gazed around at her new surroundings, although there wasn't much to see. The air inside the room smelled stale and dusty, like a trunk that had been opened after a long winter. It didn't sound as though the countess had many guests. Of course, there had been at least two other girls at the castle before her. Dorïce and Margareta, they'd said at the laundry. Years before. Had they slept in this room?

The rain sounded louder than Vivi had ever known, like fingers drumming on a table. Maybe the circular room made it echo or maybe she was simply closer to the sky than she'd ever been. She stood on tiptoes on the bed and peeked through the curtains at the high window. She could just about see out, but there was nothing except rain and darkness.

She explored the rest of the room. On the washstand stood an empty porcelain pitcher – white with a delicate pink pattern – and matching bowl. She peeked under the bed. Nothing to be found except a chamber pot in the usual place.

It didn't take her long to prepare for bed and, when she was ready, she stood shivering in her shift, eyeing the bed suspiciously. It probably hadn't been slept in for years and, although the sheets were pulled tightly across the mattress, anything could have crept inside. Insects. Mice. Bats even. She untucked the sheets and pulled them back to check. No bedwarmer, but all clean and crisp, at least. Reassured, she put out the lamp. As she snuggled down and pulled the sheet up to her chin, a flash of lightning lit up the room, giving its contents an eerie blueish glow.

Would this really be her home for the next year? Countess Marozny seemed to have accepted her, but the notice had mentioned an interview. The conversation at the dining table had felt a bit like an interview, but there were no other applicants as far as she could tell. It was always possible the countess would change her mind and call for a coach to take Vivi home the next day. Vivi hoped not. She had no desire to go back to her aunt's. Despite the cold and the strangeness, this was a wonderful chance for her to be whoever she wanted. To create opportunities for a brand-new future. Vivi wasn't going to run away before her adventure had even started. Besides, the castle would surely look much less creepy when the sun came out the next day.

Rain continued to pelt the window and the occasional thunderclap rattled the walls. She whisked the blanket off the stool and put the extra layer over her. Would she ever sleep in these conditions?

But within moments she was sleeping the sleep of the dead.

CHAPTER SEVEN
CASTLE BEZNA

The air was awhirl with flapping black wings. Airborne intruders – dozens of them, as many as a hundred, filling the room. Bats! How did they get in? The window was shut – the door locked.

"Get away! Get out!" she tried to shout, but her voice had gone. She held her hands in front of her face to protect herself. The creatures whirled closer, beating their wings, screeching at such a high pitch her eardrums threatened to burst. One was bigger than the rest, with pointed fangs and piercing eyes. It was

moving its mouth as though it was speaking. It had a message for her...

"Breakfast!"

Vivi opened her eyes. She sat up fast, heart racing. Someone was knocking on a door.

"Breakfast, Miss DeRose!"

Where was she? She looked around at the unfamiliar room, with its curved walls. A pale hint of daylight was shining through the drapes at the high window. Of course, in Castle Bezna. She'd slept deeply. The bats were just a dream.

Heavy rain was still pattering against the windowpane. The knocking on the door came again.

"Just a moment!" Vivi rubbed her hands over her face to wake herself fully, crawled out of bed and went to open the door. The key. She nearly forgot it was on her nightstand. She grabbed it and fumbled about until she'd managed to insert it in the unfamiliar keyhole and unlock the door. Feeling underdressed and frozen in just her shift, she hid behind the door and peeped around.

It was a plump-cheeked woman with curly grey hair. She wore a grey day dress and a white apron and cap, with a shawl draped around her shoulders. Everything about her looked plump and puffy, from her face to her cap to her sleeves. Next to her was a wheeled trolley. She reached towards it and passed Vivi a jug of fresh water for the washstand. Vivi must have looked unsettled because the woman smiled at her kindly. "Strange dream, was it, my dear?" she asked.

Vivi blinked, her eyes gritty. "A little strange, yes."

"That'll just be the long journey and the unfamiliar place. You'll soon settle in. Visitors always do."

Vivi crossed the room to put the jug on the washstand, then hurried back to the door. "So, you're the housekeeper?"

The woman chuckled. "Oh yes, I'm the housekeeper – or castle keeper as I like to say. Also, chief cook and bottlewasher, seamstress, laundress and butler. Madam Varney at your service."

"Oh. Good morning, Madam Varney. I'm Viviana … erm … DeRose."

"Well, I know that already, Miss DeRose." Madam Varney lifted a tray with a silver dome from the trolley. "I also hear you like kippers?" Madam Varney removed the plate cover and the familiar smoky smell wafted through into the room.

Vivi smiled. "Oh yes."

The housekeeper handed her the tray. "I can see you're not dressed yet, so I won't come in. There's a housecoat in the armoire which you can wear until I've finished your new outfit. It shouldn't take much longer. I'll bring it up later."

"You've nearly finished making a whole outfit? But how?"

Madam Varney chuckled again. "I've been up since sunrise. It's nearly eleven o'clock now. You had a lie-in, my dear! Anyway, I didn't make the outfit from scratch. I'm adjusting one of the countess's for you. She felt you needed some practical garments to wear around the castle. A sort of uniform."

A uniform. Vivi had never had a uniform and she wasn't sure she wanted one. She pictured the shapeless woollen dresses of the children in the Ingusport workhouse. She could have been wearing one of those dresses herself if Aunt Ina hadn't taken her in. And now look at her, waking up in a real-life castle at whatever time she chose. If she had to don a jester's outfit in order to stay here, then she'd oblige. She realized with a little surge of glee, if the countess was going to the effort and expense of dressing her, she probably wasn't planning to send Vivi back to Valesti any time soon.

"Do you know your waist measurement, my dear?"

Vivi put her hands to her waist. "No, I—"

"Not to worry! I can see from here you're taller than her ladyship and a little bigger around the middle. Which is just as she said. Mind you, anyone would be bigger around the waist than her ladyship – she has the measurements of a fire poker. No matter. If I don't get it exactly right first time, I can always adjust the outfit again once it's on you."

"Thank you—"

"That's enough chit-chat," said Madam Varney, with the air of someone who had important work to be getting on with. "You eat your breakfast while it's hot, then freshen up, and I'll bring you your clothes."

Madam Varney wheeled her serving trolley down the corridor, leaving Vivi feeling stunned. Eleven o'clock in the morning. She hadn't slept that late in … well, she'd never slept that late. She clicked the door shut and put the breakfast tray on her nightstand. She sat on the bed with the plate of kippers balanced on her knees and ate listening to the rain on the window. Breakfast in bed wasn't something she'd ever experienced before either, and she wondered if it would be like this every morning. She also wondered if she'd be served kippers at every mealtime. Not that she was complaining – they were delicious and warming and a much better breakfast than she was used to. Back in Valesti, she'd have a hunk of bread, spread with butter on a good day.

It was only as she ate her meal in the quiet, knife and fork scraping the plate, that she asked herself why her host had been sitting down in front of a plate of kippers in the middle of the night. And hadn't eaten a thing.

Shortly after she finished her breakfast, there was a second knock at the door. It was Madam Varney again, holding out some clothes and beaming proudly. "Shall we swap? Your old breakfast tray for this new outfit?"

"Oh yes," said Vivi, handing over the tray. "It looks beautiful." It did. Much better than the sort of uniform she'd pictured. It was simple yet elegant – an ankle-length dark green skirt with matching fitted waistcoat over a simple white button-through blouse. Vivi would never have known it wasn't brand-new.

The housekeeper smiled and put the tray down on her trolley. "I'll wait out here while you try them on, in case they're in need of alteration."

Vivi closed the door, discarded the housecoat and began to put on the new outfit over her shift. The fabric was much thicker than the thin cotton dresses she wore at the laundry. The skirt fitted neatly over her hips and the blouse buttoned up nicely. At her collar there was a necktie in the same colour green as the skirt. She tied it in a relaxed bow, doing the best she could without a looking glass.

"How does it look?" Madam Varney called through the door.

Vivi didn't know how it looked, but it felt perfect – fitted enough without being restrictive and not too flouncy like last night's attire. She felt older and so much more sophisticated than in her usual clothes. There were deep pockets in the skirt and she sunk her hands into them and twirled around once, watching the skirt swirl around her. Then she removed her hands from the pockets and attempted to appear more sedate.

"It all fits great," she said, opening the door so Madam Varney could take a look. Then she remembered her new persona. "I mean it's dil-ayt-ful."

Madam Varney smiled. "Oh yes. Don't you look a picture? A real beauty. No adjustments needed?"

Vivi shook her head. "I don't think so."

"I told you I had a good eye for these things. Then you're all ready. I'm sure you'll want to explore today to get your bearings."

Exploring a castle! Vivi could hardly believe her luck. "Where am I allowed to go?"

"Anywhere you like, my dear."

"Anywhere?"

"Yes – the countess said to treat this place like your home. Just make sure you avoid her ladyship's bedchamber, which is the first room you'll find in the south wing. Be quiet around that part of the castle, too. The countess'll still be asleep. Other than that, you are free to explore wherever you like."

"Be quiet in the south wing," repeated Vivi, trying to make sure she remembered everything. She'd have to figure out where all these different places were. "When *will* I see the countess?"

"At dinner time. She has asked you await her in the dining room at seven o'clock this evening, once she's awoken."

"I see," said Vivi. She didn't really see at all. Would Countess Marozny sleep all day? Was this normal countess behaviour?

"One more thing – don't draw back the drapes," added Madam Varney.

"In which room?"

"In any room."

"Oh. Even in the daytime?"

"At any time, my dear."

Vivi stared at her. She'd been hoping that the castle would look more cheerful in the daylight. "May I ask why? It must make it dreadfully dark and gloomy."

"It's just one of the Castle Bezna rules. The countess isn't well and finds sunlight triggers her headaches."

"Oh." This was strange to Vivi, whose mother always used to talk about the benefits of air and sunlight. When Ma had been ill, she'd often asked Vivi to open the window or to let her look at the sky.

But it didn't matter what Vivi's ma used to think, or even what Vivi herself thought. Things worked differently at Castle Bezna and Vivi was going to have to get used to a new way of life. At least she knew she was capable of that.

Madam Varney didn't issue any more rules. She trundled off with her trolley once again. "Make yourself at home, my dear, and I'll be down in the kitchen if you need anything."

CHAPTER EIGHT

THE LETTER

Once she'd freshened up, Vivi finally left the bedchamber, ready to discover what Castle Bezna looked like during the day. Daylight, however, was in short supply. Vivi had been right about the castle being dark and gloomy. The windowless stone corridor leading from her bedchamber was lit with flickering candles, so it could have been the middle of the night. It was also freezing – even colder than her room. Despite the lack of windows, a draught whistled in from somewhere and it felt like January rather than September.

This wasn't normal, was it? If Vivi didn't know better, she'd start to think that her host was displaying some remarkably vampire-like behaviour. Awake all night and sleeping all day. Not touching her dinner. But Vivi knew she was only thinking this because of the gossip she'd heard in Valesti. She reminded herself of the facts: there had been twelve vampires, all dead and gone. The countess's behaviour was strange, yes, but maybe all lonely old countesses acted that way. She'd not met one before and she was unlikely to meet another.

Vivi would try to put any thoughts of vampires out of her mind. She walked as briskly as she could to warm herself up. She marched down the corridor, through the workshop and into the gallery.

Here, too, there was no sign of daylight. At least the candles flickering in sconces made the room brighter than it had been the night before. What a room it was! It was twice as big as her aunt's laundry, yet this room was for nothing but paintings. It was the sort of room where Aunt Ina would tell you to keep quiet, behave and touch nothing. The sort of room that made Vivi want to do the opposite.

The big expanse of polished floor would be perfect for turning cartwheels. *Make yourself at home*, Madam Varney had instructed. And, seeing as there was no sign of Madam Varney or the countess, she did just that, springing wobblily on to her hands, then collapsing in a heap, banging her knee. She never had been any good at cartwheels – Dol was much better.

She got to her feet, rubbing her knee, thinking of her fall from Mister Vrdoljak's plum tree. That felt like a long, long time ago, not just two days.

Limping, she examined the paintings on the wall. The golden frames were all a similar size and contained portraits of people in old-fashioned clothes. There was a name painted in the bottom corner of each picture, in fancy curly script. They were all different, so they must be the names of the subjects rather than the painter. Interested for a moment, she looked at the first picture. She wasn't very good at reading and the flickering candlelight made it even harder to make out the letters. S-E-L-I-G. Selig.

He was a serious-looking man with a pale face, thin twisted moustache and dark hair. He looked as though he could be a distant ancestor of Countess Marozny. Maybe they were all Maroznys. Maybe they were the long dead vampires! She stopped. Despite her best efforts, she was thinking about vampires again. They didn't look at all scary, though.

She moved on to the next one, which was more difficult to read. N-I-K-A-L-A-U-S. No. N-I-K-L-A-U-S. Niklaus. He looked particularly smart with a hat and stripy cravat. His skin tone was darker than Selig's and he didn't look at all related to the countess.

Reading every name would no doubt take her ages. If Dol was here, she'd read the names for her. Vivi didn't bother looking at the rest: long dead people who had nothing to do with her anyway. She skipped past them and headed for the door on the south side of the gallery. There was more exploring to do.

Vivi found herself in another corridor, with doorways at regular intervals. She almost tried the first one but stopped herself just in time. Hadn't Madam Varney said the first room was the countess's bedchamber? She had to keep quiet around here.

Vivi explored all the other rooms. All bedchambers, although they didn't appear to be in use. The drapes were drawn shut and a musty smell emanated from each. White dust covers were draped over the furniture and, peeking under some of them, Vivi found little of interest.

These rooms were all much bigger than the one where Vivi had spent the night. Why hadn't she been offered one of these, rather than the strange, circular room in the north tower? Maybe they weren't ready for guests, or maybe the countess didn't like visitors too close to her own sleeping quarters.

Vivi shrugged and kept exploring. She climbed a spiral

staircase leading up to the second floor and discovered a room that looked like an old nursery. This room was also draped in dust covers, but she found many more interesting items. She uncovered a doll's house – Castle Bezna in miniature! – but quickly covered it back up again. She found anything in miniature to be rather creepy.

Behind it was the unmistakable shape of a rocking horse. She used to see them in the window of the big houses in Ingusport and always wondered what it would be like to ride one. She threw back the dust cover and admired its smooth body, painted dappled grey, its lifelike wiry mane and golden-brown glass eyes. It was still in pristine condition and looked as though it had barely been played with.

"Hello horsey," she said, shifting it back and forth, but she found herself checking over her shoulder as she did so, checking no one was watching. She couldn't bring herself to actually ride on the horse. If Dol had been here, they would have ridden it and Vivi would have made up a galloping song. Vivi drew the dust cover back over the horse's head. She couldn't think of any songs right now.

Vivi left the nursery and made her way back down the spiral staircase to the first floor. She then completed the loop back round to the workshop, glancing in one more room on the way – the library. It was, unsurprisingly, stacked full of old books. Dol would have definitely investigated that room, but Vivi was quite happy to give it a miss. Instead, she skipped past, through to the workshop and back through the gallery, taking the stairs back down to the ground floor.

She headed down the corridor but instead of taking the door on the right, which led to the dining room, she took the one on the left.

Straight away, she knew this part of the castle was different to the others. It was the smell that hit her first – this time, there wasn't a hint of mustiness. The smells that filled her nostrils were delightful and unmistakably foody. Tarragon drying on racks, onions frying in butter and cakes browning in the oven. She must be nearing the kitchen. She walked through a shelved area, with labelled bottles and jars on one side and folded linens and doilies on the other. Above the shelves hung ham hocks, pheasants and bunches of herbs.

The little pantry area led into a huge kitchen, bigger and better stocked than Vivi could have imagined. Like the rest of the castle, the windows were shuttered, but the fire was blazing and oil lamps hung from the ceiling, making it the brightest room Vivi had encountered yet. A long scrubbed wooden table and chairs were at the centre of the room. On the right was a large dresser filled with patterned china. Vivi would love to own something like that if she was ever lucky enough to have a house of her own. Or a castle.

Next to the dresser, various-shaped jelly moulds hung from the wall, like barnacles clinging to a rock. A clock ticked on the mantelpiece. A pot bubbled on the stove. And working away at the stove was Madam Varney, humming as she stirred.

Behind the bubbling, ticking and humming, Vivi realized that music was playing at a low volume. It was coming from an odd device on the side: a wooden box with a handle and a great brass horn, like a trumpet. Vivi knew the tune. A music hall comedy favourite – one Ma and their friends used to sing at the fish market. Snippets of words and phrases came back to her, and she began to sing along.

"Oh, how I miss you when you're out at sea
Won't you bring a little something back for me?"

Madam Varney turned, her hand flying to her chest. "Oh, Miss DeRose, you gave me a shock!" She chuckled. "You must think me a silly old lady, humming along to these songs when I think no one's listening. This gramophone was gathering dust, so her ladyship let me bring it down to the kitchen. Here, let me turn it off."

The housekeeper wiped her hands on her apron and made to turn off the machine, but Vivi crossed the room and put out a hand to stop her. "No, please leave it. I like this one!" She turned the volume dial up, and put on her best music hall voice.

*"A memory of our love when you are gone
And if that something's gold you can't go wrong!"*

Madam Varney laughed, grabbed the corners of her apron and danced along, swishing the apron in time to the tune.

*"Porcelain or silk will do just fine
But diamonds, pearls and rubies are divine!"*

They sang along to the whole of the song, then listened to a couple more tunes, both singing any words they happened to know. They flung out their arms theatrically. Vivi grabbed a couple of tea towels and spun them around in her hands like ribbons.

Afterwards, when the music stopped, Madam Varney was laughing so hard tears ran down her face. "Oh, my dear! I haven't sung like that for years!"

Vivi grinned. "I love to sing. And dance."

"So did I, when I was your age," said the housekeeper. "I've always thought how marvellous it would be to see the gallery restored to a ballroom for parties and dances."

"Yes," agreed Vivi, smiling. That's what she'd do if this were her castle.

"But it's not the music that brought you down to the kitchen – you must be ready for luncheon?"

"Luncheon?" Vivi couldn't believe it was that time already. "I've only just eaten breakfast!"

"Well, this is true, my dear, but are you sure I can't tempt you to a bite of something? How about a slice of fruit cake and some tea?"

Vivi accepted happily, pulling up a chair at the table. Madam Varney cut her a generous wedge of cake, which she placed in front of her. "Fresh out of the oven," she said.

The cake was warm, moist and crumbly. Vivi munched away while Madam Varney fetched a pot of tea, then went back to her work.

"Do you need help with anything?" asked Vivi.

"Help? Bless you, my dear. A kind sentiment, but it wouldn't do for you to be helping in the kitchen now, would it? What would her ladyship say?"

Vivi shrugged, her mouth full. She didn't know what the

countess would say if she found her peeling carrots. She wasn't sure what her position here was at all. She was supposed to be a lady's companion, but the countess slept all day. She had a uniform and her bedchamber was tucked away in the north tower like a servant's, yet she hadn't been allocated any work. The notice had also mentioned an 'education'. It was all very confusing. Vivi hoped the countess would explain it all when she saw her later on.

Madam Varney brought a spoonful of the bubbling sauce from the pan up to her nose, smelled it, then added more seasoning. While the housekeeper's back was turned, Vivi finished her cake, dabbing at the leftover crumbs with her fingertip. She wondered if it would be rude to ask for another slice, but decided against it. Instead, she wandered back over to the gramophone and put on the record once again, at a low volume.

The housekeeper turned back to face Vivi, red and sweaty from the steam of the stove. She fanned her face with some oven gloves. "We clearly share a taste in music, my dear! How is it you know those old songs?"

Vivi thought of all the women at the fish market, linking arms and singing along raucously. "My ma…" She stopped. Was that what well-to-do folk called their mothers? "My mama used to enjoy them," she said cautiously.

"I see." It looked as though Madam Varney might ask her another question but she just smiled, put on the oven gloves and then turned again to open the oven door. She lifted the pot and transferred it to the oven.

Vivi continued to gaze around the room. A deep butler's sink was fitted into an alcove with a drying rack above, blue-and-white china plates slotted into it.

Next to the sink, a grisly sight caught her by surprise. A headless chicken lay on the counter, its neck hanging limply over the side, blood draining from its lifeless body. Vivi was mesmerized by the steady dripping of blood into the basin below. Where was its head? Her stomach turned and she wrinkled her nose. Madam Varney chuckled. "Not squeamish, are you, my dear?"

"No!" said Vivi defensively. "I'm not squeamish about anything. I've gutted more fish than you've had hot dinners! And I've prepared chickens for the table at my aunt's. I'll kill one now if you like!"

Vivi realized she'd let her well-to-do voice slip and revealed more about herself than she'd intended.

Madam Varney raised an eyebrow. "That won't be necessary. One chicken for dinner should be quite sufficient, don't you think?"

"Yes," replied Vivi, looking down at her empty plate. The blood dripping into the basin sounded so loud, Vivi couldn't believe she hadn't noticed it earlier.

Madam Varney put her hands on her hips. "I hope you don't think me impertinent, but I wonder if we share more than a taste in music? If our backgrounds are perhaps more similar than you would lead people to believe?"

Vivi drank the last dregs of her tea, pointing to her mouth to show she couldn't speak while she was drinking. As Vivi replaced her cup on the saucer, Madam Varney spoke again. "You can trust me, Miss DeRose. I understand sometimes people like us have to take opportunities where we can. I wouldn't tell her ladyship a thing about it, but it would be nice to know the real you."

Vivi believed her. And it would be a relief if she didn't have to keep up her act everywhere in the castle. She swallowed the tea and let the words flow out of her. "I'm from Ingusport. My family were poor and I worked at the fish market."

"I see," said Madam Varney. "And your real name?"

"Viviana Peste. But everyone calls me Vivi."

Madam Varney nodded and patted Vivi's arm. "A lovely name, my dear. It's good to know the real you. I shall, however, continue to call you Miss DeRose and treat you just as I would any other lady's companion. I wouldn't want to make any slip-ups in front of her ladyship. But I'm here if you need me. You can come and ask me anything at all."

"Thank you, Madam Varney." Vivi wondered if she really could ask *anything*. She wondered what the housekeeper would say if she mentioned vampires. Had Madam Varney heard any rumours about a thirteenth vampire on the loose? No doubt she'd think it silly. But Vivi didn't get a chance to ask. Madam Varney was already clearing away the plate and cup.

"It won't do for you to sit here in the kitchen all afternoon – you must leave me to my work and continue to explore the castle."

Vivi pushed back her chair and stood up. "Do you think I could come and have breakfast down here tomorrow?" As luxurious as a tray in her bedchamber had been, she'd felt lonely eating alone.

"Of course you can, my dear. And there is always a piece of fruitcake in the tin if you fancy company and a chat."

"Thank you, Madam Varney," said Vivi again. She was grateful there was at least one place in this cold and lonely castle where she could feel warm.

*

After her visit to the kitchen, there wasn't much castle left to explore. She longed to go outside, but the rain still hadn't stopped and the thought of getting cold and wet again was too much to bear. Instead, she retreated to her bedchamber and lay on the bed. It was hours until dinner. Not that she was hungry – she was simply unsure how to fill her time. Who'd have thought you could be in a castle, with twenty rooms or more, yet still be bored? No wonder the countess wanted a companion.

As she lay there, Vivi remembered she'd promised to write Dol a letter. But she had no paper or writing equipment. That was the problem with promises: they slipped out so easily, before you had a chance to think them through. Still, it couldn't be that difficult to find some stationery somewhere in this place. She seemed to remember that one of the rooms in the south wing had a writing bureau hidden under a dust cover.

She found the bureau in the second room along from Countess Marozny's bedchamber, just inside the door. She pulled off the dust cover. The bureau was made of shiny mahogany, and smelled of furniture polish. Vivi turned the little brass key in the sloped front, which dropped open on its hinges, extending into a gilded burgundy leather writing desk. Inside were various drawers and shelves with everything one might need to write a letter. On one side was paper, sealing wax and a seal depicting a scrolling 'M' – for *Marozny*, she guessed. On the other side was a pen and a couple of cut-glass inkwells that reminded her of the wine glasses from the dining room.

In one of the drawers was a small cardboard box, just big enough to sit in the palm of her hand. It rattled when she shook it and had some writing on the side. She sighed at the sight of it. Quite long words. *Fl-a-ming F-u-ses.* Flaming fuses. She opened the box to reveal little wooden sticks with black ends. She knew what they were – chemical matches that ignited by themselves. The castle was full of luxuries like these, which saved you having to light candles from the fire. Unable to resist, Vivi leaned over and struck one of the matches on the rough stone wall. The tip flamed into a bright ball of light. Panicking, she dropped it on to the writing desk, blowing at the same time. Luckily, the flame was quickly extinguished. She picked up the burnt-out match and put it back in the box, then thrust the box into her right pocket. Nobody would miss them.

She quite fancied sitting here at the desk to write her letter to Dol, but she needed more light. Who was going to know if she opened the curtains? She'd draw them back when she'd finished.

The ceilings were high and the heavy curtains were made of floor-length grey velvet. She dragged one of them to the side, hoping for a spectacular view of the mountains, but was disappointed. The windows were latticed and so filthy she could barely see through them. She supposed if you kept your curtains shut all year round, there was probably little reason to wash the windows. What Vivi could see through the grime and the steady rain was mainly just trees, of the same sort she'd gazed at on the journey the day before.

Just enough daylight filtered in for her to write. Vivi crossed back to the bureau and drew up a stool. She ran her hand along the padded leather of the writing desk. The match had luckily made no mark. She wondered who the desk had belonged to. One of the Marozny family? Or perhaps one of the resident vampires? She shivered. Did vampires write letters? She found it hard to believe they had really been here in the castle. She'd definitely ask Madam Varney about them next time.

Vivi took a piece of paper, which was satisfyingly thick, white and smooth. She dipped the expensive-looking pen in the inkwell, but the blue-black ink had dried in a crusty layer. The only inkwell she could find that was full contained bright red ink. That would have to do. She dipped her pen in, but as she brought it out, she spattered tiny red spots over the whiteness before she'd even put pen to paper. Now it did look like a vampire's letter. Maybe they wrote in human blood. The thought made her shudder, although she was certain from the colour and smell that this was ink, not blood. She started writing, leaving a new trail of inky blobs.

How she disliked writing. Did people really do this for amusement?

She wrote Dol's name, trying hard to join up the last two letters as Dol had shown her.

Dol,

She knew she should have started with a different salutation, like 'my dearest cousin', or at least 'Dear Dol', but what a waste of words that would be, plus she wasn't sure she could spell them all correctly. Dol knew who she was, after all.

What should she write next? Dol had asked Vivi to let her know she was safe, so maybe that's how her letter should begin. She dipped her pen again and formed the next few words.

Got hir as pland.

What else would Dol want to know? Vivi would have liked to have told her about the bats on the journey, the strange weather and her first view of Castle Bezna. She'd have liked to tell her about the enormous rooms and the long, dark corridors and her unusual host.

But that was a lot of hard words.

Vivi decided a picture might tell her story better, so she drew the mountains with the castle at the top. She drew the coach travelling up a steep path, surrounded by bats. It wasn't a very skilful drawing, but was still much better than any of her writing. The horses looked like long-legged sheep. She drew the full moon, the hail and pelting rain and Countess Marozny in her doorway. She liked the idea of drawing Madam Varney in the kitchen, but decided that could wait until her next letter. Then she thought a drawing on its own wouldn't do – she still needed to write something.

People always talked about the food on their travels, didn't they? The weather and the food. She wrote one last sentence:

Hav iten lots of kipprs.

She drew a small fish and then signed her name at the bottom, like Dol had taught her.

Vivi

Vivi stared at her writing on the page. The red ink was hideous and the words looked large and badly formed, as though written by a young child. The drawing was plain bad. Dol would only laugh at it. No, Dol *wouldn't* laugh at it because she was too nice, but she *should* laugh. Vivi would laugh if she were Dol and received a letter like this one. She scrunched the paper into a ball and threw it on to the floor.

She went back to the open curtain and dragged it across the window. Then she stuffed the writing tools into her pockets – paper and pen in one side, ink, wax and the seal in the other. She'd take it all away with her and then maybe, when she was in the privacy of her bedchamber, she'd write to Dol again. Properly.

CHAPTER NINE

AN EDUCATION

Finally, the clock in the hall chimed seven. Vivi made her way to the dining room as instructed, but there was no sign of the countess. She wasn't sure if she should sit at the table or not, so she stayed on her feet, pacing around the room.

This time, there were two places set at the table, with sparkling glasses as before. The countess's glass was filled with wine and Vivi's with water. In the centre was a plate of tiny slices of toast.

Vivi had been hungry for most of the afternoon. Madam Varney's delicious cake had been hours ago.

She would have been tempted to swipe some toast from the table, but her appetite vanished as her nerves took over. She wasn't sure exactly what she was nervous for: she'd already met the countess and survived the experience of a meal and the accompanying questions. Perhaps she was unsettled because last night felt like such a long time ago, almost as if it had been part of her strange dream. Would she finally find out what she was here for? And when would her education begin? What would it look like? Her mind drifted off as she imagined walking across the gallery with books on her head.

"Please, take a seat."

Vivi jumped. Countess Marozny stood in the doorway, her voice projecting across the room. Vivi hadn't heard her ladyship's boot-heels clicking down the corridor.

The countess looked as Vivi remembered. She was even wearing the same black, high-collared dress as the night before, or at least a very similar one. Vivi wondered if she was in mourning and, if so, who had died.

The countess smiled wryly. "Do excuse me, I didn't mean to startle you." She looked Vivi up and down in much the same way as she'd done the evening before. "Ah yes, the uniform quite becomes you. Less ostentatious than the garment you were wearing yesterday."

Vivi had no idea what *ostentatious* meant, but she was pleased the countess liked her new clothes. "Thank you. I like the uniform too … my lady." She was still so nervous she'd almost forgotten how to address the countess.

The countess inclined her head to acknowledge Vivi's words, then gestured to the table. "Let us sit and eat," she said.

They sat.

The countess pointed to the centre of the table. "Please, have some pâté."

Vivi hadn't realized there was anything inside the small ceramic pot. She took two slices of toast and spread them with the thick brown paste. The countess ignored the food altogether, so Vivi held back from taking any more, not wanting to appear greedy in contrast. The slices were very small, though, and she was worried she might be hungry in the night. She tried to savour each one, nibbling away and enjoying the rich, salty flavours. The countess was distracted, gazing into the flickering flames of the candles and tapping her long nails on the plate, then the table.

The minutes ticked by and Vivi wondered if she should be the one to start a conversation. She was supposed to be an entertaining companion after all.

"Countess Marozny? I mean … my lady?" (She pronounced it 'my laydee', doing her best to sound like the rich clients at the laundry.)

The countess looked up sharply. "Yes, Miss DeRose?"

"I was wondering … what is expected of me here at the castle? That is, what should I *do* all day?"

The countess tapped her nails again. "Of course. I should have explained your role. You will be expected to sit with me every evening at dinner and converse as we are doing now. You will receive formal lessons from me, and I have some expectation that you will pursue self-study during the daytime. Other than that, you are free to explore and do whatever it is that young people enjoy." She smiled thinly and Vivi nodded, swallowing another piece of toast. Formal education. Self-study. She still didn't really know what it all meant.

The door swung open and Madam Varney arrived in the room with a whole roast chicken, its crisp skin golden in the candlelight. Vivi realized then that the pâté was just the first course and not the entire meal.

Of course. Chicken. Vivi should have remembered. It looked

much more appetizing circled with roast potatoes than it had with its neck dangling over the counter. Madam Varney bent to carve and Vivi grinned conspiratorially at her new friend. The housekeeper didn't return the smile. It was as if Vivi's earlier trip to the kitchen had never happened. Madam Varney had said she would treat Vivi as she would any other lady's companion, but Vivi still felt inexplicably bereft.

Madam Varney brought out more bowls of food, side dishes of cabbage and carrots, and heaped spoonfuls on to Vivi's plate until it was full. A jug of herby sauce stood on the table and Vivi poured it liberally over her meat and vegetables.

They ate in silence to begin with, or rather, Vivi ate, whereas the countess spooned tiny portions of food on to her own plate and ignored them. She swirled the wine in its crystal glass. "Do you find the food to your liking, Viviana?" she asked.

"Oh, yes, it's delicious," said Vivi, automatically. It *was* delicious. The sort of food she would only normally eat on a special occasion. "I pah-ticulah-ly love the sauce." It was different to the garlic sauce her aunt served with chicken, but almost as good.

The countess smiled and dragged the tip of one of her slender fingers through the sauce on her plate in a decidedly un-aristocratic sort of way. She licked it off. "Mmm, yes, I have to agree. Garlic sauce is my favourite."

A laugh burst out from Vivi and the countess smiled back. The countess probably thought Vivi was surprised at her table manners. In fact, Vivi was laughing with relief – the countess couldn't possibly be a vampire if she liked garlic so much.

Vivi gulped back more laughter and went back to eating the meal, taking much daintier bites than she would have done at home. Apart from the sauce, the countess ate nothing. She just continued to take small sips of wine.

Perhaps confusion showed on Vivi's face, because Countess Marozny remarked, "You must excuse my meagre appetite, Viviana. I have lived alone for many years and I have habits some might think strange."

Vivi was pretty sure *anyone*, not just *some* people, would find the behaviour strange. "Er, maybe a little," she said. " I s'pose … I mean I suh-pose it seems a shame not to pah-take in this delicious fare."

The countess nodded. "I haven't been feeling quite my best lately and prefer a simple meal in my chamber before I retire for bed. Madam Varney continues to try and tempt me with dishes like these, but I find them increasingly too rich for my liking.

However, I do enjoy the lively conversation that takes place across the dinner table." The countess smiled and looked straight at Vivi. "What are your interests, Viviana? Do you have any particular accomplishments?"

Vivi had a feeling her own accomplishments, which included gutting fish and stealing plums, would not be what the countess had in mind. She took her time to chew her mouthful while she considered the question. Watercolour and needlework, while suitable, would be risky answers to give. She might be asked to demonstrate her skills. She needed a safer option, something closer to the truth.

She swallowed and smiled. "I enjoy … music." (True.)

The countess tipped her head to one side. "Really? How interesting. I must confess to having very little musical ability myself."

Vivi breathed an inward sigh of relief.

"What do you play?" asked the countess.

Vivi took another mouthful and chewed slowly. Of course the countess would assume she played an instrument, rather than just listened to music. What answer could she give? Not the piano – there could well be a grand piano under a dust sheet somewhere. Those other girls before her had probably been perfect pianists.

Something less common, that was less likely to be at hand. "Piccolo," said Vivi. "I play the piccolo."

The countess raised both eyebrows. "How unusual. I don't believe I've met a piccolo player before. I don't suppose you have the instrument here at the castle with you?"

"Sadly not. It was in my other bag," replied Vivi, who wasn't entirely sure what a piccolo even was.

"Your other bag ... yes, of course," replied the countess, going quiet and staring at some nondescript part of the wall behind Vivi's right ear.

There was a long pause, where the only sound was the clock ticking and Vivi's cutlery scraping on her porcelain plate as she finished her meal. The countess stared at the flickering candle flames until she appeared to remember once again she had a guest.

"So, Viviana ... Madam Varney tells me you reside in Valesti? Our valley town. Please, tell me about it. I believe the town is known for its fluffy plum dumplings?"

Vivi was relieved by this new topic of conversation, with which she was unable to trip herself up with lies. Countess Marozny explained she'd never visited Valesti or any of the other local villages and towns. Vivi did her best to provide entertaining and informative answers to the countess's questions, even when pauses between were drawn out and painful.

Madam Varney cleared away the plates and brought out yet another course: raspberry syllabub in delicate twin-handled glasses. It was creamy and sweet. Although Vivi was already full, she found she was able to finish all of hers – in fact, she had to restrain herself from scraping the glass absolutely clean. Afterwards, coffee was served, so strong and bitter that Vivi heaped in four spoonfuls of sugar. The countess left her dessert and coffee untouched.

When the meal was over, the countess smiled and said, "I have appreciated your company this evening, Viviana. It has been a long time since I've enjoyed lively conversation."

Vivi took another sip of water and swallowed down her automatic response, which was "*Really?!*" If *that* was lively conversation, then she wouldn't want to hear the dull kind. "I enjoyed our discussion, too," she said politely.

The countess stood, indicating that Vivi should do the same. "You've probably been wondering when your education will begin?"

"Yes, a little." Finally!

"Well, there's no time like the present. Let us take a trip to the library and I'll show you around."

Vivi followed the countess down the corridor, up the stairs and through the gallery. When they reached the library, the countess grew more animated. Vivi wasn't quite sure why, as it smelled as musty as the rest of the castle and all that was in the room was books. Hundreds and hundreds of them, on bookshelves that ran from floor to ceiling, around every wall and on further bookcases. There was an occasional chair and table amongst the freestanding bookshelves. Unlike the other rooms, it was lit by oil lamps rather than candlelight, which was presumably better for reading.

"Have you already explored the collections?" asked the countess.

"No…" Vivi hadn't given the library a second glance. "I, er, thought there might be items of value here and I didn't want to handle the books without checking first."

"Ah, yes." The countess seemed pleased at this. "The Maroznys were great scholars and collected books on all manner of subjects. Some of the collections *are* quite valuable. Unique, in their way. Still, there is nothing that is out of bounds for you, as long as you take good care."

"Of course, my lady."

The countess led Vivi to a bookcase in the middle of the room. She trailed one hand along each shelf, seemingly looking for something. She stopped and removed a slim book. It was bound in red leather, with gilt letters embossed along the spine. "This. This would be the perfect start to our discussions."

She held out the book in her bony hand. Vivi stared at it.

"Go on then, take it!" instructed the countess, somewhat impatiently. Vivi took the book, which was surprisingly heavy for its size, hoping she wouldn't have to read it.

"We will sit over here." The countess moved swiftly over to a pair of easy chairs, facing each other across a table in an alcove. A bronze reading lamp with a green shade cast out a gentle glow. The countess lowered herself into one of the chairs and indicated that Vivi should sit in front of her.

Vivi obliged and perched on the edge of the seat, as a lady might, with the book held neatly in her hands.

The lamp bathed them both in a circular pool of light. The countess sat forward in her seat. Vivi could see the powder on her cheeks and the creases around her eyes. The top half of her face was lit, the whites of her eyes bright and expectant, whereas the bottom half was in shadow. She nodded at the book. "Well, then?"

Vivi remained motionless, her hands gripping the book tighter. She hadn't expected reading to be part of her education. Along with balancing-books-on-her-head, she'd thought there might be curtseying classes and elocution lessons. She scratched her arm, wondering how she might excuse herself from the situation.

"You don't enjoy poetry, Viviana?"

So this was a book of poetry. She'd never heard a poem in her life. Poems were rhymes, though, weren't they? Songs. Like the ones Madam Varney was playing earlier. Or the ones the women sang in the fish market. Or the ones her father sang after a night at the inn. Just with fancier words.

"Yes, I ... er ... enjoy poetry," she said.

The countess smiled. "Good. That is something. Read me a poem of your choice. Any one you like." She sat back in her seat, hands folded in her lap.

Vivi opened the musty-smelling book. She turned the gilt-edged pages slowly, stalling for time. Most pages were covered in words. Long, indecipherable words. Every ten pages or so there was a full-page illustration, detailed in black and white. Vivi paused to look at each one. There was a picture of a donkey, some geese and a basket of flowers. One of an old man in a tall hat.

The countess waited patiently for a time, then the fingers of one hand began to tap on the heavy fabric of her dress.

Vivi had to pick a poem. She turned a page to see a ship sailing beneath a beautifully drawn full moon, its whiteness taking up most of the page. It was a short poem, of just a few lines. "I will read this one," she said, flexing the spine of the book to open it wider.

"Very well," said the countess.

Vivi was sure she could read this poem. It would just take her a long time, as she sounded out each syllable of every word. That wouldn't impress the countess. She wanted to do better.

Two letters jumped out at her: a sharp 'V', followed by a dotted 'i', like the repeated pattern of her name, 'Vivi'. She forced herself to focus. V-I-L-L-A-I-N.

The countess cleared her throat.

"Villain!" blurted out Vivi.

The countess looked at her keenly. Vivi couldn't think with her watching like that. It would be easier just to make up some words. She took a deep breath.

"Villainous Moon."

The countess raised her eyebrows with interest, so Vivi said it again, slowly and calmly.

"Villainous moon"

What had she told Dol? The secret was to start with a sliver of truth and then twist it. If she could make up songs on the spot, then she could make up a rhyme. Something with long words. She could ignore the words on the page and make up anything – she just had to be confident.

She licked her lips and continued.

> *"Villainous moon*
> *Playing your tune"*
> (This didn't make much sense, but at least it sort of rhymed.)

She thought of Ma then, how the moon had shone brightly the night she passed away. She felt an unexpected rush of sadness and had to clear her throat before she made up the next lines.

> *"Taken too soon*
> *That night in June"*

It hadn't been June. It had been November. But November didn't rhyme with moon or soon.

> *"My misfortune*
> *Villainous moon"*

The poem in the book was no longer than that. Besides, surely the countess didn't know every poem in every book?

"THE END"

Vivi closed the book, hard, forcing out a small cloud of dust. She smiled confidently. Had she done enough to convince Countess Marozny, or would she be travelling back to Valesti before she'd even spent a second night in the castle?

The countess fixed her eyes on Vivi. "An interesting poem, indeed. What do you think the poet intended by the personification of the moon?"

Vivi had no idea what *personification* was but guessed the countess was asking her what the poem meant. She felt her cheeks grow pink and hoped it didn't show in the low light. "I think the ship in the picture is about to be wrecked…"

"Yes…?"

"… and maybe it's the moon's fault."

"Even more interesting. Of course, you have some personal experience of this."

Vivi wrinkled her brow. Personal experience? How could the countess have known she was thinking about her ma? "I…"

The countess leaned forward and patted Vivi's arm. "You told me how your father was taken by the sea."

Ah. Vivi had almost forgotten about her father the 'captain'. That was the only problem with spinning elaborate stories – one had to keep track of all the threads. She nodded sadly and Countess Marozny went back to tapping her knees and staring at Vivi. Vivi wasn't sure where to look, so she stared at the book in her hands, running her finger over the embossed gold details on the cover.

At last, the countess said, "I think I know the poet's name."

Vivi looked up. Had she fooled her?

But the countess's expression was shrewd. "It's Viviana DeRose, isn't it?"

Vivi nodded sheepishly. She knew when to admit a lie.

"I see. And can you tell me why you made up the poem?"

Vivi said nothing.

The countess went back to tapping her fingers, then stopped. "Sometimes, we tell a tale for a good reason. Perhaps to protect another, or to protect ourselves. Sometimes we tell an untruth out of fear. Yet the truth is important. Sometimes truth can be all we have. Truth can be the difference between life and death. Do you understand?"

Vivi nodded again. She considered telling the whole truth.

That she'd never been to school and had learned her letters at her mother's knee. That her wide range of vocabulary had been picked up at the fish market and by listening to bawdy music hall songs. So far, the countess had seemed to like her, but Vivi suspected if the countess knew the truth about her background, she wouldn't be so pleasant. Maybe she'd even call Jarv at first light to have Vivi taken swiftly back to Valesti. In fact, Countess Marozny would probably don a top hat and drive the coach herself.

Vivi made her decision. "I'm sorry, my lady. I made up the poem because I couldn't read the words on the page."

The countess tipped her head to one side. "You couldn't read them?"

"No…" Vivi kept her gaze lowered. The castle might be gloomy and strange, but it was also exciting and new. She had a room of her own and was eating better than she'd done in her whole life. She wasn't yet ready to return home to the laundry and to a life of not having very much at all. She'd be pleased to see Dol, but that was about it. The thought of Dol gave her an idea. She looked up and met the piercing gaze of the countess. "I need spectacles, you see."

The countess pursed her lips. "Spectacles. This is unusual for a child of your age."

"Yes, but I have terrible eyesight. Just terrible." Vivi held up her hand close to her face. "I can see my hand here ... but when I move it here" – she moved it a few inches nearer the countess – "it's a blur."

"Interesting," said the countess for the third time that evening. "And do you own a pair of reading glasses?"

"Yes..." said Vivi, knowing the countess would offer to send for them. "But they are broken. Broken beyond repair."

"How inconvenient." The countess pushed her chair back and stood, taking the poetry book out of Vivi's hands. She started making her way back over to the shelves where they'd found it. Vivi jumped up to follow. The countess placed the book back on the shelf. "You didn't think to inform me of this incapacity?" she asked, in a somewhat irritated tone.

"No. I didn't realize we'd be reading books."

Countess Marozny frowned. She pushed in the other books on the shelf so that the spines were all level. "If you didn't expect my lessons to involve books, then what were you expecting? Perhaps you'd envisaged deportment lessons? Piano? Lessons on how to find a suitable husband?"

Vivi shook her head, although those had been exactly the sorts of classes she'd envisaged. "No, I—"

"Because if that is the case, then you are in the wrong place.

The education I offer involves books and lots of them. I expect you to open your mind. To absorb knowledge and to create. Is that understood?"

"Yes," muttered Vivi.

"A good education is the only way for a young lady to better herself – to have a life of her own."

Vivi nodded. She was almost convinced by what the countess was saying, although inheriting a castle would be an even quicker way of bettering oneself.

Countess Marozny ran her finger along the neat row of books. "As it happens, I enjoyed your ... poem very much. We will get you some reading glasses if that is what is required. In the meantime, I wonder if this might suit you better."

The countess reached down to a lower shelf and brought out a large book with far fewer pages. "Poetry again, but the letters are bigger and easier to read. Read at least a page every day."

When Vivi opened the book, her heart sank. She could see from the illustrations and the small number of words that this was a book for a small child. She could read better than that.

Still, she thanked the countess and took the book away with her.

As they left the library, Vivi thought she would quite like to read the real poem about the moon on her own, taking all the time she needed. And, if there were fifty poems in that one book, then how many stories, poems and articles must there be in the whole library?

She had a deep desire to find out.

Back in her chilly bedchamber, Vivi got ready for bed as quickly as possible and then climbed in. It was almost midnight and she yawned, but her head was still buzzing from her lessons. Still, the pillow was soft and the mattress supportive. She was going to sleep well tonight.

She closed her eyes.

Then she remembered she'd forgotten to lock the door.

Vivi opened her eyes in the darkness and turned over.

Must she really lock it?

The countess had informed her it was essential, but hadn't said why.

Maybe she'd leave it open tonight and lock it tomorrow.

She closed her eyes again.

All she could think about was the door.

She'd better just lock it, then it was done.

Muttering to herself about why this was strictly necessary, she picked up the key from her nightstand, got out of bed and turned the key in the lock, freezing her toes on the way. She jumped back into bed, put the key back in its place and snuggled under the covers.

Vivi lay on her back, but the sheets felt too tight. She kicked her legs to untuck them and then curled up on her side.

Her feet were still cold and she couldn't quieten her brain. Why, in a virtually empty castle, containing just three people, did she have to keep her door locked?

She tried to think of rational explanations. Maybe it was in case robbers came in the night. Or an even more simple solution than that. Maybe the door wasn't secure and could be blown open by a strong wind. Whatever it was, it definitely couldn't be vampires. They were all dead and gone, she reminded herself.

As she turned on to her back, there was a noise from high up above her bed. Something knocked against the window. Just once, but loudly, like a thump. Her heart thumped in response and Vivi sat bolt upright. How could something be knocking on the window when she was all the way up here in the north tower? There were no trees that tall. She held the blankets up to her chin and listened.

Another thump.

It was no good – she was going to have to take a look. No doubt there was a simple explanation. She stood up on the bed, on her tiptoes, and opened the curtains.

Peering out, she could see nothing. Just pitch black. Not even the moon or stars were visible. And no lightning tonight – the storm had eased and the rain was now falling softly.

Then out of nowhere came a loud screech. A tiny, yet hideous face appeared, with sharp teeth in an open mouth and a pig-like nose. Vivi screeched herself, from the shock, and jumped away from the window.

There was another thump and, as Vivi's brain caught up, she realized it had been a bat. The poor little creature had flown into the window and fallen away. There must have been a few of them. Maybe they were part of a larger group, like the ones that had swarmed around the coach on her journey here. They must have lost their way. They might not even have survived after knocking into the window like that. She pulled the curtains back across and slid down the wall. Crouching on her bed, she shivered from the cold and the shock.

There was no point in even trying to get to sleep until she recovered, so she remained as she was, with the sheet wrapped around her. She was fully awake, her senses attuned to any little sound.

And the next thing she heard was the sound of footsteps in the stone corridor outside her room.

At first she thought she must be imagining it. The bats had startled her, that was all.

But the more she listened, the more she was sure it was footsteps. Someone outside her room was moving slowly as if they didn't want to be heard.

Vivi could think of no good reason why she would hear footsteps in the middle of the night, in this isolated part of the castle where only she slept. She held her breath so she could listen better.

Her first thought was the countess, who did keep strange hours, but Vivi recognized the sharp click of her boot-heels by now.

Vivi exhaled slowly.

No, it wasn't the countess. Or Madam Varney, who either shuffled along or wheeled her trolley. This was a slower, softer tread. Tiptoeing. Then a sniff, followed by a gentle *step, step, step*. After a pause, it began again, as if the person was looking for something. Vivi swallowed. She got off the bed and stumbled over to the wall, where she plucked the housecoat from its hook. She wrapped it around her and knotted the waist tie.

Were the footsteps coming nearer? It was difficult to tell.

In the dark, she fumbled for the chamberstick on her

nightstand. She found the matches from earlier in the pocket of her discarded skirt, and struck one. There was a sudden fizz and a blaze of white light as she lit the candle. She took the key to the door in her right hand and the chamberstick in her left, and crossed the room.

Holding the candle away from her, she put her ear to the door.

As she leaned against it, there was a slight rattle. She gasped and brought her trembling hand to the handle, which jiggled under her touch. Someone was trying to get in!

She froze for a moment, then gathered herself.

"Who is it?" she whispered.

There was no reply, but the door handle stopped rattling. She should be frightened, but instead she felt suddenly angry. How dare this person come to her room in the night and scare her? She wasn't afraid of anything!

"Who is it?" she repeated, more loudly and insistently. No answer. Fine. She would confront them and demand some answers.

She aimed to put the key in the lock, but her shaking hand betrayed her and she missed the keyhole. As she scrabbled around, the footsteps started up again, more quickly this time, back down the corridor.

Vivi finally managed to unlock the door. She wrenched it open.

The moonlit corridor was empty, but a long shadow of a figure running was cast on the wall, then the floor, before disappearing.

She gasped and drew back shaking for a moment. Then she gathered together all her nerves and tiptoed down the corridor. She looked down the staircase at the end, but her anger had made way for a chilly kind of fear and she really didn't want to go searching around the empty castle at this hour.

She retreated back to her bedchamber, closed the door behind her and locked it, checking it twice afterwards.

CHAPTER TEN

A BREATH OF AIR

Vivi wasn't sure what time she finally got to sleep, but it must have been in the small hours. Without any alarm, she slept in late again. If she carried on that way, she'd end up nocturnal like a bat. Or the countess.

When she did finally wake, the first thing she noticed was that the sound of the rain had stopped. It had been falling steadily for two nights and one day and she'd grown used to the background noise. Without it, the castle was strangely silent.

The good news was she would now be able to explore outside. Her body was craving daylight and fresh air. This place was so dark, and the events of the previous night had disturbed her. Had it all been a dream? No – it had been too real for that. The laundry gossip, that she'd been trying so hard to forget, came right back to her:

"… *some* folk think there was a vampire up in those mountains that was never found. A *thirteenth* vampire. And that it still hides in the forest somewhere, waiting for the right time to strike."

What if it wasn't a silly story, after all?

What if there really was a thirteenth vampire out there, looking for its next victim? She thought of the bat knocking into her window, its sharp teeth on display. The unexplained footsteps.

She headed down to the kitchen, hoping Madam Varney had remembered that Vivi wanted her breakfast down there. Music played softly from the gramophone. It was a tune Vivi didn't recognize, but Madam Varney hummed along as she gathered a mixing bowl and steel whisk. "Did you come to see me last night?" asked Vivi.

Madam Varney cracked two eggs into the bowl. "I did not." She narrowed her eyes. "Why, did you see someone, my dear?"

"Yes. Well, I heard footsteps. And I saw a shadow. Of a person running."

Madam Varney laughed. "A shadow, was it? This castle has a habit of frightening people. Shadows start to look like men or monsters. Bats in the attic sound like footsteps." She smiled sympathetically. "You'll get used to it."

Vivi smiled back uncertainly. She was pretty sure that she *had* seen someone but she didn't want to push things. Besides, she had another more burning question. "May I ask you something else?"

The housekeeper paused, whisk in hand. "Of course, my dear."

"It's about vampires."

Madam Varney began to beat the eggs into a froth. "Oh yes?"

"It's just, when I was thinking of coming to Castle Bezna, people warned me against it. According to the townsfolk, this place used to be filled to the rafters with bloodthirsty vampires. They call it Vampire Towers, and even though all the vampires were killed, there's a rumour that one may have escaped and is still roaming around these parts."

Madam Varney rested the whisk on the side of the bowl and turned to face Vivi, hands on her hips. "You should be careful about listening to gossip."

"I know, but is there any truth in it?"

Madam Varney pursed her lips. "All that vampire business was a very long time ago. Take a look at me – I've been up here for almost as long as Countess Marozny. I haven't been attacked, have I? And I've never met anything untoward roaming the corridors. Doesn't that tell you something?"

"I suppose so. I just wondered…"

"You would do well not to suppose or to wonder, and certainly not to mention anything about vampires to our dear ladyship. The past has nothing to do with her and yet she has paid the price for people's narrow minds. You've seen how few visitors we have – how lonely it is. Now, let's stop this chit-chat, otherwise your breakfast will never be ready."

Madam turned and gave her full attention to the sizzling pan on the stove top, leaving Vivi feeling somewhat deflated. She was sure she'd seen someone in the night and she'd hoped that Madam Varney would be able to offer some sort of explanation, but the housekeeper seemed keen to shut down that subject of conversation.

Conversation aside, breakfast was very satisfying, the eggs tasty and filling. After eating, Vivi felt an almost desperate need to get outside – to walk off the breakfast and to feel the sun on her skin. She left Madam Varney in the kitchen and headed for the front hallway, where she retrieved her borrowed parasol from the umbrella stand, in case of more rain.

Dol's mantle was hanging on the hook where she'd left it. It was dry now, although it had acquired a somewhat unsavoury, fusty smell. Nevertheless, it felt good to put it on, almost like wrapping a part of home around herself.

As she opened the front door, Vivi wondered if she should be seeking permission. But the countess had said she was allowed to explore the castle grounds. So she stepped outside, feeling free.

She pulled the door closed behind her and stood in the stone porch surveying her location. So much for feeling the sun on her skin. As far as she could see, there was no sun. It was neither hot nor cold, and there wasn't a breath of wind. The sky was white and a light mist hung low in the air, so although it wasn't raining, it still felt damp.

Vivi hoped the weather wasn't like this every day, although it was better than darkness and candlelight. She breathed deeply, letting cool air fill her lungs.

Everything outside looked different to how she remembered from her arrival. The gargoyles in the porch seemed comical rather than frightening. The forest was full of autumnal colour, no longer a looming black. And there wasn't a single bat in sight.

She considered a walk in the forest but, despite its beauty, the tall lines of trunks reminded her of the dark corridors of the castle. And there could be wolves hiding away out there. Or bears. Not vampires, she told herself strictly. All the vampires were dead and gone. Madam Varney should know, after all.

"Twelve dead vampires don't scare me like working in this laund-uh-ry," muttered Vivi.

Still, she'd leave the forest for another day. On this occasion, she would stay close to the castle and explore the gardens.

She followed a narrow walkway with a balustrade right around the castle until she'd reached the south side, where it opened out into a terrace spanning the whole of the back of the castle. Despite the damp gloom, it was a great vantage point for the gardens, which stretched out below.

From the looks of things, this must have once been a special place, perfect for entertaining. Vivi could almost hear the throngs of guests in ballgowns laughing as they sipped their drinks. But today, the flagstones were speckled with lichen, and the balustrade and ornamental stonework had all seen better days. A statue of a man in a draping cloak had some orangey brown growth on his face that looked like a beard, Vivi thought with a smile. Next to him was a stone animal so worn away Vivi couldn't tell what it was supposed to be.

The gardens themselves were expansive and split-level. A pathway ran right down the middle to a fountain, with sculptures and untidy topiaries dotted on each side. Sadly, it looked as though a gardener hadn't been to Castle Bezna for years. Nothing was in bloom, and the trees and shrubs were overgrown and neglected, just like the terrace.

If Vivi owned the castle, she'd scrub the lichen off the stone. She'd put out dainty tables and string up glowing lanterns, ready for those grand parties she'd imagined. She'd employ teams of gardeners to trim the hedges, restore the lawns and plant flowers in every colour of the rainbow.

A sound of loud scuffling below the terrace snapped her out of her grand imaginings. She leaned over the balustrade to see what – or who – was making the noise. There was nothing there.

At the bottom of the steps, she began walking down the pathway in the direction of the fountain, when she heard the sound of footsteps again. A soft tread, like the night before, but very faint. She looked over her shoulder, but there was nothing.

Could Madam Varney be right? Was this peculiar place getting to her, along with the darkness and the lack of sleep? Could she really be imagining footsteps where there were none? Either way, a bit of exercise and fresh air would get her back to her usual sprightly self.

She sprinted the rest of the way along the path, leapt down the steps to the lower garden, and continued to the circular stone fountain. It was a grand feature, with four sculpted tiers at its centre, and topped with a trumpet-blowing cherub. It was empty of water, and weeds grew in a crack in the basin. Vivi stepped up on to the rim, taking tiny heel-to-toe steps around the fountain. She held the parasol horizontally and at arm's length, like a tightrope walker.

She tried to imagine she was high up in the air, in a stripy big top, and if she put a toe out of place, then she'd plummet down to the sawdust-scattered ring below. She sped up her circles, making up a new song, which she sang at just above a whisper.

> *"Viviana Rosa Peste*
> *You are better than the rest*
> *You're not scared of candlelight*
> *Or funny noises in the night*
> *You're not scared of bats or rain—"*

Her foot slipped off the edge and she went over on her ankle. Not badly, just enough to make her cry out.

A rustle came from the nearby hedge. And a sniff. Vivi stopped, heart thumping. Someone *was* watching her. "Who's there?" she called. Nobody answered. She swallowed and lifted her chin.

Anything could make a rustling sound: little birds in the hedges. Rabbits. Or bats.

She stood on the side of the fountain, flexing her foot to test her ankle. It was fine. She couldn't decide where to go next. She was tempted to run across the lawn, but the grass was sodden from all the rain. To her right was a neglected maze, with hedges that looked brown and sparse. She'd leave that for another day. She went in the other direction, following the path back up towards the upper gardens and the castle.

Slightly off the pathway, through a vine-choked arbour, was a large wooden chicken coop. Half a dozen chickens were pecking about in the attached run. They were plump, friendly looking creatures, clucking softly to one another. She felt sorry for them: it must have been one of these poor birds that ended up with its neck hanging over the kitchen counter.

"Thanks for my breakfast," she called lightly to distract herself and sped back to the main garden.

Near the back door, beneath the terrace, there was a small, fenced-off kitchen garden. Vivi went to have a closer look, glancing over her shoulder before unlatching the iron gate and stepping inside. Compared to the rest of the castle grounds, this area was actually in quite good shape. A neat cobblestone path led around the perimeter. To the left were well-tended raised beds stocked with vegetables – some rows of tufty leaves, and others, peas or beans, climbing poles. In the centre was a square knot garden, the gaps in its symmetrical design filled with aromatic herbs. Vivi recognized thyme and parsley, but there were plenty of others, too.

An ornate iron bench with a design of intertwined flowers faced the knot garden and a couple of trees stood to the side. The only one that appeared to have anything growing in it was a pear tree. Vivi reached up and twisted off a pear, thinking of Dol and Mister Vrdoljak's plum tree. At least this one was easier to reach. She bit into the fruit, but it was as hard as hailstones and she spat it into the herb bed. A mouse would be glad of the meal.

A rustle came again from just outside the kitchen garden. An angry rustle. An angry rustle? She really was imagining things now.

She leaned over the gate and called out, "Who is it?"

There was no response, but in the gloomy quiet she heard

another sound coming from around the front of the castle. Horses' hooves and wheels on stones.

A carriage.

Which meant a visitor! If there was someone out here, then at least she was no longer alone. She could have cried with relief at the thought of it.

CHAPTER ELEVEN

THE VISITOR

Vivi left the kitchen garden, skipped up to the terrace and around the castle. She ran to the top of the stone steps and squinted into the distance. She recognized the dilapidated coach and its top-hatted driver, drawing up in the road.

"Jarv!" she called, giving a giant wave, as if greeting a long-lost friend. Jarv tipped her hat in response and Vivi began running down to greet her. She wondered who Jarv was bringing to the castle today. Perhaps another girl had replied late to the notice. Perhaps it was even Dol deciding to join her. Her heart leapt at the thought, although she doubted it could be true.

Vivi stopped at the gateposts and waited. She smiled at the mysterious stone creatures crouching on each post. How monstrous they'd seemed that first night, guarding their territory and looking ready to pounce. Now, in the daylight, she saw half their faces had weathered away. They could hardly have been staring at her in a menacing fashion. "Poor old things," she said, giving them each a pat on the head.

She dropped the parasol on the ground, leaving her free to climb on to the unlatched gate. It creaked as though it was protesting at her weight, and she swung back and forth for a few moments, trying to make it creak some more. The creak sounded so eerie, but the gate just needed oiling.

Meanwhile, Jarv climbed down from the coach, settled the horses and opened the carriage door. Vivi realized there was no passenger at all – the seats were piled with parcels and packages. She tried not to feel too disappointed.

Jarv retrieved a large basket and a couple of brown paper-wrapped boxes and started up the stony path towards the castle. She was wearing exactly the same outfit as before – top hat, coat and eyeglasses – despite the change in weather. Vivi could imagine her dressing that way even in high summer.

As Jarv drew near, Vivi jumped off the gate and grinned.

"Morning, Miss DeRose," said the coachwoman.

Vivi opened the gate wide. She waved Jarv through with a flourish of her hand, in the same way the coachwoman had ushered Vivi on board the coach. "I wasn't expecting to see you again," said Vivi.

"Weren't you?" asked Jarv in a flat tone, amusement flickering around her mouth.

"No. I thought you'd abandoned me here."

Jarv raised her eyebrows. "Well, you seem to be doing fine for an abandoned urchin. Are you?"

"Am I what?"

"Getting on well?"

"Very well, thank you." Vivi closed the gate behind them and they continued to walk up the steps together.

"No bumps in the night or eerie footsteps keeping you awake?" asked Jarv.

Vivi cringed inwardly as she thought of the literal bumps on the window and the mysterious shadow in the corridor, but she wasn't going to tell Jarv about her strange night. Jarv would only think she was scared. "No."

"You don't need me to take you back to town, then?"

Vivi felt a brief rush of relief at the offer. The thought of heading back to Valesti, seeing Dol and sleeping in familiar surroundings was so comforting. But there was no way Vivi would go back to her old life. Who knew if she'd be welcome, and besides – she'd only just got here! While she had hot food in her belly and new opportunities, Vivi was staying put. She would be the only companion to the countess who managed to stick it out the whole year. Perhaps that would give her certain advantages.

She shook her head. "I am planning to stay. As I believe I have explained already. Multiple times."

Jarv chuckled. "You are a one-off, Miss DeRose. And I'm sorry if you were hoping to see the last of me, but I am at Castle Bezna regularly with food parcels for the kitchen and the like." Vivi noticed then that the basket was full of groceries: she spotted butter, salt and flour in amongst various other tins. Of course, the residents of the castle wouldn't be able to exist on a few chickens and produce from the kitchen gardens. It made sense that Madam Varney bought food and other items from elsewhere.

"Would you like me to carry anything?" Vivi offered.

"No, that wouldn't do for a lady," said Jarv with a smile. "And your arms should already be occupied with carrying the parasol you left by the gate. Or should I say *my* parasol?"

"Oops!" Vivi rushed back to retrieve it and tucked it under her arm. "Thank you – it's most useful – it's always raining up here or looking as if it's about to. You don't happen to have one without holes, do you?"

Jarv laughed. "I'm afraid this is the best I've got. But it won't do you any good if you keep leaving it by the gatepost. In fact, you'd do well to keep it on your person at all times."

An odd suggestion, but it did seem to rain a lot up here. "I promise not to let it out of my sight," said Vivi. She began heading in the direction of the porch, but Jarv stopped her.

"It also wouldn't do for me to use the front door," Jarv said.

Of course. Castle staff, delivery people and presumably coachwomen should never use the front door. Vivi really needed to start thinking like a lady. The girls before her – Dorïce and Margareta – would have no doubt known these things instinctively. Jarv led the way around the castle to the back door and placed the basket and parcels down.

"Shall I fetch Madam Varney?" asked Vivi.

"No, don't bother her. Our usual arrangement is I leave the groceries here on the step and put any letters in this box." Jarv rapped her gloved hand on the metal postbox to the side of the door. "Speaking of which, if you've decided to stay here at Castle Bezna, rather than travel back home with me today, I should give you this." The coachwoman reached inside her coat pocket and brought out a crisply folded letter. "It's from your little friend."

Vivi pounced upon it eagerly. She instantly recognized the neat, compact handwriting spelling out her name on the front. She held it close to her heart. "From Dol! However did she track you down?"

"She didn't. I tracked her down, as it happens. I know it can get lonely up in these parts and letters from friends and family are some comfort."

"Where did you find her?"

"It didn't take long. You don't have to ask too many questions in Valesti to find who you're looking for. I asked a little freckled boy in the town square if he knew of a Viviana and he said you were his cousin!"

"That will have been Ralph. Or Eddie," said Vivi, with a smile.

"Well, Ralph-or-Eddie took me straight to the laundry, which is where I met Dol."

"Oh." Vivi swallowed. That meant Jarv, like Madam Varney, knew that Vivi wasn't a lady. She never really thought the coachwoman had believed her anyway. It seemed nobody did. Not that it mattered now. She was here at the castle, wasn't she? And there was no talk (yet) of sending her back. In fact, the countess seemed to be growing rather fond of her.

Vivi thrust the letter into her pocket. She would read it later, when she was on her own. She dropped any pretence of a well-to-do voice. "Thanks," she said.

Jarv smiled kindly. "You're welcome. And do you have anything you'd like me to take to Valesti? Your cousin thought you'd be writing back."

Vivi thought of the scrunched-up letter on the floor of the room in the south wing. "I will have a letter for her. Next time you come. Tell her I'll reply to this one – I've been busy since I got here."

"Busy, eh? Looks like it. Swinging-on-the-gate sort of busy."

Vivi turned pink. "I might not appear to be occupied right at this very moment, but I've been working very hard at pursuing my education during the evenings."

Jarv held up her hands as if surrendering. "You don't have to give *me* any excuses – I'm just the messenger. If there's a letter, then I take it. If not, I don't." Jarv tipped her hat again. "In that case, that's everything. I'll be off now, Miss DeRose. I'll leave you to *pursue your education.*"

At the thought of the coachwoman leaving, Vivi had a sudden sinking feeling. She didn't want to be left on her own.

"I'll see you back to the gate," Vivi said, running after Jarv as she took the path back to the front of the castle.

"As you wish." Jarv took such long strides, Vivi found herself scurrying along to keep up. The coachwoman seemed to be in a hurry to set off.

When they reached the gate, Vivi put her hand lightly on Jarv's shoulder. "Can I ask you a question?"

The coachwoman turned to face her, with a faint smile. "Something makes me think I couldn't stop you."

Why couldn't people just say yes when she asked them that? "Have you ever seen anything suspicious out in the forest? At night, I mean."

"Are you asking me about vampires, Miss DeRose?"

Vivi flinched at the directness of the question. "I suppose so."

"Well, in that case, no. I know how people talk about this place. All the 'thirteenth vampire' gossip. I haven't seen anything – yet – but I'll keep looking!" Jarv lifted her eyebrows above her eyeglasses.

Vivi smiled. There couldn't really be vampires up here without Jarv's knowledge.

Jarv began to walk away.

"One more thing!" called Vivi, wanting to keep her visitor just a little longer. She knew, though, her next question probably sounded peculiar. "Were you watching me earlier?"

"*Watching* you?"

"By the fountain, just before you arrived. I was walking around the edge and I sensed someone there. It happened again later by the kitchen garden."

Jarv wrinkled her brow. "No. How could it have been me? You heard the coach, didn't you? You saw me arrive."

Vivi felt her cheeks grow hot – she knew none of this was rational. She didn't want to sound like one of those flighty girls who begged to be taken home the minute they left Valesti. She also knew deep down it hadn't been Jarv watching her. "Yes, I heard the coach. But before that, someone was here in the gardens. I'm sure of it."

Jarv paused for a moment and cocked her head to the side, as if she were listening for footsteps. For a moment, Vivi thought Jarv was about to say something to shed some light on the situation – but she didn't. She straightened her top hat and opened the gate.

"It wasn't me, Miss DeRose. I've got better things to do than watch a countess's companion dance around an empty fountain with her imaginary friends. I've got a feeling you're going to be just fine. You're a bold young lady. Just keep your wits about you – and don't lose that parasol."

Jarv waved farewell, then began to walk back down the steps.

Vivi watched until the coach and horses disappeared into the distance, then made her way back to the gardens. Seeing Jarv had given her a jolt of confidence. Jarv had said she was a *bold young lady* and, of course, she was right. Looking nervously over her shoulder? Shaking in her boots? That wasn't the real Vivi. And she was going to prove it.

Whoever it was that was following Vivi was counting on her playing the scared victim. Earlier, every time Vivi had heard a rustle, she'd reacted by calling out or looking around. It was time for a new strategy: Vivi needed to pretend she thought she was alone. She would lull her pursuer into a false sense of security by acting oblivious to their presence. Then she'd have the upper hand. Like a good game of hide-and-seek. And Vivi knew the perfect place to play.

CHAPTER TWELVE
THE MAZE

In order to lay her trap, Vivi spoke as if to herself, but loudly enough for anyone else to hear. "Ah, it was lovely to see Jarv. I wonder if I should head to the kitchen and let Madam Varney know the provisions are here."

She stood for a moment, scratching her chin. "No, on second thoughts, I'll go and play in the maze."

An answering rustle informed Vivi that her pursuer had left their hiding spot by the kitchen. Whoever it was, they were bad at keeping quiet. They had clearly not played much hide-and-seek in their time, whereas Vivi was somewhat of an expert after multiple games with her cousins. She didn't plan on losing. She was going to draw them nearer and nearer, then she was going to pounce.

As she approached the maze, she called out the odd comment in case the stalker thought she'd changed her mind.

"I love mazes," she said. "What beautiful gardens these are."

As she drew closer, she saw the maze wasn't in quite as bad shape as she'd thought. On one side, the hedge appeared to be dying. The leaves were brown, dry and crispy and there were clear gaps between the plants. But whatever disease had affected this part of the hedge hadn't quite reached the other side. There, the hedges were overgrown and needed a good prune, but for the most part looked green and healthy.

She walked in through the entranceway and began following the passages, laughing to herself whenever she reached a dead end. Vivi had a pretty good idea her pursuer would be hiding somewhere on the green side, where the coverage was better. All she had to do was lure them closer, which was easy. A person playing in a maze would always reach one place eventually – the centre.

She took her time to get there, aware the mystery person would be following. She smiled as she heard what sounded like a muffled sneeze from the hedge.

She had them right where she wanted them.

At the centre of the maze was a small cobbled area with a sundial and a little stone bench. It looked as though it had once been pretty, planted with roses and other blooms in pots, but these plants had either died or grown rampant. The bench was perfectly positioned for Vivi's purposes, facing away from the green hedge. A couple of overgrown bushes, covered in clusters of red rose hips, obscured the view to the centre. She sat on the bench and drew up her feet so no part of her was in view.

"Oh, I'm worn out now! What a night it was last night. I think I'll rest here for a moment and regain my energy."

This was her chance. Vivi rose from the bench and, as quietly as she could, sidled over to the brown side of the hedge. She squeezed through a gap in the dead plants, using her parasol to help, then through another, until she reached one of the outer passages. She skipped lightly along, following the passage over to the green side.

Vivi hadn't quite decided what she was going to do with this person once she found them. Depending on how big and scary – or bloodthirsty – they were, she would either confront them, there and then, or run back to the kitchen and tell Madam Varney. At least she'd have something more concrete to report than a rustle and a sniff.

When she reached the green section of the hedge, she slowed down to a tiptoe. She followed the inner passages, peeping through as best she could.

Then she saw the shape of a person.

She held back a cry and tightened her grip on her parasol. Someone *was* there!

She moved nearer and saw him clearly, hiding in the hedge and peering through the foliage as he tried to get a glimpse of her sitting on the bench.

But she couldn't have been more surprised at her pursuer's appearance.

This was no vampire. No monster. The person hiding in the hedge wasn't scary at all. He was a boy. Small and slight – younger than her even – wearing a ridiculously large straw hat that cast his face in shadow.

He was dressed in a long-sleeved shirt somewhere between white and grey, with a waistcoat buttoned over the top. Below that were knee breeches and stout boots. One long sock had bunched at the top of his boot, revealing a slim brown leg, which looked very much like a knobbly twig.

Any thoughts of running back to the castle evaporated. In fact, Vivi had to stop herself from laughing.

"Got you!" shouted Vivi, louder than even she'd intended, holding her parasol like a rifle. The boy whipped around, grabbing at his hat to stop it from flying off. His jaw dropped, the shock on his face as pronounced as if the parasol had been a real weapon.

She lowered the parasol. He had plump cheeks and big dark eyes and his chin wobbled as though he might cry. His eyes darted right and left, and for a moment, she thought he was going to run. Vivi put her hand on his shoulder as if she were arresting him.

He shook her off. "What are you doing?" he asked in a high-pitched voice. He blinked rapidly. "You took me by surprise – creeping up on me like that."

"Creeping up on *you*? *You're* the one who's been creeping about the place. Why were you following me?" she demanded.

"I don't know." He stared down at his feet, scuffing the toe of his boot in the stony path. "I was working in the garden—"

"You *work* here? I didn't think there were any staff here. Only Madam Varney. And Jarv sometimes."

"No, I work here, too. Outside mainly," he said, avoiding eye contact, looking down at the ground.

Vivi shook her head in disbelief. Why had no one told her this? "Why were you following me?" she repeated, more gently.

The boy looked up and managed to finally look her in the eye. "I saw you playing. Your games looked fun. And I liked your songs. I wanted to watch, that's all."

Vivi became less defensive. He was just lonely, like her. "Why didn't you step forward and introduce yourself?"

"I didn't think I should. I was told to keep away from you."

"By whom – the countess?"

There was a pause, then he nodded. "Yes, that's right, Countess Marozny."

He looked right and left whenever he spoke, as if worried he'd said the wrong thing. Why would the countess tell him not to talk to Vivi?

"What's your name?" she asked.

"Kurt."

"And how old are you?"

"Eleven. Nearly twelve."

She raised her eyebrows. Not much younger than her, then.

"Well, Kurt, we've established why you've been watching me this morning. But what about last night?"

Kurt opened his mouth but Vivi put up her hand to stop him.

"Don't even think of denying it," she said. "I know it was you – I heard you sniff and saw you running off down the corridor."

"I didn't mean to scare you," he said, miserably.

"What were you doing?"

"Working. I was … erm … polishing the door handles."

Vivi folded her arms. She, of all people, knew what a lie sounded like. "In the middle of the night? I don't believe you. What were you up to?"

Kurt wriggled. He clearly was not enjoying the conversation. He looked around for an escape route to no avail.

"You might as well tell me now, otherwise I'll tell Madam Varney and we can see what she thinks about it."

Kurt looked horrified. "No! Don't tell Ma Varney!"

"*Ma* Varney? She's your *mother*?" They looked nothing alike.

He looked at the ground. "No, not my real mother. I don't remember my real mother. I've worked here since I can remember. But I call Ma Varney that. She looks after me. And she's good to me. But she'd be cross if she knew."

"If she knew *what*?" It was hard to believe that the wrath of cuddly Madam Varney was anything worth worrying about.

Kurt twisted his hands together awkwardly. "I sometimes sleep in the rooms up in the south wing. I'm not supposed to. But I can't always get to sleep in my bed – it's a mattress on the kitchen floor. The beds upstairs are so much comfier."

"Oh," said Vivi, remembering the curtain in the kitchen. She felt bad that she had a proper bed and a room of her own. She could understand why he'd been wandering around the castle looking for somewhere more comfortable. "Does Madam Varney sleep in the kitchen, too?"

"No. She has her own annexe, with a bedroom and living area. But I'm not allowed in there. She doesn't know I sometimes explore at night."

"Still, what were you doing in the north tower? Mine's the only room up there."

Kurt smiled weakly. "I didn't think the countess would put you there."

"Why?"

"Because it's the worst room. It used to be a prison cell."

"A *prison cell?*" Come to think of it, it did look like a prison, thought Vivi. The circular shape, the single high window, hidden away in a tower all by itself. She supposed it was normal for an isolated castle to have a prison cell, but it seemed odd to put the companion to the countess in there.

"Yes, so you gave me a shock when you called out," said Kurt.

"I gave *you* a shock? What about *me*? I was woken up in the night by a rattling door handle." She didn't mention that she'd already been disturbed by the bat. It felt silly.

"Sorry," said Kurt. "I won't do it again."

"You'd better not!" said Vivi. "We are living at Vampire Towers after all – what do you expect me to think?"

Kurt looked wounded. "Don't call it that. It's Castle Bezna now."

"Very well, I won't call it that as long as you stop following me in the gardens and roaming around the corridors at night. Come on, let's get out of this miserable maze."

Kurt sniffed. "Miserable? I thought you liked it?"

Vivi didn't have the heart to admit her earlier comments were a trap. "The green side is lovely," she said, and he smiled proudly.

They left the maze and walked past the chicken coop in the direction of the castle.

"What exactly do you do here?" Vivi asked.

"I do a little bit out in the gardens."

Vivi looked around at the overgrown hedges and out-of-control rose bushes. "A *very* little, by the look of things."

Kurt appeared crestfallen, shrinking away beneath the wide

brim of his hat. "The gardens are big," he muttered and Vivi felt immediately bad for laughing at him.

"You're right. It's an awful lot for one person. I wouldn't know where to start."

"I try to look after the kitchen gardens, mostly. We use those every day."

"Ah yes, I noticed that they were particularly well cared for," said Vivi. To her surprise, Kurt looked cross rather than proud.

"I saw you there. You shouldn't have taken the pear. It wasn't ripe," he said.

Vivi smiled. So she *had* heard an angry rustle when she stole the pear. "I nearly lost a tooth."

"Pears ripen from the inside out," said Kurt solemnly, "so you can't tell from the look of them. I always pick them first, then let them ripen indoors. If you try to ripen them on the tree, the middle will grow rotten and mushy."

"Do any of them need picking now?" asked Vivi, as they passed the kitchen garden.

Kurt nodded. "I was about to pick some before I saw you. You can help, if you like," he said.

Vivi agreed and he fetched a basket and crate from the shed, putting them under the tree between them. He turned the crate over and stood on it so he could reach the higher branches.

"When they're ready to be picked they let you know. Like this one." He took a large pear and tilted it away from the branch. It broke off easily. "But this one" – he tilted a smaller pear in the same way – "is holding on for now."

He put the large pear in the basket with a smile.

"Easy when you know how," said Vivi. She put down her parasol and began picking alongside him. As she picked, she made up a song.

> *"Kurt knows how to pick a pear*
> *You have to leave it hanging there*
> *Until it wants to leave its branch…"*

Vivi closed her eyes momentarily, trying to think of the next line.

"Nothing rhymes with branch!" said Kurt.

"I can make anything rhyme," countered Vivi, and after a few moments she started up again.

> *"Until it wants to leave its branch.*
> *But not until it's like blancmange!"*

Kurt laughed, his eyes crinkling under his hat. He looked like a completely different person when he was happy.

They continued their work until all the pears that were ready were placed in the basket. Vivi rotated her arms in large circles to ease her shoulders, which were aching from all the stretching. "What next?" she asked, looking around the garden.

Kurt's eyes widened. "You really don't mind helping?"

Vivi grinned. "There's nothing more pressing for me to do this morning."

"Well, I need to pot up some of the mint and parsley from the herb garden to keep it warm over winter."

"Show me how," said Vivi.

Kurt gave her the pots and showed her how to divide the plants without damaging them. They worked side-by-side, Vivi stealing little glances at Kurt, trying to figure him out. There were many unusual things about him. His nervousness. The constant sniffing. The fact that she'd only just found out about his existence. And the straw hat.

The hat was particularly difficult to ignore.

It was enormous, with a flat top and a wide brim, which may or may not have once been stiff, but now drooped down at both sides. Black chin straps were knotted loosely below his neck. To Vivi it looked like a woman's hat, although she was hardly a fashion guru. The effect was one of a much younger child playing at dressing up with their mother's clothes.

She didn't want to offend him. He was quite sensitive and she could do with a friend at Castle Bezna. But she couldn't help asking the question. "Why are you wearing that hat?"

He put down his flowerpot and trowel for a moment and brought his hand to the brim.

"It's a gardening hat," he declared, somewhat proudly.

"To keep all this lovely sunshine out of your eyes?" she asked, indicating the general mist and gloom with a sweep of her hand.

Kurt lowered his head so that his face was completely hidden by the brim of the hat. "You're mocking me," he muttered.

Vivi smiled. "Perhaps a little. But I like the hat. I love it, in fact. May I try it on?"

Kurt eyed her suspiciously and shook his head. "At least I don't carry a tatty old black parasol around with me."

Vivi laughed good-naturedly and said no more about the hat.

CHAPTER THIRTEEN
CASTLE LIFE

Vivi and Kurt continued to chat as they planted the herbs, lining up terracotta pots on the low wall surrounding the garden.

"Kurt, why didn't you want me to call this place Vampire Towers?"

Kurt continued digging. "Because there aren't any vampires here. That was all a long time ago."

"But how can you be sure they didn't miss one? That there isn't a thirteenth vampire on the loose?"

He stopped planting and knelt there, motionless, with clumps of earth dropping from his trowel. "A *thirteenth vampire*?" he whispered.

"Yes," said Vivi. "That's what some people say, anyway."

"Is it?" Kurt went back to his digging, shaking his head. "I don't know anything about all that."

Vivi hadn't been expecting that reaction. He'd looked genuinely shocked, as if he'd never heard the rumours. He can't have seen anything sinister, then. She stopped her questioning and they worked in silence. After a few minutes, Kurt put down his trowel and said, "I need to take these to the greenhouse now, and the pears to the kitchen."

Between them, they'd filled eight pots with the mint and parsley plants.

"Let me help," said Vivi. "I'll take the pears."

"Thanks," said Kurt. "Leave them just inside the door."

She tucked the parasol under her right arm and then picked up the basket of fruit in her left. She managed to open the gate and shuffle through, leaving Kurt to carry the flowerpots to the greenhouse.

Vivi left the pears where she was instructed, then walked into the kitchen.

Madam Varney turned from the stove. "Hello, my dear. What did you think of the gardens?"

Vivi laughed. "They were..."

"Rambling and untidy – I know!" said Madam Varney. "Such a shame. In the old days they were magnificent."

"I can imagine," said Vivi. "I was just thinking how grand the terrace would look if it was restored. I can just picture tables and little lanterns out there—"

"People joking and laughing—" added Madam Varney.

"—even dancing!" Vivi grabbed Madam Varney's arms and spun around the kitchen in time to the music. The housekeeper laughed. She was surprisingly light on her feet.

Just as Vivi was spinning Madam Varney around, their waltz was interrupted by a cough. Kurt was standing there in the kitchen, holding a single pot of parsley. "I thought this might be needed in here," he said.

Madam Varney's round cheeks were red from the exertion. She tutted and drew her eyebrows together. "I hope you're not trailing mud into my clean kitchen." She turned to Vivi, who was smiling at Kurt. "Miss DeRose! You didn't mention that you'd met Kurt." It was a mild observation, but Vivi thought she could detect a sharpness behind the words. Was it disapproval? Madam Varney had hinted that Countess Marozny wouldn't want Vivi to mix with the staff.

"You must be hungry after all that fresh air, Miss DeRose," she continued, taking the pot of parsley from Kurt. Any hint of annoyance had disappeared. "Would you like a spot of luncheon?"

"Luncheon?" Vivi hadn't realized it was anywhere close to lunchtime but, as if on cue, her stomach began to rumble. There must be something in the mountain air that made her permanently hungry.

"It's soup," said Madam Varney, bustling back to the stove. "You can wash your hands at that sink over there."

"Thank you – it smells delicious," said Vivi, washing her hands and sitting at her usual spot at the table. Kurt was still by the doorway, pulling up his wrinkled sock. For the first time since Vivi had met him, he removed his hat, chin straps holding it in place at the base of his neck. He ran his hand through his black hair, which was cropped short. He looked different without the hat – maybe a little older. He smiled self-consciously when he caught Vivi looking.

"Are you going to join me for lunch?" Vivi asked him.

Madam Varney turned and threw up her hands in horror. "I'm not having dirty gardening boots and breeches at this table!"

Kurt sniffed, replaced his hat and brought a pocket watch on a chain out from his waistcoat pocket. "It's a bit early for me," he said. "Anyway, I eat outside. I prefer it."

"Very well," said Vivi. "Just stay away from the unripe pears – you don't want to lose a tooth!"

He left with a polite nod to each of them. Vivi glanced over at Madam Varney, who held a spoonful of the soup up to her nose, then added more seasoning.

"I was surprised to bump into Kurt in the gardens," Vivi commented. "I thought it was just you and the countess here at Castle Bezna."

"I didn't say that, surely?" Madam Varney ladled some of the soup into a bowl.

"Well, no. But you didn't mention him, either."

Madam Varney put the steaming bowl in front of Vivi and wiped her hands on her apron. "I find it difficult enough to do all the cooking and cleaning for the countess and yourself. And the laundry. I'm not sure how I'd have time to do a thing out in the garden, let alone run errands down to the village, do you?"

"No, I hadn't really thought about it…"

"Not to mention the chickens – feeding them and putting them away at night. That's why Kurt's here."

Vivi blew on her soup to cool it, then ate a spoonful. Chicken and potato. Delicious as always. It was no doubt made up of leftovers from last night's dinner, but Vivi didn't mind. She'd never eaten so well.

"So would it be acceptable for us – for Kurt and me – to be friends?"

"Well, that's not for me to say, now, is it, my dear? You must put that question to her ladyship."

Madam Varney turned back to the stove and picked up the empty pan, muttering to herself. "As if I'd keep young Kurt hidden away! You forget you've only been here a couple of days. I won't have thought to tell you every little thing. I'm sure there'll be plenty more surprises hidden away for you within these walls."

Vivi continued to eat her soup as the housekeeper clattered and clanged about the kitchen.

Plenty more surprises.

Later that day, up in her bedchamber, Vivi reached into her pocket and pulled out the letter from Dol. In the excitement of meeting Kurt, Vivi had almost forgotten about it. The paper was a bit more crumpled than it had been when Jarv gave it to her, but the folds were still sharp.

There was no seal. As Vivi unfolded the paper, she noticed that it was written on the back of one of the Castle Bezna notices that Ralph had brought to the laundry. There was no writing bureau stocked with blank paper at her aunt's house, so Dol would have to make do with what she could find. Vivi felt a pang of guilt that she now had access to all the luxury of the castle and Dol didn't.

Dol had put two of the notices back-to-back so that the print didn't show from the outside. Vivi smiled. Her cousin was always so resourceful. Vivi lay down on the bed and held the letter in front of her with straight arms. Dol's writing was neat and clear and there weren't too many tricky words. Vivi read the whole thing slowly but surely, sometimes mixing up the words or having to re-read them, whispering them aloud to herself.

Dearest Vivi,

You've been gone for just two days but oh how I miss you! I miss your songs and your jokes and the way you brighten up the laundry. I don't know how I'm going to last the week, let alone a whole year without you.

You were wrong about Ma. She wasn't glad that you'd left. She wasn't angry either – just sad. She cried and said, "I've failed my dear sister," and "Whatever possessed Viviana to go to such a dismal place?"

It's not a dismal place, is it, Vivi?

The nice coachwoman said she dropped you safely

at Castle Bezna. All I can imagine is a dark and dreary place with stone walls and echoing chambers. And those rumours about vampires! I know it can't really be like that. It's probably bright and modern and cheerful and I'm sure you're having such fun!

Please, please write and let me know you're safe and happy.

Your cousin (and best friend),
Dol xxx

Vivi could hear Dol's voice in the letter. She could see her writing, leaning on the back of a book, glasses slipping down her nose, shooing away her small siblings. Vivi's eyes prickled with tears at the thought. Was Aunt Ina really sad? Maybe Dol was lying to make her come back. Vivi doubted it. Dol would never make anything up.

She would write back straight away.

There was so much to tell her cousin. All the things she'd wanted to put in her first letter about her journey here, the countess and the castle. But then there were all last night's events and the morning's, too.

The writing paraphernalia from the south wing was tucked in her old carpet bag in the armoire. She removed it all and laid it out on the washstand, which would be her desk. The candle from her nightstand was always lit when she was in her bedchamber, because of the dim light. She brought that over to her washstand, too, and wrote sitting on her stool.

Dol

Got hir as pland. Hop yur kipin well and not lettin old Ivette push you araund. Dont you wory your hed about the casel. Its a bit dark but nais. Countes is as we thort. She slips at funny taims and never sims to eat. I did wondr if vampairs wer hir but it turnd out to be a boi with a big hat called Kurt. His my frend now. His like half littl gentlman, half gardner, half I dont no what. That makes thri halfs but you no what I min. Madam Varny the housekipr is also nais and looks after me. She says there are no vampairs hir and I believe her. I have new clos that are nais and not ostentashus like the other dress.

Vivi

X

She held it out at arm's length. Her writing would never be as good as Dol's, and she hadn't said half the things she'd wanted to, but she was getting used to the red ink and there were fewer blots. She'd even used the brand-new word she'd learned from the countess. She folded the paper, trying to make the edges line up and the folds as crisp as Dol's. Then she softened her sealing wax over the candle flame, rubbed it on the join to make an almost-circle, and sealed the letter with the Marozny stamp.

She would give it to Jarv when she next saw her.

After the letter-writing, Vivi read her book of children's poems. In fact, she read it multiple times. The poems were as dull as she'd expected. Kittens chasing balls of wool and warning tales about children burning their fingers on the stove. Still, Vivi was determined that she shouldn't be caught out again. She took the book down with her to dinner, ready to swap it for a new one.

Dinner was served once again at seven o'clock. The countess was in a dark purple dress this evening, which made her look paler than ever and brought out the dark circles under her eyes.

As Vivi tucked into the meal – chicken and mushroom pie with layers of flaky golden pastry – she told the countess about her exploration of the castle grounds. "I met Kurt this morning," she added, wondering how the countess would react.

The countess sliced her pie into tiny pieces but didn't bring any to her mouth. "Kurt. Kurt … who might that be?"

"Kurt! The Kurt who works in the garden, for Madam Varney."

The countess wrinkled her nose as if the meal smelled bad, and said dismissively, "Oh – the errand boy. We've had so many errand boys over the years and they all seem to have been called Kurt or Bert or something like that…"

Vivi thought of the pride in his voice as he'd explained to her what he did. "Isn't Kurt – this Kurt – more of a gardener than an errand boy?"

"Who knows what he does out there. A strange child. And why does he wear that hat?"

Vivi felt hurt on his behalf, even though she, too, had found the hat strange. "It's a gardener's hat. I like it. And it was nice to have someone to talk to during the day," she said.

"During the day…" said the countess, in a tone of wonder. "Well, I suppose it won't hurt for you to have the company of someone young. As long as you don't keep him from his work and as long as he doesn't distract you from your studies."

Vivi grinned. "Thank you, my lady." She'd been worried that Countess Marozny might forbid any contact.

There was a long pause, during which the countess folded and unfolded the corner of her napkin. Then the door swung open and Madam Varney swept in with the next course. This time, Vivi didn't make any eye contact.

"How are you sleeping at night, Viviana?" asked the countess once the housekeeper had left the room.

"Extremely well, thank you, my lady," she replied, not wanting to get Kurt into trouble.

The countess raised her eyebrows but looked pleased with the response. "Good, good. And I hope you are remembering to lock the door."

"Of course, my lady."

"Good, good," the countess repeated, then her eyes glazed over.

Afterwards, they retired to the library. They sat on the same seats as before and Vivi opened her book on the table. Vivi half-expected the countess to produce a pair of reading glasses, but she didn't. The countess took the book for a moment, flicked through the pages and, as Vivi had hoped, asked her to read a poem aloud. "This one," she demanded, tapping one of her sharp fingernails on the picture of the kitten.

Ah, yes, the kitten poem. By now, Vivi knew the poem upside down and standing on her head. She raced through the words, to show the countess how easy she found it.

"Stop, stop!" said Countess Marozny after the first stanza.

Vivi stopped abruptly, unsure what she'd done wrong.

"You are ploughing through without even listening to the

words. Try again, from the top, and, this time, try to pronounce every sound in every word. C-a-t. Understand?"

"C-a-t," repeated Vivi, dutifully.

"Very good. Continue."

"The c-a-t is chas-ing down the hall.
Can kitt-y cat-ch the wool-ly ball?"

The countess nodded along. "Much better. You have a natural ear for rhythm. I'd like to hear another poem. Try this one next."

Vivi did as she was asked, reading the familiar warning tale about the children and the matches. She pronounced every word as clearly as possible. The countess seemed pleased. "Wonderful. Tell me, what do you think about the poems?"

"Well, the kitten seemed like a strange subject choice."

"Go on. Why?" The countess was much more animated than she'd been at the dinner table, looking directly into Vivi's eyes.

"Because ... there's not much to be said, is there? If the kitten was playing with a live mouse, then there might be a bit more ... tension."

Vivi wasn't sure if she'd been a bit too honest, but the countess smiled. "Indeed. What about the second poem? There was more tension there, wouldn't you agree?"

"You mean because they got burned?"

The countess nodded encouragingly and Vivi continued. "I thought the children in the poem were quite, well, foolish. Most children, at least the children I know, would know not to do that. If the children decided to put their hands on a hot stove, then they deserved to get their fingers burned, as far as I'm concerned."

The countess laughed. "Ha! Very true. I do like your company, Viviana. You are like a breath of fresh air. And fresh air is much needed in this old place. You entertain me."

Vivi agreed about the fresh air but was unsure about being a form of entertainment. At least she hadn't been asked to play the piccolo.

The countess closed the book of poetry and held it under her hands. "You certainly rose to that challenge, Viviana. The teaching part of this evening is finished. Next, you should choose your own reading material. But I would like you to promise me that you will read at least a chapter or the equivalent every evening. That way, your reading will soon improve."

Great – no more kitten and wool books. "Thank you, my lady."

The countess left Vivi alone with the choice of all the books in the library.

No more was said about reading glasses and Vivi was left suspecting that the countess had seen right through her story all along.

CHAPTER FOURTEEN

THE LIBRARY

Vivi missed her old life at the laundry. Not the knotted muscles in her shoulders, or the smell of ammonia. Not the heat or the harsh words from her aunt. But she missed the friendly chatter and the laughter, and the shape of her day. She and her cousins had been woken early by her aunt, even on a Sunday. Breakfast was small but sustaining. She and Dol would walk to the laundry, work, work, work until their hands were red raw, then home again to help prepare the evening meal. There was barely a moment to oneself, let alone time to question their schedule.

At the castle, things were different. Vivi had to seek her own pursuits in the day, as her lessons never began until well after dinner and sometimes not until late in the evening. Gradually, she made a routine for herself. Very different to the one she had in Valesti, of course. She would rise late, breakfast with Madam Varney, then help Kurt in the garden. The long, drawn-out days began to pass more quickly.

She sometimes thought about going further afield, or exploring the forest, but when she asked Kurt to accompany her one morning, he was very clear on that matter. His eyes went wide. "No!"

"Why not?" asked Vivi, although she could guess the answer.

"There are animals in there," he said. "Wolves and bears."

Vivi knew he was probably right, and she certainly didn't want to meet a wolf or a bear while out on her own, so they kept close to the castle.

Afternoons were spent in the library.

Vivi found that her reading promise to the countess was actually a very easy one to keep. She was soon getting through much more than the required daily chapter. The more she read, the more she enjoyed it, and she found herself actually looking forward to opening a new book. As her reading and writing improved, the library became her favourite place. The countess was delighted at her progress and would ask her to read longer and longer passages during their evening lessons.

There was more to the world of books than Vivi had realized and she explored the library shelves with great enthusiasm. She found a whole bookshelf dedicated to maps and another that was full of recipe books. There was a book to suit any mood.

Before she knew it, weeks had passed and the days grew colder and shorter. One afternoon, on a particularly chilly day that felt more like winter than mid-autumn, she cosied up in the library, which was warmer than some of the larger rooms. She'd explored most of the bookshelves on the ground floor and decided to have a quick look around the upper level before dinner. She climbed the short spiral staircase and, as she did so, a word jumped out at her from the spine of one of the books: VALESTI.

Who would write a book about Valesti, of all places? Nothing ever happened there. She made a beeline for the book. Her reading had grown so good she could scan the full title quickly. VALESTI AND ITS SUNFLOWER FIELDS.

She took the book from the shelf and flicked through the pages. Most of the books had words only, or printed illustrations, so she was amazed to find photographs in this one. They depicted places that she knew: the sunflower fields and parts of the town.

The grainy black-and-white images didn't do the town justice, but it was fun seeing familiar spots; the laundry even appeared in one. Vivi smiled at the thought of little old Valesti being in a book. She put it back on the shelf, then had a look at the titles on either side.

THE FALNIC MOUNTAINS, THEN AND NOW

And,

THE HISTORY OF CASTLE BEZNA

These shelves obviously held books about the local area. She was particularly excited to see the one about the castle. She pulled it from the shelf, and sat cross-legged on the floor with the book resting in her lap. She hoped there might be information about the castle's dark past. Some actual facts, rather than laundry gossip. Sadly, it was full of plans and construction details with no word about vampires. Nevertheless, she began to wonder if there was something hidden away up here about the castle's tumultuous past.

There was one book that looked different, with no title on its dark red spine. Vivi eased it off the shelf, noticing that the front cover was also title-free. The whole of the dust cover looked rough at the edges and not quite even, as if it was handmade. Vivi opened it up. It was hand-lettered, rather than printed, and the words on the title page were drawn out in fancy capitals. They were trickier to decipher than Vivi's usual books, and she traced each letter slowly with her finger, pulse quickening as she read them aloud.

THE TWELVE VAMPIRES OF CASTLE BEZNA

By Dr Arnel Arvesson

This was it. This was where she would find the real history, maybe some gruesome details to share with Dol. The title was interesting in itself. Twelve vampires. Nothing to suggest a thirteenth, just as Madam Varney had assured her. The book was unusual: pages of handwritten notes and sketches bound together. Some pages were scruffy and written hurriedly with spelling mistakes that even Vivi could now detect. Others had clearly been better planned and were written in neat type.

She started at the beginning, where a sort of introduction read almost like a letter.

Dear Reader,

This is an account of what took place at Castle Bezna, in the Falnic Mountains, in the most difficult time in our history. It describes how, after years of persecution by vampires, the people decided they would take no more and rose up to meet their enemy. Details are recorded so that none of this shall be forgotten. If (heaven forbid) such events should come to pass again, the good people of the Falnic Mountains shall have a record to consult.

Vivi opened a page at random. There was a name at the top, a sketched portrait and some notes.

EDWIN

The illustration had been rendered in black ink by someone with a certain amount of drawing skill. Edwin was a white-wigged gentleman with hair tied in a black ribbon. He wore a waistcoat, jacket and shirt with a neck ruffle. All very smart, but with a shocking twist. Edwin's smile was wide and sinister, with sharp, protruding fangs, like those of a fox or wolf. Beside him, on a bed, lay his unfortunate victim, a pale woman, eyes closed and one arm stretched above her head.

Most disturbing was that the artist had used red ink on the black and white drawing to depict blood. It dripped from Edwin's fangs and from the wound at the poor victim's neck.

The result was horrifying, yet Vivi found herself unable to look away.

She read some of the notes on the facing page.

Lazy eye

Wears a gentleman's clothes.

One female survivor reported that he seemed worried by daylight.

Vivi thought back to what the laundresses had told her about the historical vampire hunt. How the townsfolk got to know their enemy and found out everything they could about them.

So, these were the notes that the hunters had made. The notes that had helped them fight back.

Vivi turned to a new page.

Selig

This page wasn't as gruesome as the first, and Selig seemed not quite as frightening as Edwin. The notes even reported him showing mercy on a couple of occasions. Apparently, he'd been responsible for multiple deaths yet, in the illustration, he looked like a proper gentleman, with his neat moustache and serious expression, despite the fangs. He looked familiar but Vivi couldn't remember where from.

Vivi scanned the pages, taking it all in. The book had her hooked. Adriana could turn into a wolf. Novak had two fingers missing on his left hand. It was like a scary story but real: the best book Vivi had come across in the library. Then she thought of the monument in Valesti, the people who'd been lost, and felt bad about her excitement.

Towards the back was a family tree, drawn as an actual tree, its leafless branches spreading across the pages. All the vampires and their relationships sketched out:

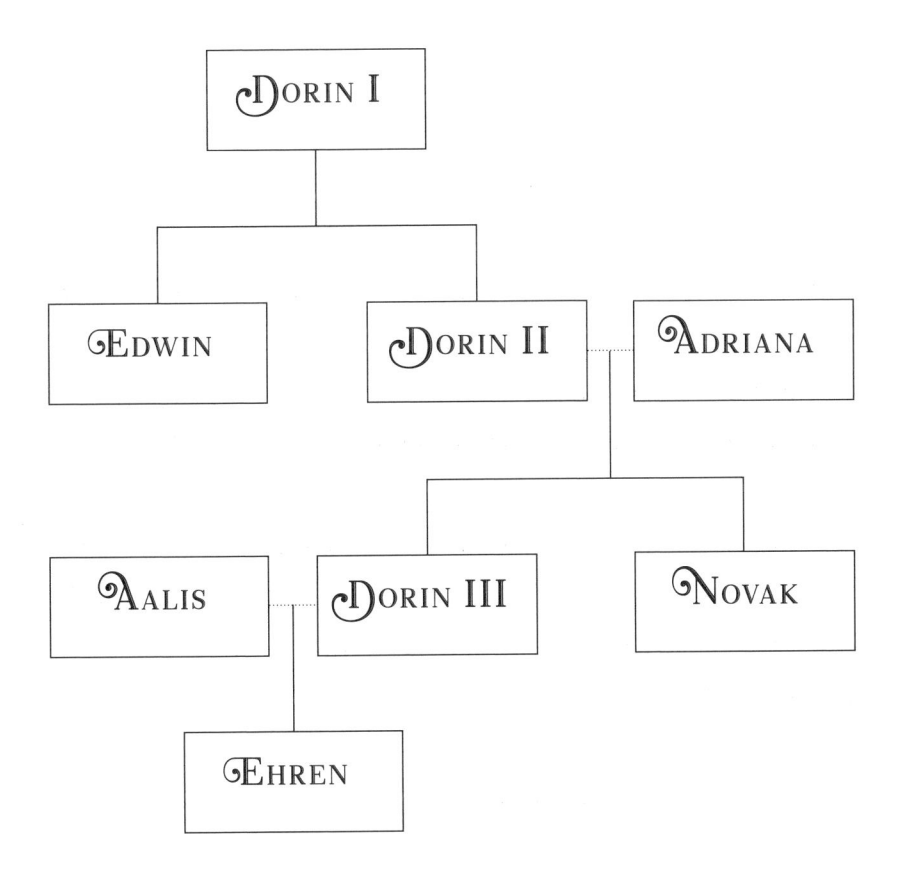

```
                    ┌─────────┐
                    │ Dorin I │
                    └─────────┘
                         │
         ┌───────────────┼───────────────┐
    ┌────────┐      ┌──────────┐    ┌──────────┐
    │ Edwin  │      │ Dorin II │····│ Adriana  │
    └────────┘      └──────────┘    └──────────┘
                         │
              ┌──────────┼──────────┐
         ┌────────┐ ┌───────────┐ ┌────────┐
         │ Aalis  │·│ Dorin III │ │ Novak  │
         └────────┘ └───────────┘ └────────┘
              │
         ┌────────┐
         │ Ehren  │
         └────────┘
```

Then, off to one side, under the heading *Origins Unknown* were some additional names:

GRISELDA
OTTILIE
SELIG
NIKLAUS

Something about this page made Vivi pause. The names were familiar. Therese at the laundry had spoken of three generations, all called Dorin, but Vivi couldn't remember if she'd mentioned any other names. Yet she recognized them from somewhere. Niklaus… Selig…

She flicked to the end of the book, feeling proud of how her reading had improved over her time at Castle Bezna. Just weeks ago, reading felt like an impossible feat. And now she was reading an entire history book.

WHAT HAPPENED TO THE TWELVE?

All twelve vampires were given a proper burial (see 'The End of the Castle Bezna Vampires'). At the time, this was controversial, given their reign of terror. It must be remembered that, apart from the original vampires, these monstrous creatures didn't choose this path for themselves. Some of the twelve were, it is assumed, innocent people taken from the villages and towns nearby. Killing them was to protect the people of the Falnic Mountains, but a merciful act in itself. May all these lost souls find peace.

Here ends the terrible story of the Castle Bezna vampires. As the author of this book, who lived through these terrible times, I can only hope, on this occasion, history does not repeat itself.

Dr Arnel Arvesson

Far away in the hallway, the clock chimed the half hour, making Vivi jump. She was due at dinner with the countess in half an hour. She slammed the book shut guiltily, knowing Madam Varney would disapprove of her reading about vampires. She pushed it back into its gap on the shelf, thinking it was better to leave it there, rather than take it up to her bedchamber.

She'd come back tomorrow to read more.

What was it about those names that felt so familiar? Vivi pondered the question as she left the library and made her way back to her bedchamber.

It was only later, when she was walking through the gallery to dinner, that it struck her as clearly as the chiming clock. The portraits. Each one had a name painted on it. She rushed to the pictures to check, and read the names speedily this time, unlike that first morning. She was still amazed at how quickly her reading had improved after only a few weeks. *Selig* and *Niklaus*. Just as she'd thought. Next to them, a person who was even more familiar to her now, with a white wig and a flouncy shirt. *Edwin*. The portrait artist was more accomplished than the author of the book. Edwin looked less ferocious, with a closed mouth and no garish red blood. Nevertheless, he was recognizable.

They *were* vampires. All of them.

The clock chimed again for seven o'clock: Vivi really did need to hurry down to the dining room if she didn't want to be late. But she couldn't stop herself from checking the other portraits.

Could these twelve smart people with pleasant smiles *really* be the monsters that had terrorized the area? And if they were vampires, then why were they hanging proudly on the gallery walls when almost everything else in the castle was hidden under a dust sheet?

Vivi was desperate to find the answers and hoped that dinner would provide an opportunity to discover the truth. Unfortunately,

Countess Marozny was in a dreamier mood than ever. Beetroot soup was on the menu. Vivi did her best to eat it daintily, keeping the spoon horizontal as she moved it from dish to mouth. The countess stared into her own dish, eyes fixed on the cream swirl and parsley garnish.

But Vivi couldn't wait until the countess was looking more alert. "I found myself taking a good look at the portraits in the gallery this afternoon, my lady," she began. "I wondered if you could tell me a little more about them."

The countess glanced up with renewed interest. "Ah, the portraits. They are my ancestors. All members of the Marozny family, may they rest in peace."

"I thought so," said Vivi smoothly, careful not to react to the countess's answer. "Fascinating to think they all lived their lives here, as we are doing now. When was that, exactly?"

"The last of my ancestors died around seventy years ago."

Yes, thought Vivi. *When they were killed off by the vampires, according to the laundry gossip.* Was the countess going to mention that? Or was she deliberately keeping the information from Vivi? She pushed a little further. "Do you know much about them?"

"No, I'm afraid I don't." The countess took her spoon and

mixed the cream into the soup. "I've always meant to research my family but somehow I've never got around to it. There is a local history section on the mezzanine floor of the library if you're interested in finding out more."

"Yes, I've already discovered it," said Vivi, scrutinizing the countess's face for any reaction.

The countess hovered the spoon close to her chin and then lowered it, staring at the contents as if surprised. "In that case, you will be able to educate me, Viviana," she said, in a dull voice.

Vivi thought about it. What would the countess say if Vivi raised the subject of vampires right here and now? But Madam Varney had made it very clear that Countess Marozny didn't want to discuss it. And Vivi wanted to stay on her good side.

"Perhaps we can look together during my lesson?" suggested Vivi.

The countess shook her head. "This evening's lesson will focus on handwriting. Your cursive script leaves a lot to be desired."

That evening's lesson was the longest and most tedious yet, with what felt like hours of perfecting letters to Countess Marozny's exacting standards. Afterwards, Vivi couldn't sleep. This was not at all unusual at Castle Bezna. She had gone from being someone who fell asleep as soon as her head touched the pillow, to someone who barely slept at all. The noises in the north tower didn't help. When it rained, it sounded like it was raining inside her bedchamber. When it was windy, she heard the ominous creaking of trees in the forest. And on a rare clear night without wind or rain, like this one, wolves howled incessantly.

Eerie noises aside, she was now used to staying up at night, with only her unresolved thoughts to keep her company. Vivi couldn't stop thinking about the countess's reaction to her mentioning the portraits. It was possible that the countess thought she was telling the truth. She'd *looked* like she was telling the truth. Maybe she'd assumed that these people were her ancestors, as Vivi had done. Or she knew perfectly well who the people were and she was telling a convincing lie. If it was the latter, what reason did the countess have to lie? Unless Countess Marozny was a vampire herself.

The thought had been niggling away at the back of Vivi's mind again. The countess was a peculiar person, with her strange sleep pattern, lack of appetite and aversion to daylight. But that was her illness, wasn't it? When she was thinking rationally, Vivi knew that the countess couldn't be a vampire. All the vampires had been finished off years ago. Plus, the countess *loved* garlic. Vivi had seen it for herself. Besides, if she wanted to attack Vivi, then surely she would have done it by now.

What Vivi needed was a good night's sleep and to put these thoughts out of her mind until the morning. The noise from the wolves died down for a moment. Vivi tried to think happy thoughts. She remembered sitting in her family cottage back in Ingusport, mending fishing nets with her parents by the glow of the fire. That was the last time she could remember them all together and content. She smiled at the memory. But then the howls began again. Her overactive brain imagined all the prisoners that had lived (and possibly died) in the north tower. Had they been chained up in this very room? What crimes had they committed? She put the pillow over her head and tried not to think about any of it.

CHAPTER FIFTEEN

SECRETS

For once, after breakfast Vivi didn't go outside to see Kurt. Instead, she headed straight up to the library to read some more of the vampire book. She'd find him afterwards and tell him all about it.

But on the way there, passing through the gallery, Vivi noticed something that made her stop in her tracks. She couldn't believe she hadn't noticed it before.

There was a gap.

The framed pictures were spaced evenly along the walls. Six on each wall. But, because of the door leading to the south wing, the wall on the left-hand side was shorter. This meant that on the right-hand wall, there was space opposite the door. Space for one more picture at the end, next to the painting of the young girl, Griselda.

Vivi stared at the wall. As always, the light wasn't good. Despite that, she could see an oblong patch where the yellowing white paint was brighter than the rest of the wall. Very much as if it had been covered for some time by another painting.

Her mind spun. If there had been a thirteenth portrait, why would someone remove it?

She'd been so relieved when she'd found that book. The title had been decidedly clear: *The* Twelve Vampires *of Castle Bezna.* But if these twelve portraits matched the twelve names in the vampire book, then why would there have been a thirteenth painting?

What if all the gossip was true and the author of the book was missing an important piece of information? Suddenly the gallery seemed smaller than ever, the eyes of the vampires upon her.

Heart racing, she ran to the south wing. Forget about the library – why would she want to read about twelve dead vampires, if there was a thirteenth on the loose?

She had to find the missing portrait.

When she imagined what it might look like, she couldn't help picturing Countess Marozny, in her high-necked dress, staring out of the frame. She would love to be able to put that image out of her mind, but until she found the painting she suspected she wouldn't be able to.

Was it possible the missing painting had been hung elsewhere in the castle? She revisited every room she'd explored on her first day. She hadn't been looking at the paintings then. Most had been removed from the walls and covered with dust sheets, which Vivi whisked off now. There were fishing scenes, hunting scenes, landscape after landscape. Up in the nursery there was a framed picture of a basket of kittens, which she briefly considered moving to her room in the north tower. She raced back down to the ground floor. There was a picture of a country scene in the dining room, landscapes in the corridors, and an impressive depiction of Castle Bezna in the hall. But not a single portrait.

When Vivi had looked in all the obvious places, she began to wonder if the portrait had been hidden away intentionally. She could ask Madam Varney, but the housekeeper would never approve of Vivi meddling in the countess's business. And Kurt wouldn't want to upset Madam Varney. Vivi would prefer to find it herself.

So she decided to look in the less obvious places. She couldn't check the countess's bedchamber so she started with her own.

Her room was small, and it was unlikely a large painting could be hidden away in there, but anything was possible.

She felt under the mattress. A couple of broken springs were no surprise as she'd already felt those during her sleepless nights. Under the bed – nothing. She checked for loose floorboards and secret drawers in the washstand. Nothing. She stood on the bed to get a better look on top of the armoire. There did seem to be something up there but she couldn't quite see, so she dragged the stool over and climbed from there on to the top of the washstand. Hoping it would hold her weight, she stood on tiptoes and peered over the top. Right at the back, pushed into the corner by the wall, was a large leather trunk, and on top of it a carpet bag not unlike her own. It was doubtful a painting would fit inside either of them, but she couldn't be sure.

She couldn't reach them so she jumped down from the washstand, looking for some kind of long object she could use to reach them.

Jarv's parasol! It would be ideal. They'd had relatively dry weather lately, so Vivi had stashed it in the armoire. She found it and clambered back on the washstand. From there, she was able to hook the curved handle of the parasol through the leather handles of the trunk. The trunk edged forward with the carpet bag resting on top, bringing with it clouds of dust. Vivi coughed and looked away while it settled.

Once the two bags were close to the edge, Vivi was able to move from the washstand back to the bed and heave the cases one at a time off the armoire. The weight of the bags made them drop heavily from her hands. Not empty then.

She looked in the trunk first, as it was the only one big enough to hold a painting (if the painting had been removed from its frame and rolled up). The case was the sort someone with money might take if they were going to stay away for a while. It was made of fashionable brown leather with rounded brass caps at the corners. On the top of the case near the handles, also in brass, were the initials M L-M. She stared at them for a moment, then polished them with the cuff of her sleeve until they were shiny.

Next, Vivi slid the clasps to the side. They were stiff, but they unlocked and clicked open easily. She lifted the lid and gasped. The interior looked like something from a newspaper advertisement. The lid and main compartment were lined with oyster-coloured silk, and the contents all perfectly arranged. She ran her fingers along the folded edges of the clothes. Crisp white nightgowns and matching caps with frills. Cotton drawers. It all smelled faintly musty and soapy.

She pulled out a silk stocking, which was soft and embroidered. What was the point of embroidery when no one ever saw it? She knew from her time at the laundry that the folk with embroidered stockings were the ones with all the riches. The stockings were about her size. A little smaller if anything. Did they belong, or had they belonged, to someone her age?

A small matching leather case was tucked inside the top corner. Vivi opened that, too. Inside it were some vanity items. A hairbrush, similar to Vivi's but shinier – better. Hair slides and scarf pins, tweezers, nail scissors, tiny brushes with specialist yet unknown purposes. Little glass lidded bottles and compacts, filled with creams and powders, some dried up now, but each with its own place. This was the sort of case it would be fun to unpack and pack up again, for the joy of seeing the items arranged so prettily. She took out a silver hair comb, made of the finest filigree and dotted with blue and silver sparkling stones. It made Vivi think of butterfly wings. She slid it back and found something else, too, tucked inside the lid of the vanity case. A flat, hinged object in shining silver. At first, Vivi thought it might be a pocket mirror, which would come in useful. But when she slid it open, she saw a photograph of a family inside, and realized it was a travelling frame. It was a clever design, which folded back and stood by itself. Vivi placed it on the washstand and examined the photograph.

A girl of around Vivi's age looked out. She was wearing a fancy white frock with voluminous sleeves, and was seated with a couple who must have been her parents. It was unusual to see a small family group like this one, without at least a couple of siblings. It reminded Vivi for a moment of her own family. But apart from the size of the family, there were few similarities. This photograph showed what a 'good' family looked like. They were all dressed splendidly, the father in a suit and the mother in a long-sleeved stripy dress and a neat hair turban. The mother and daughter looked directly at the camera with the same expressions – particularly striking was their identical, very slight smile. The father's smile (or lack thereof) was hidden behind an impressive moustache.

"Who *are* you?" Vivi asked the girl, as though she might speak back. And then, as if in answer to her question, something came back to her – a memory from the laundry. Lilith and Therese's gossipy tones when they told her about the other companions to the countess.

"... *Dorïce Engel and Margareta something.*"
"*Lang-Mayer... Lived at the big house on the edge of town.*"

"One married a rich man, didn't she? And the other one went travelling around the world."

M L-M. The initials were unusual. Plenty of people's first names began with 'M', and plenty of people's surnames began with 'L' or 'M', but not both together like that. Vivi had only ever heard of one person, and that was Margareta Lang-Mayer. One of the girls who came before her. The type of girl the countess had been hoping for.

This was what the case of such a girl looked like. This was what the countess had been expecting when Vivi's own scruffy bag fell open in the hallway. This was the type of case girls like she and Dol could only dream of. Yet here it was, forgotten on the top of a wardrobe, left behind when Margareta Lang-Mayer went on to her next glamorous adventure. Typical – it was only people who had so much who could disregard their possessions in such a way. Vivi decided she wouldn't have liked Margareta. At all.

As a child, Vivi had been envious of a friend's doll's house. The friend's father had made it and it had been perfect, with miniature tables, chairs and even teapots. Yet her friend had never played with the house – she'd become so used to her toys she'd stopped marvelling at them and had forgotten how lucky she was. Seven-year-old Vivi had been so enraged by this that she'd purposefully tipped over the house. She remembered watching with satisfaction as the contents rolled across the nursery floor and the chimney broke off.

She felt that same rage now. With no one even there to see, she upturned the case in one sweeping motion, watching the cotton drawers, perfume bottles and nightgowns fall. They still looked too tidy – too perfect in their folded rectangles – so she churned them up with her hand as if they were in the dolly tub at the laundry. When all the things were in one mixed up heap, Vivi stopped.

There. That's what Vivi thought of Margareta and her precious travelling case.

She breathed out. As she stared at the pile on the bed, she didn't feel better at all. It was sad, seeing the once ordered items in such a state of disarray, and Vivi knew she'd never be able to fold them like that herself. She began to put them back in the case, Vivi-style, in no particular order.

But before she'd even finished, she became distracted by the other bag on the bed. The carpet bag. It looked like her own but newer, with a brown houndstooth pattern. Did this bag belong to Margareta, too? Upon opening it, Vivi knew straight away it didn't. It contained similar items to the fancier trunk: clothes, underwear and vanity items, but with some noticeable differences.

The nightgowns weren't quite as crisp. The stockings were cotton, not silk, and not embroidered. They were all nicer than Vivi's own possessions, but not quite as nice as Margareta's. And this time the family photograph was in a leather travel frame rather than a silver one. In this photograph, there were siblings. Two boys in matching jackets with smart buttons, a baby on its mother's knee and a girl of Vivi's age. The girl had neat plaits and freckles. Dorïce Engel. It must be.

How strange that both girls had left the castle without bothering to take their family photographs with them. Photographs that had been important enough to take with them for a year away, but not, it seemed, into a new marriage or travels around the world. Photographs of the families they would perhaps never see again.

Vivi's heart began to race. She packed up all the clothes and items on the bed and stashed the case and bag back where she'd found them. Margareta's vanity case with its bottles and powders was too alluring to put back. She put it at the back of the armoire in case she wanted to have another peek.

She felt sure she wasn't supposed to have discovered these things. One abandoned bag would have been strange, but two? Two seemed suspicious.

CHAPTER SIXTEEN

THE OTHER GIRLS

For the whole of that afternoon, Vivi felt jittery and jumpy. Margareta and Dorïce were on her mind, and she no longer felt in the mood to search for the missing painting. She began to wonder what the other girls had experienced at Castle Bezna. Had they slept in the north tower, like her? Presumably so, since that's where their things had been left. Could they read and write? Did they wear uniforms? And, above all, why had they abandoned their treasured possessions?

She decided to put some of the questions to the countess at dinner that evening.

At the first opportunity, before the starter had even been served, Vivi blurted out her question. "My lady, what happened to the other girls?"

The countess's eyes widened. "The *other girls*?"

"The ones who replied to your notice. Before me."

Countess Marozny blinked. "Ah, but that was all a long time ago."

"Still, you must remember them. What were their names? What were they like?"

"Let me see now." The countess peered into her water, as if it might help her remember. "They were quite different from each other. The first one, Margareta, was a slight, dainty thing. Walked with such poise, like a ballerina."

Vivi snorted. "Of course she did," she muttered.

The countess raised an eyebrow, but continued. "Her voice, however, could be rather piercing." She laughed. "The other one, the Engel girl, was quite the opposite. She stomped around the place like an elephant. Neither of them was here for long."

Madam Varney came in with two plates: a large unidentifiable vegetable on each one. "Artichokes for you this evening."

Vivi stared at hers. She'd never seen anything quite like it. It resembled a prickly ball. When Madam Varney had left the room, the countess seemed to realize Vivi's confusion and smiled. "You remove a leaf at a time, dip it in the vinaigrette and scrape off the soft part. Like so." Countess Marozny demonstrated the process with her own artichoke. Vivi was surprised to see her actually bite into the vegetable. She had grown used to eating alone in the countess's company. She watched the countess subtly, looking for extra-sharp teeth, but they looked perfectly normal. Then she imitated the action and left the leaf at the side of her plate as the countess had done.

"Where did they go? The girls?" Vivi asked.

One artichoke leaf had satisfied the countess and she leaned back in her chair. "Margareta married, I believe, although how she met her beau while living here, I have no idea. Perhaps he was someone she knew before she arrived. Dorïce went off to see the world by train."

Vivi nodded. The story fitted with the gossip she'd heard in the laundry.

The countess sighed. "I tried my best to make them feel at home, but perhaps hospitality isn't my strong point."

Etiquette rules probably dictated Vivi should disagree – to

argue that Countess Marozny was an excellent host. But that would be difficult to do with a straight face. Vivi didn't see her for hours at a time and, if it weren't for Madam Varney, she would have no hot food or clean clothes. So instead, she said, "You promised opportunities, my lady. They took the opportunities and left..." If Vivi were to speak the whole truth, she'd add, "Which is exactly what I plan to do."

The countess looked up from her water glass and stared at Vivi for such a long time Vivi began to wonder if she'd spoken the words aloud.

"The other girls ... they were quite different to you, Viviana."

Vivi almost spat out her tiny mouthful of artichoke at this understatement of the century. "Really?" she managed to say.

"Yes, in many ways you compare favourably. There are, however, a few areas you might want to address. Your handwriting, of course. And your general presentation. The uniform is an improvement on your previous clothes, but you are sixteen years old, are you not?"

Vivi almost laughed and shook her head – she wouldn't be sixteen for just over two years – but then she remembered to keep up her pretence and her head shake became a nod. "Yes. Yes, I'm sixteen."

"At your age, in polite society, you would be expected to wear your hair up, not cascading down your back. It is perhaps a habit you should begin to adopt here at the castle as the other girls did."

Vivi nodded. "Of course." Vivi wasn't sure how the conversation had moved on from her careful questioning about Margareta and Dorïce, and ended up being about hairstyles.

She stared at her plate. After much ripping and dipping of leaves, she had reached the core of this strange vegetable, which was fuzzy and ugly. She had no idea what to do with it, so she placed her cutlery neatly on her plate and folded her hands in her lap. Countess Marozny had gone very quiet, and Vivi knew from experience she was unlikely to say much else for the rest of the meal. It was doubtful the countess would notice whether or not Vivi had finished her first course. She probably wouldn't notice if Vivi jumped up on the table and bashed the fine plates together like cymbals. Vivi guessed that was what happened when a person lived on their own for so many years.

"A curse on polite society!"

It was late in the afternoon. Vivi had tackled another artichoke for lunch and she was now trying to put her hair up, as requested by the countess. After ten minutes of trying, Vivi felt like throwing her hairbrush and hairpins from the high window. How did respectable ladies manage to pile their hair so neatly and elegantly on the tops of their heads? Until she'd come to the castle, Vivi had been a thirteen-year-old laundry maid. No one had cared whether she wore her hair up, down or stuffed into a mop cap, but now she had to think about being *respectable.*

She put her head on the washstand and moaned, much as she used to on the ironing board.

"Can I help you with that, my dear?"

Vivi jumped. "Madam Varney! I'd been concentrating so hard I didn't hear you come in."

Madam Varney laughed. "I've brought some fresh water for your washstand. But then I saw you battling with that hairbrush. It looks like you're losing. Am I right?"

"Yes," said Vivi, sadly.

"It might be easier if you let me do it," said Madam Varney, putting the jug down on the side.

"Oh, would you?" said Vivi, handing over the hairbrush and pins. "You're my saviour!"

Madam Varney took the brush and began deftly running it through Vivi's hair from root to tip. She held the hair bunched up in her hand near Vivi's head so the brush didn't pull and hurt her scalp. It was what her ma used to do and she felt unexpected sadness rising in her chest.

"No one's brushed my hair for a very long time," said Vivi.

"You don't have a ma?" asked Madam Varney. Vivi shook her head and Madam Varney didn't ask any more. The brushing continued, steadily.

"I always wanted a daughter, but it wasn't to be," said the housekeeper.

"Was there ever a Mister Varney?" Vivi bit her bottom lip, unsure if she should ask a question like that, but Madam Varney didn't seem to mind.

"No, my dear, I've never had a husband. It's just me. It's been just me for years. I grew up in Bezna village, nearby. My parents and sister died when I was young and I had no idea what the future held for me."

Vivi nodded. She could relate to what Madam Varney was saying.

The housekeeper continued, still brushing. "I was still quite a young woman – a girl – when the advertisement for a housekeeper for the new countess was posted in the village square. Nobody wanted to know. Not after the vampires – the fear and hatred stayed with people."

Vivi willed her to keep talking. "But for you, it was an opportunity?"

Madam Varney smiled. "Yes. An opportunity to live in a castle and find a new home doesn't come up every day. I had to take the chance while I could. I'm sure you understand?"

"Yes." Vivi did understand. It was exactly what she'd done herself.

"But the opportunities I found here meant that meeting a husband was out of the question. You don't meet many people at all up in these parts. And over the years, I have become loyal to her ladyship alone. She and I have grown old together. Don't misunderstand me – we aren't close. I am her servant and she treats me as such, but we both know a thing or two about being alone."

"How long have you worked for the countess?"

"For years now, my dear, years and years." Madam Varney spoke slowly, brushing to the rhythm of her words.

Vivi tried to imagine being in this place for 'years and years'. She couldn't.

"I suppose you have had visitors occasionally. The other girls, before me."

"The other girls, yes. But that was a long time ago." Madam Varney swept all Vivi's hair to one side, so it fell over her shoulder.

"What were they like? If you remember?"

"Yes, I remember." She rolled up Vivi's hair tightly, pinning as she went. A couple of the pins came close to Vivi's head, but didn't hurt her. "Truth be told, they were both such flighty girls. I never expected them to stay for long."

"The countess said they left without any warning, but I was wondering … did they tell you where they were going?"

Madam Varney shook her head. "Sadly, neither of them told a soul. They both just left letters. Would you like to see them?"

"Yes please!" Vivi hoped she didn't sound too nosey or desperate, and added, "If you don't mind."

The housekeeper chuckled. "I don't have them on me at this very moment! I'll find them next time we're in the kitchen."

"Can you remember what the girls wrote?"

"Oh no, my dear. I'm sorry to say I never learned to read or write."

"I'm only now learning properly," confessed Vivi.

"Yet another thing we have in common, Miss DeRose."

Vivi smiled. Madam Varney so rarely referred to their conversation that first day. It was like their little secret.

"But I don't understand; if you're unable to read, then why do you have the letters?"

"The countess gave them to me. She told me to throw them

on the fire, but I didn't feel that was something I could do. Not knowing the girls had families out there. Families that might ask about them one day. And I suppose, for me, they were a reminder the girls were once here."

Throw them on the fire! Why would Countess Marozny have suggested that? Unless she had something to hide. Vivi would make sure she asked to see the notes at breakfast time. They could explain everything. Madam Varney tapped her on the shoulder to signal she'd finished pinning, and Vivi swivelled around on her stool to face her. The older woman's eyes were red and Vivi hoped the conversation hadn't upset her too much.

"I suppose you have Kurt for company now," said Vivi, in an attempt to cheer her up.

The housekeeper beamed. "That I do, Mistress DeRose. And now we both have you, too." She paused. "You know, you could always call me Ma Varney too, as Kurt does."

"Call you Ma Varney...?" Vivi was rather taken aback. Her own mother had gone and she couldn't imagine ever calling anyone else 'Ma'. Not even Aunt Ina, who might not be the most maternal figure but had looked after Vivi. Vivi wasn't quite sure what to say. "I … er … think I'd better stick to Madam Varney for now, so as not to confuse the countess."

As she said it, she wondered briefly if Dorïce and Margareta had called Madam Varney 'Ma'. She hoped Madam Varney wouldn't be offended by her refusal, but the housekeeper didn't seem to mind. She nodded with some satisfaction at the finished hairstyle. With her forefinger, she teased one lock of hair out from the pins, its softness brushing against Vivi's cheek. Then she smiled. "It suits you. It shows off your neck, my dear, so long and elegant."

"Thank you," said Vivi, touching her hair, which felt neat and secure in its new style. She moved her chin from side to side. "My hair feels heavier, piled up on my head like this."

Madam Varney put Vivi's brush and leftover hairpins back on the washstand, lining them up neatly. "It will feel strange at first, but you'll soon get used to it. I'm sure you'd love to take a look at it yourself, wouldn't you?"

"Yes," said Vivi, trying not to sound too eager to admire herself, but Madam Varney shrugged apologetically.

"You've probably noticed we have no mirrors here at the castle."

"Yes. Why is that?" Vivi wasn't used to being surrounded by mirrors at home, but she'd have thought in a big castle like this, they'd have spared no expense.

"It's just the way the countess likes it."

Another odd rule. Hadn't Vivi heard somewhere that vampires couldn't be seen in mirrors? "But why?"

"It's not my place to question the castle rules. Now, I must get back to the kitchen. But I'm always happy to help with your hair again if you're still finding it tricky."

Madam Varney bustled out of the room to do whatever job was next on the list and Vivi called after her, "Thank you. Again!"

Vivi was fond of the housekeeper and hoped she didn't mind her reluctance to call her 'Ma'. Maybe it would be something Vivi would consider one day – just not yet.

Vivi patted her hair again, and stood up, holding her head stiffly. This must be how ladies felt all the time. She rather liked it. No one had ever told Vivi she had a long neck before, but she thought Madam Varney was probably right. Her ma's neck had been long and elegant – Vivi must have inherited it along with her love of singing. There may have been no looking glasses but Vivi knew she was looking her best.

Feeling confident, she took Margareta's vanity case from the back of the armoire and opened it up. She knew exactly what she was looking for. The decorative hair comb she'd discovered when she first opened the case. It was a distinctive accessory and she guessed anyone would recognize it as Margareta's. She wondered what the countess would say if she wore it to dinner. Would she realize then that Vivi had found the abandoned cases? If so, Vivi might get a sense of how the countess felt about the girls and if she'd had anything to do with their sudden disappearances. With a smile, she ran the teeth of the comb through her coiffed hair, flipped it over and secured it at the side of her head, above her ear.

Vivi sashayed down to dinner with her heavy head of hair held high.

Countess Marozny nodded approvingly across the soup tureen. "You are looking most elegant."

"Madam Varney helped me," said Vivi, as the housekeeper came in to serve.

The countess smiled at her housekeeper as she ladled yellowy orange soup into two bowls. "She has done a fine job and you look well for it."

Madam Varney made a modest, dismissive gesture with her hand and hurried out of the door, although as she did so, her eyes settled on Vivi's hair comb. Vivi thought she saw her purse her lips.

Vivi ate her soup, trying not to slurp. Pumpkin. Delicious.

Her hairstyle must be beautiful to attract a compliment from the countess. "My lady, why are there no looking glasses at Castle Bezna?" she asked.

"No looking glasses? Surely that's not true! You'll probably find one under a dust cover in one of the rooms on the south wing. Ask Madam Varney and I'm sure she'll arrange for one to be brought to the north tower for you. Or get her to ask the boy..."

Vivi shook her head as she swallowed another mouthful of soup. "There are none. I've checked." She wondered when the countess might notice the hair comb.

"Oh, Viviana, you've looked under every dust cover in the castle? This issue must be terribly important to you. Oh, to be young!" She began to laugh – a low, wheezing chuckle that made her cough. "Forgive me," she said, holding a napkin up to her mouth. "At my age, one tends to run from mirrors rather than seek them out."

The countess had another short fit of coughing. Once she'd recovered, she asked, "Any other peculiar questions for me this evening?"

It was possibly a rhetorical question, but Vivi took the opportunity anyway to ask about something else that was on her mind. "Well ... I was wondering if you have any pictures on the walls of your bedchamber?"

"None at all. I find plain décor much more calming. Why on Earth would you ask me that?"

Vivi shrugged and placed her soup spoon carefully back in the empty bowl. "I was just wondering."

The countess looked baffled. "Hmmm. Now tell me, Viviana, why is it you chose to learn the piccolo, rather than a more traditional instrument?"

This was a classic Countess Marozny question which, Vivi had learned, signified the previous conversation was over. The new line of questioning wasn't welcome, as she still wasn't entirely sure what a piccolo was. Did one bang it, blow it or play it with a bow? She finished the soup and placed her spoon down gently in the bowl while she thought. "My father played the piccolo and his father before him. There was really no other option for me."

"Indeed," said the countess, a faint smile on her lips.

Later, as they left the dining table, the countess said again, "I do like your hair like that. A definite improvement."

Vivi smiled coyly. They walked through the dining room door

and Vivi stepped to the other side of the countess so the butterfly hair comb was in clear view. The countess spotted it immediately and pointed to it with a long pale finger. "What's that adornment?"

Vivi's hand shot up to the sparkling stones. "This?"

"Yes – the hair comb. I didn't see it at the dinner table. I don't believe it's yours."

They stopped in the corridor for a moment, each meeting the other's gaze. It was one of those moments where Vivi could choose between the truth and a lie. But which one would allow her to extract the most information? She chose a half-truth. "You're right – it's not mine. I found it, tucked between the skirting board and the floorboards." She smiled again.

Countess Marozny shook her head. "How strange. Margareta was such a careful girl. So neat and precise. It would have been unlike her to misplace such a valuable item."

"Oh, I didn't realize." Vivi wiggled the comb loose from her hair, releasing a few stray locks. "Would you like it back? To send on to her?"

The countess stared at it for a long moment, then waved her hand dismissively. "No. No, I have no idea where the foolish girl is now. You may keep it. But please, save it for special occasions. Keep it somewhere safe, with your precious things."

What precious things? Vivi tucked the comb into the pocket of her dress. "No losing it under the skirting board for me!"

The countess stared at her with eyes as cold as the stones in the hair comb. "Quite."

*

To my dear cousin Vivi,

How my heart soared when I received your wonderful letter! What smooth white paper! And red ink! I've never seen coloured ink before.

Everyone at the laundry has been asking about you. I'm so pleased and proud to be able to tell them you're happy at Castle Bezna and you're receiving a proper education.

Vivi, you'll never guess what! Miss Winterburn came into the laundry looking for her pink dress – the one you borrowed for your trip. We all said we didn't know what had happened to it, but then Ivette came straight out and told them you'd taken it. I wish I'd never told Ivette. I said you must have packed it by mistake but Miss Winterburn insisted she'll have to be compensated. Ma has stopped being sad about you leaving and is now angry. In fact, she's angrier than I've ever seen her. She's coming down hard on us at the laundry. She asked me to write and tell you to come home <u>right away</u>. Failing that, if you could possibly send the dress back then it would make life a lot easier.

With so much love,
Dol xxx

Dear Dol,

I woud love to return the dress to Miss Winterburn and to make her and Aunt Ina happy. Unfortunatly, the dress doesnt look quite the same as it did wen it left Valesti. It got wet and riped on the way. Tell her it woudnt do to be wearing last years fashun and to get a new dress. Like me. You woudnt recognize me these days with my hair in a new fancy style and my new uniform making me look like one of them maids up at the hotel. I hope for your sake Aunt Ina doesnt stay too angry but you can tell her Im not coming back any time soon.

Im getting better at writing – see? Reading, too. The countess will make a lady of me yet. The countess likes *me! She said as much. Shell be riting me into her will before I know it! All is going to plan so far! I am happy even if I dont sleep too good. Its something about this casel. Evryone here is yawning all the time.*

The only thing is, I quite like the countess, too. I dont actually want her ded. Not that I woudnt want the casel, but shes not going anywhere yet. She is old, as we thort, but still walking about the place. Maybe shell give me a big present wen I leave at the end of the yir ...

I started reading all about the twelve vampires at the libry. There are twelve picturs to match in the gallery tho I found a blank space for another one at the end. I started looking for it. Then I found some luggige that used to belong to them other girls before me. I wonder where they went. Interesting isnt it? I bet youd have an idea with your big brain. Anyway got to go,

Vivi

X

Dearest Vivi,

Thank you for writing back so soon. I can see that

your writing is improving, and so quickly! If I'm not able to see you in person, then a letter from you is the next best thing. I'm sorry to say that Ma is <u>still</u> angry. She has such a hot temper. She thinks you are ungrateful for going and she's still cross about the dress. She says you're no longer welcome here and doesn't want to hear your name mentioned at home or in the laundry. Perhaps if you could write to say how sorry you are, then she might calm down and forgive you.

The mystery of the missing painting is interesting. I don't have any ideas where it could be, but don't give up searching, will you? This could be evidence that the thirteenth vampire is more than just a rumour.

It's funny you should mention the luggage. Ivette had been asking if you'd found out any more about the other girls before you. She's still convinced there's some mystery about their disappearance. What do you think? Oh, I do worry about you, Vivi, so far away from home.

I hope you continue to be safe, warm and happy.
Your very own,
Cousin Dol XXX

Dol,

Sorry for your sake that Aunt Inas stil angry. Im not going to rite and say sorry to her becos how can I be sorry for trying to bettr myself? Also for giving her one less mouth to feed?

For wunce I think Ivettes rite and that there is some mystry about the girls and the luggige. Madam Varney said there were some letters and shes going to show them to me. And your rite about the pictur. Im not going to give up. Ill serch evrywhere! This casel is full of mystries, that's for sure, and Im going to do my best to get to the bottom of some of them!

Vivi X

CHAPTER SEVENTEEN
THE CHICKENS

Over the next couple of days, Vivi thought a great deal about Dol's latest letter. It seemed Vivi had been right: she was no longer welcome in Valesti. This was exactly what she'd thought Aunt Ina would say, but it still hurt to read the words. Vivi did everything she could to put it out of her mind. She scoured the castle for the missing painting but found nothing. She even ventured into the attic above the south wing, which was empty and damp, with beams that looked ready to crumble. There was nothing at all up there. The only rooms she didn't search were Countess Marozny's bedchamber and the servants' quarters, but Madam Varney confirmed there were no paintings in either location. She wasn't sure where to try next and decided it was probably time to ask Kurt next time she saw him. In the meantime, Dol's letter had got Vivi wondering afresh about Dorïce and Margareta. She decided to find out what she could from Madam Varney.

Breakfast was always the best time to quiz the housekeeper, when she wasn't yet distracted by other jobs. Vivi waited until Madam Varney had placed her porridge and tea in front of her before beginning the questioning.

"Did Dorïce and Margareta eat breakfast down here with you, or up in their rooms?"

"I don't remember."

Vivi topped up her cup of tea from the pot. "Did they go outside very much, or did they prefer to spend time in the library?"

"I don't remember that, either." The housekeeper chuckled and shook her head. "You have so many questions this morning, my dear! What is it you really want to know? Are you comparing yourself to them?"

"I don't know. I—"

"Because, those other girls … they never fitted in here like you do. They didn't *want* to stay. Whereas you're different." The housekeeper patted Vivi's hand. "You and I are alike in so many ways."

Vivi smiled. "You did tell me you'd show me the letters that they left."

"That I did," said Madam Varney. "If I do, do you promise to stop with all the other questions?"

Vivi nodded, and Madam Varney wiped her hands on her apron and crossed the kitchen to the dresser. She opened the drawer and rustled through some papers. As she rummaged, Vivi called out, "Madam Varney, you told me you kept the letters to show the families, but *did* the families ever ask about them?"

"I'm sure they did, but they would have asked her ladyship, not me. Even if they had asked, the letters are so short that I doubt they'd have given much away. Look."

Madam Varney came back to the table and passed the letters to Vivi. They were brief and to the point, giving no more information than Vivi knew already. Margareta explained she was going to get married, but provided no details about her future husband. Dorïce's was even more vague, explaining that she was going to travel around the word but didn't specify where, or how long she'd be away.

The letters didn't put Vivi's mind at rest. If the girls were *really* starting brand-new lives, wouldn't they leave a forwarding address or details of what they were planning to do? Excuses, or at least reasons for going?

The lack of information was strange to Vivi.

But there was one more thing that was even stranger...

The handwriting in each letter was exactly the same.

Vivi would have liked to stay in the kitchen to gather more information, but the minute she had put her empty cup on her saucer, the housekeeper clapped her hands together. "It's lovely weather today. You should be outside – not up in that library with your nose stuck in a book."

Vivi did as she was told and went out into the gardens via the back door. Maybe Kurt would know more. She was also hoping, now she'd exhausted her own search, that he'd be able to help her locate the missing portrait.

But Kurt was nowhere to be found.

He usually had a habit of appearing whenever Vivi went outside. But not today. She looked in the kitchen garden, all around the rest of the grounds, then headed back to the kitchen garden again.

"Kurt!" she called, but there was no answer. Maybe he was upset with her for not coming out to see him for a little while. She'd meant to, but she'd been distracted by the book and the painting and the suitcases.

She couldn't think of anywhere else to look so she sat on the iron bench by the knot garden and waited.

A blackbird flew down to the vegetable patch, cocked his head to one side as if surprised by her presence, then flew off again.

It was quiet. Quieter than usual, even.

She couldn't put her finger on what was different. It was always quiet out here, after all. All she could hear was the rustle of leaves in the wind. Then she realized.

The chickens weren't clucking.

Maybe they'd wandered off, but that wasn't like them; they usually stayed close to their coop.

As Vivi unlatched the gate and approached the archway through to the coop, she noticed scattered feathers. Small fluffy white feathers blew about in the breeze and longer shiny brown feathers caught in the grass.

Her stomach rolled.

She saw the first bodies. Two of the gentle birds lay outside the door to the run, blood smeared down their breasts, heads hanging loose.

She gasped, closed her eyes and put her hands over her mouth.

Then she steeled herself to go further.

All eight chickens were there – four in the run and two in the coop.

All dead. Most decapitated.

It must have been a fox.

"Poor chickens," she said in a whisper.

A sob and a sniff came from the side of the coop. On investigation, Vivi finally found Kurt sitting in a tight ball, his legs drawn up and his face buried in his knees. He was crying hard. Vivi cleared her throat to alert him to her presence, and he immediately stopped crying and lifted his head. His cheeks were stained with tears, grime and chicken blood. He sniffed and dragged the heel of one hand across both cheeks, smearing the mess on his face so it looked even worse.

"Oh, Kurt," said Vivi. Despite the grimy cheeks, she wanted to give him a hug, but she was unsure what he might think about that. She patted him on the shoulder instead.

His chin quivered and he looked away. She knew guilt when she saw it. "It wasn't your fault, Kurt."

"It was," he said miserably. "It's all my fault."

Vivi remembered that the chickens were one of his responsibilities.

"Ah. Did you forget to shut the run last night?"

He began to shake his head, then seemed to change his mind and nodded, sobbing so hard he was unable to speak. Poor Kurt. He was sad about the chickens and no doubt he was also worried about getting into trouble with the countess, or – more likely – Madam Varney. And if anyone knew about getting into (and out of) trouble, it was Vivi.

"Come with me," said Vivi, putting out her hand to help him to his feet. She walked back round to the front of the coop and run. "Now, give me your gardening knife," she demanded.

Kurt frowned but he did as she asked, unhooking the knife from his belt and passing it to her.

Vivi unfolded the knife and tested it for sharpness on the tip of her thumb. "Foxes…" she said, kneeling in front of the open run door, "… have very sharp claws…" She put the point of the knife through the chicken wire and cut a ragged line so it flapped open. "This flimsy wire is no match for them. It's surprising no foxes have attacked before."

She stood up and closed the door to the run, sliding the bolts into place. Next she picked up one of the little bodies, trying not to look at it directly. It was stiff and light. She squashed it under the flap of chicken wire as if the fox had tried, and failed, to drag its kill out.

"There. It wasn't your fault," she repeated firmly and patted Kurt on the shoulder again.

Vivi tried all the usual things to cheer Kurt up – jokes, funny songs, asking questions about the garden – but he remained subdued and distracted. She left him harvesting green beans and went back to the library.

Vivi headed straight up to the upper level and found the book. But this time, she wasn't interested in the small details about the individual vampires. She wanted to know if there was any chance the hunters had missed one.

She opened the book and turned right to the back – to the section about the burial. It seemed an abrupt ending. There was no word about *where* the vampires were buried. Nothing to shed light on her questions. In frustration, Vivi turned the last page so violently that she dislodged the dust cover. As she went to replace it, she noticed that there *was* more writing, hidden beneath the flap of the dust cover. Vivi folded it open and began reading. It was a sort of postscript, written in the same hand as the rest of the book.

ADDENDUM

There is talk in the village. Rumours. Some believe the twelfth vampire killed was not the last. There is nothing to substantiate these claims, just stories. A sighting of an unidentified winged creature. The death of a sheep. This author, for one, does not believe there is any truth behind these stories. After the terrible years we've lived through, there will always be rumours. And yet, I have been persuaded to consider these claims – that it would be remiss of me not to include this information. I therefore record it here in case, heaven forbid, there proves to be any truth behind the idea of a thirteenth vampire and in case this book can be of help.

The author's initials were scrawled at the bottom:

AA

Vivi shut the book. So the top vampire expert acknowledged that there was a *possibility* that they hadn't found them all. Thinking about the dead sheep made her wonder again about the chickens that morning. Was it possible they'd been killed not by a fox, but by the thirteenth vampire?

Dearest cousin Vivi,

Thank you for your letter. Did you find the painting in the end? Or read the letters from the other girls? Tell me about Countess Marozny. Is she kind? Is she strict with your lessons? Does she have you working all day? She's obviously doing something right as your handwriting is so much improved. What about Madam Varney? And Kurt? He sounds nice and I'm glad there is someone there you can talk to, but I do hope you don't forget about me!

Lots of love from Dol xxx

Dol,

Im learning well and the food is the best Ive ever eaten. The countess is piculiar. There's no other word for her. She isnt as strict as she looks and sometimes I think shes kind but other times Im not so sure ... Madam Varney likes music hall songs, like me. She is kind and motherlike. Kurt even calls her Ma. Kurt is nais but looks scared all the time and is a bit sad at the moment cos all the chickens got killed on his watch.

I did read the letters from the other girls and they were short and didnt say much and the writing was the same which was odd. I still havent found the missing picture (sorry I spelled it rong last time) and I cant help thinking theres some mystry about it all. I no I keep telling you there is no vampire here and for a long time I beleeved that to be true. But the more I read and the more I discover, the more Im starting to beleeve there could be a thirteenth vampire after all. Theres this bit at the back of the vampire book where the old man says there were rumors they never found them all. I no, I no, its what you told me all along. I should always listen to you, Dol! But don't worry. If there is a thirteenth vampire, then its not going to get me. Im finding out evrything I can and Im staying one step ahead.

Love Vivi X

Dearest Vivi,

I am worried after reading your last letter that you're not as safe as I'd hoped. Please promise me that if you *do find any real evidence of a vampire on the loose then you'll come straight home.*

Even though Ma says you're no longer welcome here, I know she'd have you back if you were in real danger. She might be angry but you're still family after all.

Keep writing and keep me up-to-date with any developments as they happen.

Stay safe.

Your faithful cousin Dol xxx

CHAPTER EIGHTEEN
THE CRYPT

Two days after she'd discovered the chickens, Vivi went looking for Kurt, hoping she'd given him enough time to recover from the shock. He was in the kitchen garden, dipping a rag into a pot of blacking. "Kurt, I need to talk to you."

He looked up, startled perhaps by her abruptness. "About what?"

"I need to find the nearest burial ground."

"What? Why?"

"Because I want to see the final resting place of the twelve Castle Bezna vampires. It says in the book they were 'given a proper burial'. But it doesn't say where." She also told him what she'd discovered at the back of the book.

Kurt sniffed and shuffled his feet. "I'm not sure about any of this, Miss DeRose."

"Call me Vivi, *please*. How many times? And please tell me where the burial ground is. I can find out at the library, but it will be so much quicker if you tell me."

"There isn't a burial ground. At least, not for miles."

Vivi frowned. "Then where would they be?" She thought for a moment. Where would rich people bury their dead? "Is there a crypt anywhere on the castle grounds?"

Kurt shrugged. "I'm not sure."

"What do you mean, you're not sure?" Sometimes he could be quite frustrating. "Maybe it's that stone building that I've seen from the terrace. Come on, let's go and explore!"

Kurt and Vivi crossed the cold, hard lawn with its bare patches of earth and overgrown pebbly path, towards the wooden gate in the centre of the hedge. The sky was, as always, grey, but this time it was because the light of the day was dwindling, and not because more rain was on its way. At least, Vivi hoped so, as she'd forgotten the parasol.

Vivi unlatched the gate with ease and stepped through, with Kurt trailing along after her. The path led into a thick mass of pine trees like the ones she'd seen on the journey. "Are we still on castle grounds, or is this the forest?" asked Vivi.

"It all belongs to Castle Bezna. All the way to the river in that direction," said Kurt, pointing south.

The wooded area was darker and colder than it had been on the other side of the gate.

"I hope the wolves and bears know not to venture on to castle grounds!" joked Vivi. Vivi also hoped it was too early for a vampire to be out hunting.

They arrived at a low, single-storey stone building. It was about the size of a garden shed, with no windows. An imposing iron door stood at its centre, flanked by sturdy pillars.

"This must be it – the Marozny crypt!" exclaimed Vivi. She was thankful they hadn't had to venture further into the darkness of the trees to find it.

Kurt nodded his head for a couple of moments, then said, "Well, now you know where it is. I'd better get back to blacking that fence." He turned and began walking in the direction of the gate.

"No, no, no, no," said Vivi, catching his arm. "We're not leaving now."

"But you said you wanted to find a crypt. This is it."

"What do you mean, 'this is it'? I can't tell anything at all from the outside of the building. I need to see headstones – names – dates! All of which will be *inside*. Look – there's a great big door right in front of us. In my experience, doors tend to be for one thing – opening!"

"And closing," muttered Kurt.

"But in this case, opening. Do you know where the key might be?"

Kurt shook his head and scuffed the toe of his right boot on the ground, looking like he'd rather be anywhere else at all. This reminded Vivi of their first encounter.

"Sorry, Kurt, but I'm not getting this far only to give up. Let's take a closer look."

Vivi approached the door, which was heavy, but ornate, with floral ornaments and studs. The iron had weathered to a deep reddish brown. Above the door was the same 'M' as on the sealing stamp.

Vivi peered at the keyhole, which was very rusty – it probably hadn't been opened for years. She was surprised, then, when she pushed on the door with both hands and it opened with a loud creak. What a strange place Castle Bezna was, with the bedroom doors all locked every night, but the family crypt left open.

She beckoned to Kurt to join her. "It's unlocked! Just in need of oil, like all the hinges in this place."

Kurt shuffled over to join her by the doorway.

They peeped in together, but Vivi couldn't see much at all, apart from stone steps leading down into blackness.

"It's dark down there," said Kurt, stating the obvious. "We won't see a thing without a lamp. Let's come back another time."

Vivi tapped her pocket, which rattled. "Luckily for us, I have these matches." She was glad she'd kept hold of them.

Kurt hesitated. "The steps look terribly uneven."

"They'll be fine," said Vivi, with more confidence than she felt. "I'll go first."

She struck a match, which fizzed and blazed. "It might seem scary, but the thing about crypts is everything inside is dead. That means nothing can hurt us, doesn't it?" She knew, as she said it, that it wasn't strictly true in the case of vampires.

Kurt didn't reply, but he did follow as she descended the worn steps.

"Make sure you leave the door open," called Vivi. She heard a protesting creak as he pushed it wide open, then a clunk as he put a stone or some sort of weight in front to hold it.

She took slow, extra-careful steps as she didn't fancy tumbling down into the darkness. She made up a funny rhyme as they went.

> *"Whoops-a-daisy, nearly slipped*
> *And landed in the castle crypt.*
> *Everybody's dead in there*
> *But not us if we take care."*

Kurt didn't laugh but she felt better herself as the cold and darkness began to envelop them. There were about a dozen steps. At the bottom, the flame of the match bit at her fingertips. She dropped it and it went out instantly on the cold stone floor.

Her eyes hadn't yet adjusted to the change in light levels and, for a moment, it was too dark even for Vivi. She struck the next match and passed it to Kurt, who took it with shaking hands. His startled face looked so comical in the halo of light that she laughed as she struck her own match. "Take off your hat, Kurt. You don't want to burn it."

He pushed the hat back on its strap and they gazed around the crypt together. It was much bigger than it looked from the outside. Everything was made of stone, with five wide arches holding up the ceiling. It smelled cold, earthy and forgotten, which was much better than the rotting smell she'd expected.

Some light was filtering down the stairs from the open door but not much. White candles stood in tall, wrought iron stands by the bottom step.

"Quick, light the candles before your match burns out," said Vivi, doing the same. Once she'd lit the first candle, she dropped the match, removed the candle from its holder, and used it to light the others. She sang a new song under her breath.

"Light you first and watch you burn
Light another – it's your turn!"

"Can you stop that for one moment? The singing. Please," interrupted Kurt, sharply.

Vivi jumped. He sounded more cross than she'd ever heard him before. "I'm sorry. I didn't realize I was doing it." She was feeling jittery.

She continued lighting the candles, which were dotted around the crypt, in silence. With each new flame, a little more of the space was revealed. There was even more stone. Stone slabs on the floor, stone pillars and three stone coffins at the centre.

Vivi swallowed and bent to read the names. As expected, 'Marozny' was incised in most of them, with dates going back hundreds of years.

"Interesting. But none of them match the names on the vampire portraits."

Kurt shrugged. His eyes darted back to the doorway at the top of the stairs. He didn't have to say anything for Vivi to understand he was desperate to get out.

But Vivi hadn't finished. She had a feeling there was more to discover in this place.

And then she saw it.

Another door. It was small and hidden away in a shadowy alcove, so she'd nearly missed it.

"This is it, Kurt, I know it."

She turned the brass door ring and pushed, but it remained stubbornly shut.

"Leave it. It's locked. We'll look for the key and come back another time."

But that made no sense to Vivi. Why would the main door be

left open and this smaller secondary door locked? She kicked it hard out of frustration, not really expecting a result, but to her surprise, the door swung open. A whole new room.

Vivi gasped and peered in but could see very little without candlelight or natural light from the stairway.

She took one of the tall pillar candles from its stand and held it at arm's length, so as not to singe her hair. It provided just enough light for their purpose.

"Come on, Kurt."

He followed her through the doorway.

This annexe was smaller and more enclosed than the last, with a low ceiling and no pillars or ornamental arches. It had clearly been dug out as an afterthought. Vivi had to duck to get inside. The atmosphere was stifling and Vivi started to feel, more than ever before, that she'd been buried herself.

Straight away, she saw them. A row of coffins. Twelve, made of dark wood, and each with a brass label. Uncharacteristically, Kurt rushed towards them.

"What do the inscriptions say?" whispered Vivi, holding her candle out so he had twice as much light by which to see.

He wiped the dust off the first with the cuff of his sleeve.

"It's a name," he said in a low voice.

Vivi rushed over and Kurt stood back against the wall. She knew as she read it out what it was going to say. "Dorin the first."

The coffins were covered in layers of dust. She wiped the next label clean.

"Dorin the second."

She moved on to the next one. "This one's Adriana." She gave the lid a wiggle. Who knew what could be inside – a note from the vampire hunters or some hidden clue. She was, however, mainly relieved to find it nailed firmly shut.

The others were as expected. Dorin the third, Aalis… They were all there. The twelve vampires of Castle Bezna, given a proper burial, as it said in the book. Tears welled in Vivi's eyes, though she couldn't have said who the tears were for: the vampires, their victims, or the hunters who put them here. Maybe for all of them. She wiped her eyes with the back of her hand. This was no time for crying. She was here to find answers.

Twelve coffins. Twelve coffins for twelve vampires.

Vivi realized she'd been expecting to find thirteen.

Even if the thirteenth was on the loose, it would come back to sleep in its coffin, wouldn't it?

Maybe she had it wrong. Because really, what was the evidence for a thirteenth vampire? A missing portrait from the gallery? Dead chickens? Rumours in the book? It wasn't enough.

"They're all nailed shut," Vivi said.

Kurt nodded. He seemed frozen to the spot, his eyelids blinking rapidly in the candlelight.

There was a pause where Vivi was unsure what to do next. The excitement, combined with the stifling atmosphere, was beginning to overwhelm her. She felt a little shaky and put her hand on one of the coffin lids to steady herself.

"Have you seen everything you wanted to?" asked Kurt, shuffling over towards the door.

"Yes…" said Viv uncertainly, though she still had a feeling they had missed something important.

"There are twelve vampires, and they're all dead," said Kurt.

"Vampires are always dead."

"You know what I mean. Finished off. For ever."

She walked briskly around the annexe one last time, moving the candle up and down to check she hadn't missed anything. At the back wall, the annexe wasn't quite as small as she'd thought. The wall didn't go all the way across, and it was possible to walk behind it. She moved towards it, saying, "Kurt, how on Earth did you miss—"

But the sight in front of her made her stop mid-sentence.

There was a thirteenth coffin.

This one stood on its own, and looked newer than the others. The dark wood, free of dust, glowed in the candlelight, and the brass fixtures sparkled. Unlike the other coffins, the lid was propped open.

The most remarkable thing of all was it was empty. Empty of bodies, that is. Empty of bones. But it was lined with perfect pink silk, the colour of a dog rose in bloom. At the head end was a pillow, and bunched up below were some matching sheets.

Vivi shook her head slowly.

"What is it?" asked Kurt, making his way around the false wall to join her.

"The coffin lining should have rotted away. But this is pristine. Look, the pillow and the sheets look crumpled." She swallowed. "Someone must be sleeping here." Vivi felt shaky. Her fingers and toes fizzed with excitement and fear. "This is the proof we've been looking for. There *is* a thirteenth vampire and it sleeps right here in the castle grounds."

Kurt walked around to the lid side of the coffin, so Vivi could just see the top of his head. "It's not exactly proof though, is it – an empty coffin?"

"I'd say it's pretty convincing!" Vivi was rather glad they had found it empty, otherwise they might not be standing there having this conversation. However, she did want to know more about this vampire's identity. She had sudden inspiration. "There must be an inscription, like the others! Can you see anything, Kurt?"

Kurt didn't reply and she heard his nails scrabbling on the lid as if he was wiping it clean.

"Come on, Kurt, this is really important," said Vivi, impatiently, going over to join him.

"There isn't a brass label," he replied, pointing at the small holes in the lid where some screws had once fitted.

"It must have fallen off. Come on, let's look around."

They used their candles to illuminate every dark corner, but the floor was clear and clean. If there had been a brass label fixed to the coffin, it was now gone. Vivi may have found proof of a thirteenth vampire, but she was no closer to uncovering its identity.

CHAPTER NINETEEN
THE SECRET PASSAGEWAY

"It's time to leave," said Kurt.

Vivi was finding it difficult to drag herself away from the open coffin. She half-expected the answers she was looking for to leap right out at her. But Kurt kept checking his pocket watch, so Vivi followed him out of the annexe.

"When we get back to the castle, will you help me look for the missing portrait again?" she asked. She was closing in on the mystery, she could just feel it.

"Sorry, I can't – I've got work to be getting on with. I need to get that fence done before it gets too cold."

"Oh, come on, Kurt. Forget about the fence. It will be dark when we get back, anyway. You can't black fences in the dark, can you?"

Kurt lowered his gaze. "No."

Vivi began to snuff out the candles one by one, the main area gradually getting darker and darker. "We've just discovered there's a vampire sleeping right here in the crypt. And the coffin's empty, which means it could be flying about nearby *right now.*" Her legs felt shaky at the thought. "Don't you want to know where it is? *Who* it is?" She couldn't help thinking of the countess. Was she *really* asleep in her bedchamber right now?

The whites of Kurt's eyes looked bright in the near-darkness. "Of course – if there really is a vampire – but I don't understand how a painting's going to help."

Vivi was starting to feel the urge to take Kurt's hat and whack him round the head with it. How could he not see what they needed to do? Still, he was her only ally and she didn't want to upset him. She kept her voice steady. "Because I think whoever's in that picture *is* the thirteenth vampire. We'll know who we're looking for and if it's a stranger or … someone we know."

"Someone we know? What do you mean?"

The only portrait Vivi could imagine unveiling was of an old woman with a pale face and a high-necked collar, but she couldn't bring herself to voice her suspicions to Kurt just yet. "I just need to find the picture. I feel so sure it must be somewhere in the castle but I've looked everywhere. I've searched the storeroom from top to bottom; I've opened every drawer, looked under beds and on top of wardrobes."

Kurt folded his arms and looked away from Vivi at an uninteresting part of the stone wall. Even in the dim light, Vivi recognized that look. There was something he wasn't telling her.

"What is it?"

"Nothing."

"Kurt! What *is* it?"

He shrank back as though he thought she might hit him. She'd thought about it, but she'd never really do that and didn't mean to frighten him. She lowered her voice. "Tell me, please."

"It's just you haven't explored the whole castle yet," he said, his voice wobbly.

"I have. I've been right up to the top of the south tower. Is that what you mean?"

Kurt shook his head.

"Outside then? I suppose I haven't been into all of those ramshackle buildings. Do they house something interesting?"

Kurt wrung his hands together. "D'you promise not to tell the countess?"

"Of *course* I won't tell."

"Or Ma Varney?"

"I promise I won't tell anyone, Kurt. Where have I missed?"

"I can't tell you. I need to show you."

Kurt took his pocket watch out of his waistcoat and checked it again. "We have just enough time," he said.

"Time? Time for what?"

"You'll see."

Vivi grinned. Kurt was finally going to help her properly. She went to blow out the two candles in the final sconce, but Kurt put his hand on her arm to stop her. "We'll need those," he said, taking one candle for himself and handing one to her.

"What for?" asked Vivi, but Kurt had disappeared, dashing up the steps. She heard him closing the door, and the crypt grew awfully dark – only a small circle was illuminated by her candle flame. For a dreadful moment, she thought he'd shut her in with the coffins and the skeletons, and her legs felt weak, as though they might collapse beneath her. But soon Kurt was back, his candle flame bobbing towards her in the blackness.

"Are you coming then? There's a passageway," he explained.

Vivi's mouth dropped open. A secret passageway! Castle Bezna never stopped surprising her.

"Where?"

"Follow me." He led her back in the direction of the annexe. Almost directly in front of the alcove, in amongst all the stone, was a patch of wooden floor. Vivi was surprised she'd missed it, but then she'd been so excited to find the door, she hadn't noticed anything else.

"Remember you mustn't tell anyone about this," he said. He pushed down on a knot in the wood and a trapdoor sprang open.

"I won't," breathed Vivi, hardly believing what he was showing her. This time, Kurt went first, disappearing down some steps, and she followed, closing the trapdoor behind them. The hatch opened out into a corridor. She could barely see the walls and ceiling but the space felt small, as though she'd been swallowed by some gigantic animal. She was glad Kurt was with her; she'd hate to be down here by herself.

"We haven't got long," said Kurt. "Between six o'clock and half past, Ma Varney will be helping her ladyship get dressed. As soon as Ma Varney's done upstairs, she'll be back in the kitchen."

Vivi shook her head in confusion. "Why does it matter if Madam Varney's in the kitchen?"

"You'll see – come on."

They shuffled along, Vivi barely able to see where she was putting her feet. Did something brush past her ankle, or was it the swish of her skirt? She hoped there were no nasty surprises down here. Rats. Or worse – bats.

Vivi soon rediscovered her voice. "I can't believe I'm in an *actual* secret passageway in a castle. My cousin Dol is going to faint when I tell her this."

"You said you weren't going to tell anyone."

"Yes, but Dol doesn't even live here—"

"You promised."

Kurt looked so stern in the candlelight that Vivi laughed. "Very well, I won't tell!"

They kept walking in the near-darkness. The passageway was on a steady incline. Vivi breathed deeply. It was damp and earthy and her throat tickled. As always happened in tense moments, rhymes began to come into Vivi's thoughts.

"It's dark and damp in here, my friend—" she began, but was sharply interrupted by Kurt. "Please – no more rhymes!"

"It wasn't a rhyme," lied Vivi.

"It sounded like one. You were using your rhyming voice."

"Well it wasn't. I was just talking."

"Hmmm," said Kurt incredulously, and Vivi composed the rest in her head.

It's dark and damp in here, my friend
What's hiding at the other end?

Eventually, they reached another trapdoor, with a few steps leading up to it. By this time, Vivi had lost all sense of direction. She knew they must be somewhere under the gardens, but which part? The maze? The kitchen garden?

She felt breathless at the thought of what lay on the other side. Another crypt perhaps, or a treasure vault. Kurt climbed the steps and pulled a brass ring to open the trapdoor. Hands on either side of the hatch, he pulled himself through, then put out a hand to help Vivi do the same. Once they had made it through and closed the trapdoor, they began lighting candles.

The room itself was not as exciting as she'd expected. It was small and cluttered. It looked like an ordinary study.

Kurt shrugged, almost apologetically. "This is it."

The drapes were drawn, so the light was dim. The air was

thick and musty, like Vivi's bedchamber had been on the first day. In the middle of the room was a desk and chair of dark wood – the same wood as the thirteenth coffin. The left side of the room was dominated by a large bookcase full of books. The rest of the room looked more like elsewhere in the castle, with bulky shapes of unused furniture covered in dust sheets.

"Does this room belong to the countess?"

Kurt nodded. Vivi gaped. A secret room belonging to the countess and connected to a crypt? Didn't he find this strange? "Does she use it very often?"

"I don't think so."

The desk was polished and tidy, with no evidence of recent use. There were no paintings on the walls. Vivi cast her eyes around the room, looking at the dust sheet-covered shapes.

Kurt was standing by the bookcase, arms hanging straight by his sides.

"Can you help, please?" asked Vivi.

He sniffed. "What should I do?"

"Uncover anything that might be a painting. Let me know if you find any portraits."

Obediently, Kurt began ambling around the room, inspecting the objects beneath the dust covers.

"I'll have a quick look in here." Vivi opened the top drawer of the desk. There were more sheets of the lovely thick writing paper, and a sealing stamp, embossed with the letters 'H M'. She rolled some paper up and pocketed it, then closed the drawer.

"Here's one!" called Kurt, from near the window. Vivi looked up sharply, but the painting he was holding depicted a forlorn-looking pheasant.

"That doesn't look like a vampire to me," she said, with a smile. "Remember we're looking for portraits."

Kurt re-covered the frame, and Vivi went back to the desk. The second drawer down was empty but for a thick brown envelope. She took it out.

Neatly printed on the front, were the words:

THE LAST WILL AND TESTAMENT OF COUNTESS MAROZNY

A shiver ran through her. The countess's will! Vivi knew she shouldn't look, but it was too tempting to resist. She slid the document from the envelope and scan-read it. There was a lot of legal jargon, which she didn't understand, but her eye was drawn to one particular line at the bottom of the page:

> I give my residence, Castle Bezna, and all my tangible personal property to…

Vivi held her breath. Was it possible to imagine Countess Marozny might have left something to her, now that she'd been at the castle for a few weeks? She turned the page.

> … my faithful housekeeper, Madam Varney.
> *Signed*
> H Marozny

Madam Varney. Well, of course it would all be left to her – there was no one else, was there? Vivi had only been at Castle Bezna for just over six weeks, even if it felt like for ever. It would take longer than that for the countess to decide to change her will. If she managed to stay for the whole year then perhaps things would be different. But now she'd seen that empty coffin, Vivi's resolve was weakening for the first time. Would she manage another week at Castle Bezna, let alone a year?

She folded up the paper and put it back in the envelope, lost in her thoughts, when Kurt piped up from the other side of the study. "I've found a portrait," he said.

Kurt picked up the frame and held it up so she could see. Her heart began to race. It was not Countess Marozny. Or at least, not as she looked now. Within the frame was a young girl with dark eyes and a sullen expression, wearing a square-necked checked dress and a beaded necklace. She looked so familiar that Vivi's breath caught in her throat. Where did she recognize this face from? Could it be the countess as a child?

It took Vivi seconds to realize. "It's a copy!" she exclaimed. "It's the same as one of the pictures in the gallery. The one of the young girl – Griselda – hanging right next to the gap on the wall."

Kurt lowered the picture and Vivi's heart sank. This couldn't be the missing portrait after all; it was a copy. It made no sense. "Are there copies of any of the other paintings there?"

Vivi helped Kurt remove all the other sheets but there were no more portraits – just landscapes and animals. Vivi replaced the dust sheets. She didn't want to leave any sign they'd been there.

Kurt was looking at his pocket watch again. "We need to get back," he said, urgently. "It's nearly half past."

"I'm coming." Vivi checked that she'd left no evidence and that the desk drawer was completely shut. She had her candle at the ready, assuming they'd leave the way they came in, but to her surprise, Kurt pushed on the bookcase, and it began to move backwards – into the wall!

"It's the way out," he explained, somewhat unnecessarily. She blew out the candles, placed them on one of the shelves, and helped him push against the bookcase. It moved more easily than expected and rotated around so a gap opened up. As they tumbled through, she realized they were in the kitchen. That explained why Kurt kept wondering when Madam Varney would be back. They were standing in front of the large wooden dresser Vivi had admired. All this time, it had been hiding a doorway into the countess's study and the crypt.

"Wow!" said Vivi.

"Clever, isn't it? I just need to fix it in place again." Kurt removed the largest platter. There was a lever behind it, recessed into the back of the shelf, which he pushed shut, then put the platter back in position.

The kitchen was the same as always, music playing and pots bubbling. After the cold darkness of the crypt, it felt particularly welcoming and warm. Madam Varney appeared to have been making some rich stew for dinner and the smell of onion, paprika and cooked pork emanated from the oven. Vivi inhaled deeply.

Kurt gave the dresser a wobble to check it was secure, then stood by Vivi's side.

Without warning, Madam Varney appeared in the doorway.

"What are you two getting up to? Trouble, by the looks of things!"

"Trouble! Not at all!" said Vivi with a high laugh, and made a hasty retreat.

Dear Dol

Today, Kurt and I saw some more things that made me think the thirteenth vampire is still alive and well! Or ded and well. We visited the crypt and found thirteen coffins! The thirteenth was empty. We finally found the missing portrait! We followed a secret passagway to a secret study and found a portrait hidden. It was a copy of one of the ones in the gallery. Griselda. For a wile I was sure the thirteenth vampire was the countess but then the painting didnt prove a thing so I cant be sure.

I also found the countesses will. It said I leave everything to my faithful housekeeper Madam Varney. She hasnt left a thing to me. So for now, Im determin to stay for the year and see what changes. Madam Varney and Kurt have lived at the castle (sorry for spelling it rong before) for ages and they've never been attackd by a vampire.

You told me to come home if I see anything scary but how can I do that? Your ma might never have me back. It would be the workhouse for me. No, Im better off here, even if theres a vampire out in the woods. Im just going to keep my door locked and stay in at night.

Try not to worry.

Love from Vivi X

CHAPTER TWENTY

HELGA

Vivi did as she'd promised Dol, and kept her door locked and her head down. She slept little, but felt well apart from that. During meals and lessons with the countess, Vivi saw nothing out of the ordinary. The countess seemed in reasonable spirits and even nibbled on some carrot with garlic sauce every now and then.

A week had passed and Vivi stood in the gallery, in front of the portrait of Griselda, the dancing candlelight bringing life to her painted features. Griselda had taken on a new significance now and Vivi stopped to examine her every time she passed. Did Griselda have a secret? That morning, Vivi had brought the vampire book with her and she opened it to the Griselda page. There was very little information about her. The illustration showed a young, smiling girl who looked very much like any other girl, apart from the sharp tips of fangs protruding over her lower lip.

GRISELDA

The only child in the group of twelve, with the appearance of a ten-year-old.

Origins unknown. Perhaps the daughter of one of the other vampires.

There's no evidence that Griselda has killed a person, but she has been seen hunting with the others.

Leniency should not be shown due to her age. She is a vampire, like all the others, and it is a merciful act to put an end to her unnatural 'life'.

Origins unknown. She had been an enigma even to the vampire hunters.

"What is it you're hiding?" Vivi looked into the painting's realistic eyes. Out of all the twelve, it was most difficult to imagine Griselda as a vampire. Partly because of her age but partly because she had such a sweet expression: lips turning up slightly as if she was trying not to laugh.

Vivi was about to turn and walk away when she realized something.

A *sweet* expression? When she'd looked at the portrait in the study, she'd been struck by the *sullen* expression on the girl's face.

Was it possible the paintings weren't identical after all?

She dropped the book on the floor and ran off to get some answers.

"Kurt, Kurt!" Vivi ran into the kitchen garden, where Kurt was raking up fallen leaves. She was out of breath from running all the way. "I need your help."

Kurt stopped stiffly by the leaves, rake in hand. "What is it this time?"

"I've been looking at the picture of Griselda—"

"Who?"

"*Griselda*: the portrait in the gallery. And I'm fairly certain it's not the same as the one in the secret study! They have different expressions."

Kurt shrugged and continued with his work, the tines of the rake scraping loudly on the stone. "Maybe they painted two and hung the one they preferred."

"Then why is there an empty space on the wall? I think it's for another vampire! Don't you see? This could explain everything! Help me get the painting from the study and I'll show you."

"I can't, Miss De … Vivi… I'm busy here…"

"The leaves can wait." She took the rake from him and placed it next to the low wall. "Honestly, Kurt, this is important – all you have to do is help me carry the picture and you'll see."

Kurt looked around. "What about Ma Varney?"

"It's wash day. We're safe this morning. She won't know you've gone."

"Very well, but then I'm coming straight back out here again."

Vivi and Kurt smuggled the picture out of the study using the entrance behind the revolving dresser. Nobody could disturb them. The countess was asleep, of course, and Madam Varney would be busy with the washing until at least lunchtime.

They kept the dust cover over the painting, in case they were disturbed, then carried it up to the gallery. In its frame, the picture reached up to Vivi's shoulders, and it was heavier than it looked. Even with the two of them carrying it, they had to keep stopping to give their arms a break.

When they reached the gallery, they propped the frame on the floor, beneath the picture of Griselda. Kurt brushed his hands together and wandered off in the direction of the staircase.

"Where are you going?" Vivi asked.

"I don't belong up here," he said. "I've helped you carry the picture. I'm going back outside now."

Vivi could see what he meant. He did look out of place among the beautiful frames with his worn clothes and dirty hands.

"Please look at the portraits with me, just for a minute," asked Vivi. "I promise you'll see how they're different."

Kurt looked over his shoulder towards the stairs and then gave in to his curiosity, following her back to the painting. "One more minute."

She whisked off the sheet and they both stared. Vivi looked from one portrait to the other, comparing details. The girls were pretty much identical, with hair styled the same in both pictures, in a centre parting and scraped back from their faces. But their expressions were different. The one from the study had her mouth set in a straight line, whereas the one on the wall had that slight upturn at the corners of her mouth. She also had a mole just above her upper lip that was absent from the hidden painting.

"When you see them side by side like this you can see the differences," said Vivi. "They're very similar, but not the same."

And then she saw the biggest difference of all.

"Kurt, look at the name at the bottom of this portrait!"

The name in the corner didn't read *Griselda* at all, but,

Helga

Vivi hadn't spotted the name in the study – it had probably been covered by the sheet. Suddenly, it all became clear.

"They were sisters. Twins!"

Kurt peered at the pictures, his eyes flitting from one to the other. "I s'pose they must have been."

"All those years ago, when the townspeople came hunting, they thought they knew all the vampires. But they missed Helga. That's why she's not in the book." Maybe Helga and Griselda never hunted together so people assumed they were the same person.

A memory returned to her from the laundry gossip.

"In one of the villages, twin girls were taken from their beds and never seen again."

She couldn't remember who'd spoken, but that was definitely what they'd said. Twin girls. Griselda and Helga. Turned to vampires. It all fitted.

Kurt creased his brows together. "But if Helga is the thirteenth vampire, does that mean we're looking for a little girl? From the portrait, she looks younger than me, doesn't she?"

"Well, yes. Unless … I think there's a section about her in the book."

Vivi picked the book up from where she'd dropped it earlier and thumbed through the pages until she found the section she was looking for. She turned the book to show Kurt. "It's here, look."

She read it aloud.

VAMPIRES – APPEARANCE

When it comes to vampires, appearances can be deceptive. The first thing to remember is, of course, although vampires are dead, they don't look dead. They can appear pale or dusty-looking, but not always.

The second thing to remember is they do not age as humans do. It is often thought they cannot age at all and continue to look the same as when they died. But there are exceptions to this. Some of the vampires of Castle Bezna did appear to age. It seems this aging process can be brought about if they don't consume the required quantity of human blood. This aging, which is not reversible, does not happen at the same rate as human aging.

In addition, some vampires can shapeshift. They might become a bat, a wolf, or a fox for a time, or dramatically alter their looks to appear as a live human.

It is therefore impossible to judge the age of a vampire by their appearance.

One way to identify a vampire is to use a mirror. Because they have no soul, their reflection will not appear. However, most vampires will do their best to avoid mirrors.

"Oh. So the thirteenth vampire could look any age from about ten to a hundred. They could even look like a bat or a wolf. Not particularly helpful," said Vivi.

Kurt scratched his nose and Vivi continued to stare at the painting. The girl – Helga – looked so familiar. Something about the eyes. She'd seen the expression somewhere before. "Does she look familiar to you?"

Kurt looked towards the stairs. "I don't know... I don't think so..."

"If Helga's the thirteenth vampire, then the big question is, where is she now? Maybe she's closer than we think."

"What do you mean?" Kurt's voice was high – panicky even.

Vivi didn't answer him. She had to get the thoughts straight in her own mind first. The countess had signed her name at the bottom of the will as *H Marozny*.

What if the 'H' stood for Helga?

For a long time now she'd been thinking about it, but now she dared to ask the question aloud. She spoke in a whisper, as if the portraits might somehow report back what they'd heard. "Kurt, what if her ladyship is the thirteenth vampire?"

Kurt gawped and froze like that, in such a comical fashion Vivi nearly started giggling. "You think *Countess Marozny* is a *vampire*? But why?" he asked, in a similar whisper to her own.

"Oh, come on, Kurt, don't tell me you've not thought the same thing. The strange hours she keeps, the drapes drawn all day long, the fact we never see her eat."

"That doesn't mean she's ... one of *them*," said Kurt, his voice barely audible.

They both stared at the portrait. Could it be the countess as a young girl? It was impossible to imagine what she might have looked like all that time ago. Vivi tried to remember what she'd been told about the countess. The townspeople had searched for the heir to the Marozny fortune for years and no one came forward. Then suddenly, after the twelve vampires had all been killed, she arrived to claim her inheritance.

"It's all a bit suspicious, isn't it?" said Vivi. "What if the countess wasn't a Marozny at all? What if she was the thirteenth vampire, who had hidden away for a while and then came back? Look at the girl. Look right into her eyes. She has a *piercing* expression, don't you think? It could be the countess when she was young."

Kurt shook his head vigorously. "I don't know. I can't tell. It could be anyone." It was difficult to tell from the painting. Countess Marozny's eyes were green-grey. The eyes in the painting looked dark – almost black – which could be the lighting in the painter's studio, or the paint used, or artistic licence, or the age of the painting itself.

Kurt put his hat back on his head and rubbed the back of his neck with his hand. "I have to go now. Ma Varney will be cross if she catches me here."

"Before you go, what is the countess's first name?"

"I don't know," said Kurt.

"But you *must* know! How long have you lived here?"

"Thirteen years."

"Thirteen *years*?!"

"Months! I mean months."

"Thirteen months, and you don't know her name? Why not? What's she hiding behind that 'H'?"

"Lots of names begin with an H," said Kurt weakly.

"Name some."

"Well, there's Helga, of course, and Heidi. Horace…"

"Horace is a man's name."

"Erm, Helen. Or Helena, Hannah, Hester, Hatty, Hilda…"

Vivi waved her hands to stop him. Why couldn't he see that it all fitted her theory? "Fine, there are a few, but I still don't think it's a coincidence and I'm going to find out the countess's first name."

"You can't ask her that! It would be rude."

"I know. But I didn't say I was going to ask her, did I? I said I was going to find out."

After Kurt had left, darting down the stairs with visible relief, Vivi decided to hide the portrait of Helga in her room. She doubted anyone would miss it, plus it would come in handy if she wanted to check any details about the appearance of the thirteenth vampire. At least her bedchamber wasn't far away. Vivi managed to get the picture through the workshop and down the north corridor all by herself by resting it on the tops of her feet as she shuffled along. It only just fitted through the doors of the armoire. What with Jarv's parasol, Margareta's vanity case and her travelling dress, it meant there was little room for anything else.

She flopped back on to the bed, exhausted, and tried to get her thoughts in order. Had the countess been an identical twin who had been missed by the vampire hunters, and stayed hidden until she came and claimed Castle Bezna? What if poor Dorïce and Margareta had never left Castle Bezna at all, but had actually fallen victim to the countess? That would explain the matching handwriting in their – fake? – letters. What if the notice that Vivi had replied to had been designed to lure the thirteenth vampire's next victim to the castle? And the biggest question of all: what if Vivi was right about any of this? What would she do next?

She had only been lying there for a short time when she heard a familiar sound: horses' hooves and carriage wheels. She leapt back up, climbed on top of the bed, and attempted to look out of the window. Even on tiptoes, she couldn't see down to the ground. No matter – she could guess who it was anyway – there was only ever one visitor at Castle Bezna.

Vivi left her bedchamber and raced along the corridor, through the gallery and down the stairs, ready to greet Jarv at the back door. She opened the door at the exact moment Jarv was about to post the letters in the box.

"Anything for me?"

If the coachwoman was startled at Vivi's sudden appearance, she didn't show it. She just raised an eyebrow with her usual amused expression.

"Good morning, Miss DeRose. Yes, I've got one here for you from your little cousin and two for the countess."

Jarv handed the letter from Dol to Vivi, who tucked it in the pocket of her skirt. Vivi held out her hand for the others. "Let me take those! It will save you putting them in the post box."

Jarv raised the other eyebrow. "It's no problem to put them in the box, but if you want them, you're welcome to 'em."

Vivi read the addresses on both envelopes.

HER LADYSHIP THE COUNTESS
MAROZNY OF CASTLE BEZNA

THE RIGHT HON. COUNTESS H MAROZNY

No indication what that 'H' might stand for. She sighed. "Maybe I will put them in here after all," she said, and stuffed both envelopes in the box. "Do you know what the 'H' stands for in the countess's name?"

Jarv shook her head and laughed. "No. Your behaviour gets stranger every day, Miss DeRose."

Vivi shrugged. She had grown to like the coachwoman. Maybe she could trust her. "Jarv…?"

"Yes, Miss DeRose?"

For a moment, Vivi nearly blurted everything out. How she was sure there was a thirteenth vampire, how she was beginning to suspect it was the countess. But something stopped her. Jarv might feel like a friend, but in reality, Vivi barely knew her. The coachwoman might report Vivi's suspicions straight back to Countess Marozny.

Vivi thrust her hand into her pocket and pulled out her letter to Dol. She handed it over. "Could you please make sure this reaches Dol?"

"Yes, Miss DeRose. Are you sure you don't want to return to Valesti with me? You could give it to her yourself."

Vivi sighed. She would love to go back to Valesti. To see Dol, to feel safe. But she was on a mission. If the thirteenth vampire was flying around the mountains, then it could attack anyone at any time. She'd be no safer in Valesti than here and would be passing up the opportunity of a better life. She could even end up at the workhouse. If Vivi discovered the vampire was here at Castle Bezna, then that was a different matter. *Then* she would take Jarv up on the offer.

"No thank you, Jarv," said Vivi, although this time she didn't make a joke about it. "I'll let you know if I change my mind."

Almost as soon as she'd closed the door, Vivi ripped open the seal on Dol's letter. Before she read it, she turned the paper around. Dol always wrote on the back of the notices from Castle Bezna, and maybe – Vivi couldn't remember – the countess's name was printed on those. But no, there at the top was the usual heading:

HER LADYSHIP THE COUNTESS MAROZNY OF CASTLE BEZNA ANNOUNCES A GREAT OPPORTUNITY

No first name. Vivi turned the paper back over and immersed herself in Dol's words.

Dearest Vivi,

What an exciting life you are leading, with secret passageways and mysteries to unravel! I'm sure that this life suits you well, but I cannot lie: I am concerned about the thirteenth vampire. If it is out there, then you are in real danger. I wish you'd come home, but if you won't then please tell me everything and I'll try to help. You may think this foolish, but could the portrait depict the identical twin of the girl in the gallery? Just an idea. While you're getting to the bottom of the mystery, please don't trust anyone else with your secrets: the vampire could be closer than you think. Don't change your behaviour too suddenly. You must be doing something right, or the vampire would have attacked by now.

Keep your door locked, wear garlic and stay alert! I'm sure Ma would have you back despite what she says. Just ask Jarv to take you home. Ma would hardly turn you away if you were on the doorstep.

All my love,

Dol xxx

Vivi wasn't as sure as her cousin that Aunt Ina would have her back. If she ran back to Valesti she might find she had no home to go to. No, she couldn't return and she didn't *want* to, at least until she got to the bottom of the Helga mystery. What if Vivi ran away without checking her facts and her worries about the countess turned out to be completely unfounded? Countess Marozny would no doubt find a new companion to take her place. She might grow fond of her new companion. She might leave the castle to her! Vivi would have to be brave enough to wait a while longer. She did wish Dol could be at Castle Bezna with her, though. Dol was so clever. She'd figured out that the paintings were of twins before Vivi, and she hadn't even seen them! But now Vivi knew so much more. If only she'd penned a quick letter to Dol this morning to tell her about the name Helga. Now her cousin's advice would have to wait until the next letter. By which time everything could change again.

Vivi felt nervous about facing the countess that evening. What if she really was Helga Marozny, the thirteenth vampire? What if she suddenly flew at Vivi? Vivi would be powerless to do a thing.

But when Vivi was finally sitting at the dinner table, opposite the countess, it was impossible to feel afraid. Everything, from the ticking clock to the garlic sauce on the table, all seemed so *ordinary*. Ordinary for Castle Bezna, at least. Perhaps Kurt was right and Vivi was placing too much importance on a single initial. But Vivi would still like to know the countess's name even if it was to rule her out. When the countess didn't immediately speak, Vivi took the opportunity to lead the conversation.

"My lady, all the books I've been reading have got me thinking about names." Mentioning books usually caught the countess's attention. It had the desired effect this evening and the countess smiled while she focused her gaze on Vivi. "Really, Viviana? What exactly have you been thinking about?"

Vivi sliced through a roast potato. Had she been at home, she would have pronged it with the point of her knife and gobbled it whole, but she was still doing her best to appear elegant. "I've been wondering, if I became a writer, what I might choose as a 'nom de plume'." She'd recently learned the expression and thought it sounded sophisticated.

The countess sat up straight in her chair and her smile widened. "You have been considering writing as a profession? I have to say I'm delighted to hear that. Tell me, do you see yourself as more of a fiction or non-fiction writer?"

"I … er…" This conversation wasn't going in the direction Vivi intended. "Fiction, I suppose. I thought I would like to write under a name quite different to my own…"

"Fiction writing as a profession takes some dedication and you might find barriers in your way – particularly as a woman. Yet it is important to view these as challenges rather than obstacles—"

"Challenges, yes," interrupted Vivi. "Having a strong name would help. Names beginning with H are favourites of mine. If I do publish a book, I think I would choose a name like Hannah or Heidi, or perhaps … Helga." She paused and watched for a reaction.

The countess put down her glass and gave a small chuckle. "Helga. Really? Oh, my dear Viviana, you are a rare individual. You would do best to keep your own name, as it suits you so well."

Vivi nodded as she chewed her potato, thinking of another way to approach the subject.

"My lady, did you ever have a childhood nickname?"

The countess blinked rapidly. "What an odd question."

"It's just, I've been thinking about names—"

"So you say—"

"Yes, and I thought how strange it was my parents called me Viviana and yet they rarely called me by my full name. It was usually Vivi. And my cousin Dorothea is usually Dol…"

"I favour using a person's full name, as I'm sure you realize by now, Viviana."

"Yes, but as a child, did your parents ever call you by another name?"

The countess looked surprised at the question. Something about her intent gaze made Vivi think of Helga in the picture.

"I rarely think about my childhood. It all seems so long ago now…"

The countess's eyes glazed over and she began to drift away, in that way she sometimes did. Vivi began to think the conversation was over, when the countess started talking again. "You know, I'd almost forgotten this, but when I was quite a small child, I used to enjoy nibbling on herbs from the kitchen garden."

"Herbs?" Vivi failed to see where this story was heading.

"Yes. I was particularly fond of lovage. I'd munch on the leaves and the stalks. My favourite dish was a fragrant lovage soup. My father was amused by this and called me Little Miss Lovage. Thank you for reminding me – I'd quite forgotten."

The countess smiled happily to herself. It was confusing. At times like this it was impossible to believe she could be a vampire. But then, according to the book, vampires were masters of deception. Maybe the countess was hiding her true nature. Or maybe she was a kindly vampire who only attacked people she didn't like.

Vivi went back to eating her meal.

If only she could find out the countess's name, then she'd be able to stop asking herself all these questions.

Formal lessons with the countess weren't as regular now that Vivi was reading so proficiently. Her writing was naturally improving as a result and she barely made mistakes any more. The countess encouraged Vivi to read even more books in the library and to discuss them at dinner. But that evening, Vivi was too distracted to read. She wished with her whole heart that Dol was there to talk to. Dol would think of an easy way to find out someone's name. Instead of picking up a book, Vivi returned to her bedchamber and penned a hasty letter to her cousin.

Dear Dol

You were right about the portraits being of twins. They are almost but not quite identical and the missing one is named Helga, not Griselda. I keep wondering if it coud be the Countess Marozny when she was young. I know from the will that her first name begins with an H, but I cant find her full name printed anywhere. I am so confused. When I think about it in the daytime I feel sure the countess had something to do with the disappeernce of the other girls. Then wen Im with her in the evenings I think she cant possibly be a vampire. Shes ecksentric and lonely but not <u>evil</u>. If only I could find out her name, I would know one way or the other. Can you help?

 Your loving cousin,
 Vivi

CHAPTER TWENTY-ONE
SUSPICIONS

"We need to equip ourselves," said Vivi.

Kurt was on a ladder, pruning the pear tree, his face partly covered by the boughs.

He snipped away for a few moments, the twiggy ends of some branches falling by Vivi's feet. Then his voice floated down. "What do you mean?"

"Whether the vampire is out there in the woods or even closer than that, we need to protect ourselves. I've written to my cousin

Dol asking for help. As soon as Jarv comes, I'll give her the letter to take to Valesti, but in the meantime, we need to be prepared. Just in case. After all, the vampire could go anywhere when it's out of its coffin."

Kurt shrugged as he climbed down the ladder. "Why don't we tell Ma Varney? She'll know what to do. She always does."

Vivi shook her head vehemently. "No. Madam Varney won't hear a word about vampires. Also, she loves Countess Marozny. If we tell her, she might tell the countess, then where would we be? If the countess *is* the vampire and she finds out, she could turn on us all. We need to do this by ourselves and put into action everything we know about stopping vampires, so that we're ready."

Vivi had brought the vampire book with her out to the garden, to help persuade Kurt. She beckoned him over and they sat side by side on the bench. "Look – this is the part we need."

This section of the book made her blood run cold. But the pages contained important information. She began reading aloud.

THE END OF THE CASTLE BEZNA VAMPIRES

It is, of course, incorrect to refer to 'killing' vampires, since, by definition, vampires are neither live nor dead beings. It is really an act of mercy to put an end to the vampire's unnatural 'life'.

To ensure the Castle Bezna vampires were unable to rise again, sharpened wooden stakes were driven into the creatures' chests. This process is of course easier said than done. It requires strength of body, but also a certain inner steel. Those villagers who embarked on the hunt risked their lives. It was important, then, that we knew we would succeed. Certain steps were taken to debilitate the vampires:

1. The vampires were deprived of human blood. For two days before the attack, a decree was sent around. All the villagers were told to stay inside, with their doors locked and wreaths of garlic or roses hung outside. They were told not to venture out for any reason. Animals were locked away. Of course, the barns were less secure than the houses and we lost many sheep and cows over those nights, but no humans were taken.
2. Daylight was a key factor. The attack took place under a cloudless sky at midday in high summer to allow for the highest light levels.
3. Each hunter wore a wreath of garlic around their neck.

Coincidentally, the summer was also garlic harvesting season, so the freshest, most potent bulbs were picked.

The hunt was a necessary evil which allowed the people of the Falnic Mountains to live in peace. Still, we should not forget these vampires were once human, like all of us. Indeed, some of the twelve Castle Bezna vampires were victims of vampires themselves, who'd been turned. Families of the victims were still living in the villages. Therefore, once killed, or killed once more, all the vampires were given a proper burial.

"We need to take some of these tips and use them to defend ourselves," said Vivi.

"We haven't got any garlic," said Kurt, quickly.

"Don't tell me you've run out! Surely, somewhere in your well-stocked kitchen garden, there must be one teensy bulb."

"We don't grow it. The countess doesn't like it."

Vivi gaped. "What? She told me she loved it! Garlic sauce is one of the few things I've seen her eat." That had been one of the strongest pieces of evidence Vivi could find against her being the thirteenth vampire.

Kurt shook his head. "That's chive sauce, not garlic." He reached over into the vegetable bed next to him, snipped off a few green strands and passed them to Vivi, who chewed them, enjoying the mild, oniony flavour. It was a bit like garlic.

"I *thought* the sauce tasted different to Aunt Ina's! So the countess doesn't like garlic after all. She tricked me! Why would she have done that unless she had something to hide?" Vivi stared at Kurt, waiting for him to catch on to the importance of this, but he just shrugged. Why couldn't he see that all fingers were pointing to the countess? Vivi wasn't going to argue with him about it any more. For the first time, Vivi began to think she might leave with Jarv on her next visit. In the meantime, she needed to stay practical and follow the advice in the book.

"If garlic's not possible, what about sharpened wooden stakes – do you have any of those about?"

Kurt shook his head. Vivi sighed. "I'll have to whittle some myself. May I borrow your gardening knife?"

Kurt handed it over.

Vivi selected a sturdy-looking branch that Kurt had pruned from the pear tree and began whittling. She stripped off the bark and worked on sharpening the end, which was more difficult than it looked. She kept cutting off the point and having to start again.

The result was a not-very-sharp, bendy stick about the size of a pencil.

"I don't think I have much hope of killing anything with this," said Vivi, digging the unimpressive point into the bare vegetable patch.

She started on a new stick, which was much tougher and less bendy, but the bark was more difficult to remove. She'd only taken off about an inch's worth, when she managed to nick her thumb with the knife.

"Ow!" she cried, loud enough to make Kurt jump. It was not a large cut, but quite deep, and it throbbed. Blood trickled down her thumb and on to her wrist. She held her thumb up in the air as she'd been taught by her ma, while she searched her pockets with the other hand for something to wrap around it.

"Do you have a handkerchief?" she asked Kurt, but he didn't reply. He stood as still as one of the statues on the gateposts and stared with bright eyes at the trickles of blood dripping on to the stone paving. Then he looked away and jammed his hands into his armpits.

"Maybe there's a dressing in the kitchen?" suggested Vivi.

"I'll go and find Ma Varney," he cried, and bolted for the

kitchen.

She heard the back door slam as he ran into the castle.

Great. Her fellow vampire hunter had an aversion to blood, as well as the dark and, well, just about everything else. She wouldn't be able to rely on Kurt if things got nasty.

Eventually, her one-handed pocket search produced a handkerchief. It was crumpled, but clean enough, and she wrapped it around the cut. She sat there for a moment in the quiet of the kitchen garden. A cool breeze shook the pear tree, and a flurry of dry leaves fell to the ground. The fruit was long gone and the leaves were falling fast.

The blood had soaked through the handkerchief. Vivi refolded it so a fresh white part was facing the cut. This time just tiny red spots made their way through the material. It was still sore, but it would probably be all right without a dressing.

This was fortunate because Kurt seemed to have vanished for good. Maybe he'd been waylaid by Madam Varney with a new chore. Or maybe he'd forgotten. Either way, he wouldn't make a very good nursemaid.

Vivi wandered into the kitchen. Madam Varney beamed at the sight of her.

"Hello, my dear. Have you come for a cup of tea?" There was no cake on offer now that the chickens had gone.

"No – I was just looking for Kurt."

"Oh, you just missed him. He left through the pantry way. Seemed to be looking for something. Why don't you have a cuppa and a sing-song with me – keep me company for a few minutes? He'll no doubt be back soon."

Vivi smiled. "Very well. That would be nice. Thank you." She pulled up her usual chair and Madam Varney went to put the kettle on.

"You look a little peaky. Are you feeling well?" called the housekeeper from over by the stove.

"I'm fine!" replied Vivi. She kept her hurt hand hidden under the table. It wasn't as bad as she'd first thought and Madam Varney would only ask how she'd cut herself. Vivi didn't think she'd approve of them whittling stakes to kill vampires, even in self-defence.

"Glad to hear it. This damp mountain air doesn't suit everyone. Just look at her ladyship," said Madam Varney.

"Hmmm," replied Vivi, noncommittally. "By the way, do you know when Jarv is due to come here next?"

Madam Varney snorted. "When she's due to come here? You make it sound as though the woman runs to a timetable rather than to her own fancy."

"But she's always been such a regular visitor."

The kettle whistled and Madam Varney poured the tea. "Jarv may well have been a regular visitor over the autumn. She tells us that we'll see her at least every week, but, as the days grow shorter and the nights grow cooler, we'll have fewer visits from her or anyone else. Who knows when she'll come next."

"Oh." Vivi was surprised by the answer. Jarv had said nothing about fewer visits.

"Why are you so interested in the kitchen deliveries, anyway?" asked Madam Varney, putting a cup of tea in front of Vivi.

"It's not the deliveries. I was hoping to send a letter to my cousin."

Madam Varney's forehead creased with concern. "An important letter, is it, my dear?"

Vivi blew on the tea to cool it. "There's something I've been worrying about and I don't know what to do... I was hoping my cousin could give me some advice."

"Dear oh dear," said Madam Varney, wiping her hands and pulling up a chair. "You know you can talk to me about anything, don't you?"

Vivi nodded, feeling in a quandary. Madam Varney had asked her not to mention vampires, but she was so kind and sympathetic

Vivi had an urge to open up. She didn't know where to begin and found herself tripping over the words. "It's just I found a painting ... and a book ... and it's full of stuff about vampires... And I'm worried that the countess ... well, she can be so strange and sleeps all day..."

Madam Varney put up a hand in front of her face like a stop sign. "No. No, no, no. I can see where this is going and I won't hear of it. Miss DeRose, you and I have been friends these past few weeks. But I have spent the best years of my life at the castle with Helga Marozny. We've kept a professional distance, but we've still been close, in our own way—"

Vivi leapt up, rattling the cup in its saucer. She grabbed the housekeeper's arm. "What did you call her?"

Madam Varney looked flustered and shook her head. "I spoke out of turn. I try not to use her given name, as I avoid yours. She should remain 'her ladyship' when we talk between ourselves—"

"But her given name – it's *Helga*?"

Madam Varney creased her brows together. "Yes, but it's not the done thing to call her that. We should call her 'my lady', or 'Countess Marozny' or—"

But Vivi didn't stay around for the lecture on manners or for the tea. "I'm feeling a little unwell. I have to go!" she called, already halfway out of the kitchen door. This was the biggest news yet. And, along with the discovery about the garlic, it removed any trace of doubt. Heart racing, Vivi ran up to her bedchamber, ripped up the last letter to Dol and began a new one.

Dear Dol
    URGENT situation. You were right all along about the thirteenth vampire and the twins. The two girls were called Griselda and Helga and Ive just found out from Madam Varney that the countesses name is HELGA!! If this means what I think it means, then Im in grave danger, along with all the other members of the household. I need to get away. So does Kurt. Madam Varney, too, if shell come. Maybe shell listen to someone from outside the castle. Its not safe here. Tell Aunt Ina Im sorry. Im really sorry for everything. Pleese send help.
    Your loving cousin,
    Vivi XX

Vivi folded and sealed the new letter. She was desperate to send it straight away, but she still didn't know when Jarv was coming. She slumped on to the bed, but then sprang back up again. Why sit around and wait for Jarv to arrive, especially if she was going to take weeks? Vivi had feet, didn't she? She couldn't run away and leave Kurt and Madam Varney, but she could take the letter to Jarv's house herself: Jarv had said she lived five miles away, which was perfectly walkable. Even runnable! This was an emergency after all.

Rain clouds hovered so she grabbed Dol's mantle and the parasol. The silver tip fell off the end of the parasol and she jammed it back on. Then she raced out of her bedchamber, down the stairs, through the hall and out on to the front steps.

It was, unsurprisingly, another cold and drizzly day.

Vivi stared down the hill, planning her next move. She thought she could still remember the direction Jarv had pointed on that first night. Back down the road by which they'd come, and right. Five miles wasn't so far. She could be there in a couple of hours. As long as she could find the right path.

She put up the parasol and started making her way down the steps. After all this time, she'd still never set foot in the forest. But wolves and bears felt like small dangers now. The real threat was waiting for her in Castle Bezna itself.

She'd nearly reached the gates, when a shout from behind made her turn. "Vivi!"

It was Kurt. Running down the steps behind her, hanging on

to the front brim of his hat.

"Where did you disappear to?" called Vivi.

He caught up with her, a little out of breath. "I couldn't find a dressing. I went to see if I could find a fresh handkerchief in one of the bedchambers."

"Why did you ... never mind, it doesn't matter any more. My finger's fine. But listen, I have big news." She dropped her voice to little more than a whisper. "Countess Marozny's first name *is* Helga. I just found out from Madam Varney."

Kurt's mouth hung open for a moment and then he appeared to recover. "*Is* it?"

"Yes." She held up the letter to Dol. "I've written to my cousin to tell her all about it and to ask for her to send reinforcements. I'm going to find Jarv now. We need help, Kurt. There's no way we can manage something as big as this all by ourselves."

Kurt looked flustered. "We haven't exactly proven that she's the vampire, have we? Her name's Helga, but a lot of people have that name…"

Vivi sighed. "Oh, Kurt, when will you see? It's not just her name, it's *everything*! Her pale skin. The hours she keeps. All the strange rules about closing curtains and no mirrors. And have you ever seen her ladyship eat?"

"She just doesn't have much of an appetite."

"Look, I'm not discussing this with you any more. I'm sure. More certain than ever. It must be her."

Kurt studied his feet. "Why don't you just ask Jarv to take you home?"

"I can't abandon you and Madam Varney! Besides, if any of us just leave, it will look suspicious. Countess Marozny might know we suspect her, then she could run away herself or worse – follow us! It will be dark soon and she could track us down in the forest." A cold fear gripped Vivi. Was that what had happened to Dorïce and Margareta? "I'll be safer here, if I play along and lock my door at night."

Kurt looked up and met her gaze. "I'll take it."

"What?"

"I'll take the letter. You don't even know where Jarv lives, so I'll be much quicker. Besides, I won't be missed at dinner time like you will."

Vivi stopped in her tracks. "What about Madam Varney?"

"She'll never know – she'll just think I'm out in the gardens."

"Are you sure?"

Kurt nodded furiously and thrust out his hand. He was normally so hesitant, Vivi knew he must mean it. She handed over the letter, relieved she didn't have to make the journey after all.

"Don't tell Jarv what's in the letter," said Vivi. She wasn't sure who she could trust any more and wanted to be on the safe side. "Let her know it's urgent, though, won't you?"

Kurt nodded. She stood at the gate and watched him run down the steps and towards the forest. It was strange he was so nervous about certain things, yet when he made up his mind he was more fearless than anyone she knew.

"Thank you, Kurt!" she called, but he didn't turn around.

CHAPTER TWENTY-TWO
CLOSING IN

According to Kurt, Jarv took the letter and promised to take it to Valesti straight away. For a short time, Vivi felt less panicked, knowing that she'd hear the familiar sound of a coach and horses at any moment.

But nobody came – not Jarv or Dol or anyone.

Days passed.

Vivi couldn't understand it. Where were they? She was sure that if Dol knew Vivi was in danger, she'd be at Castle Bezna as soon as physically possible. The only explanation was that something had happened to Dol, or that something had happened to Jarv. But what? Illness? Or … she hated to even think it: a vampire attack?

Either way, the occupants of Castle Bezna were on their own. Every night they slept at the castle they were at risk.

Vivi couldn't sit across the dinner table from the countess any more. Even Vivi wasn't a good enough actress to hide the growing fear in her eyes. And if the countess caught on to the fact that Vivi knew her secret … well, Vivi didn't know what might happen. Instead, she feigned illness to Madam Varney and stayed up in her bedchamber. She even ate her meals up there. By keeping to more traditional hours, it was easy to avoid Countess Marozny. Vivi slept – not proper sleep, just dozing off – with her sharpened stake in her hand.

But she couldn't pretend to be ill for ever. When a whole week had passed since the letter, Vivi left her bedchamber after lunch and went to find Kurt.

There he was, in the garden, sweeping up leaves as usual, trying to get as much finished before darkness fell.

He furrowed his brow as she approached. "Are you feeling better now?"

Vivi rolled her eyes. "I haven't really been ill, Kurt! I've been avoiding the countess. And thinking – I've done a lot of thinking."

"Oh." Kurt stopped sweeping and leaned on his broom.

"Tell me again what Jarv said when you took her the letter?"

"Nothing. Just what I said – that she'd take it straight away."

"But she's not here, is she? No one is here to help us. We need to do something ourselves."

"What can we do?" He looked tired. More tired than usual.

"I've been thinking. You were right when you said a name isn't proof enough. If we had real evidence, then we could take it to Madam Varney and she'd know what to do. So I'm going to get the proof."

"How?" asked Kurt, biting his lower lip.

"I'm going to spy on Countess Marozny in her bedchamber."

"What?" Kurt looked pained.

"I'm fairly confident the countess doesn't sleep in there at all. That's why we're all instructed to keep away – in case we discover it's empty! I think she *actually* sleeps in the coffin in the crypt."

"The coffin was empty when we went down there…"

"Exactly! That was just before dinner. She must head back to her bedchamber just before six o'clock, before Madam Varney goes up to get her ready for the dining room."

"But how – without being seen?"

"Remember how the book says vampires can disguise themselves as other creatures? I think that's what she does. Probably a bat, seeing as there are so many about. The window is always open in the countess's bedchamber; I've seen it from outside, even though the drapes are shut. I am going to hide myself in the room and watch her fly in. Then we'll know for certain."

"Where will you hide?"

"Well, I don't know. I haven't ever seen her bedchamber, have I? Under the bed, probably. Or even on the balcony. Then I'll wait until she and Madam Varney have left the room and I'll race down to dinner. She'll never know I was in her room, but I'll have the proof we need."

"But what if she catches you there?"

Vivi whipped the sharpened stake out of the pocket of her dress and held it, pointy end up. "Then I might be forced to act."

He looked away. "You couldn't really do that, could you?"

"I could, if I had to."

"You would *kill* someone?"

Vivi considered this. She knew what Kurt meant. The thought of plunging the stake into the countess's heart was abhorrent. She couldn't begin to imagine it. But if the countess really was … one of *them*, then she'd been lying to Vivi all along. "A vampire isn't a some*one* – it's a some*thing;* it's dead already. That's what it said in the book. And if it came down to me or it, I would have to, wouldn't I?"

Kurt lowered his gaze.

"Where does the countess keep the key to her bedchamber?" she asked.

"On a hook by her bed, I think," he mumbled.

"There must be a backup key, though. There's always a backup key."

Kurt looked away.

"Kurt…?"

He sighed. "Madam Varney has them. All the duplicate keys."

"In the kitchen?"

Kurt nodded.

"Then that's where we have to go."

Kurt sighed again.

"I'll do it," said Vivi. "If Madam Varney catches me, I'll say it had nothing whatsoever to do with you."

"She'll know I was the one who told you where the keys are."

"She won't. It's obvious where they'd be if you think about it.

Anyway, we're not going to have the key for very long, so she won't find out, will she?"

The key cupboard was located next to a shelf full of preserves. While Madam Varney was busying about in the kitchen, they were able to creep in and open it. Kurt showed Vivi the key to the countess's bedchamber. It was on a large iron ring, but luckily it fitted in one of the deep pockets of Vivi's dress.

"Let's go up right away," she said, when they were safely out in the hallway.

"Now? But there's the sweeping…"

"Kurt!" Vivi put her hands on her hips. "Whatever it is you'd rather be doing, I need your help with this. Follow me."

Vivi marched down the corridor towards the stairs, with Kurt trailing behind reluctantly.

Up in the south wing, Vivi's heart began racing, but she took steady breaths and tried to stay calm for Kurt's sake. He was nervous enough already.

"You wait outside," she whispered. "But keep watching and listening. If you see Madam Varney, then call to her so I know she's there, and I'll hide."

"But what will I tell her? She'll wonder what I'm doing here."

"Oh, I don't know, Kurt. Make something up. Tell her you're polishing door handles. She won't be up here 'til later anyway – she's busy in the kitchen."

Kurt nodded and fumbled with the key in the lock. Vivi held her breath. For an awful moment, she thought they had the wrong key, but then it turned. Kurt opened the door and stepped back, closing it once Vivi had crept into the room.

It was darker than the corridor. Vivi stood rigid for a moment, heartbeat pounding in her ears. She half-expected to see severed heads on spikes, or chalices full of blood. She put her hand in her pocket, feeling the reassuringly pointed end of her wooden stick. But, as her eyes adjusted to the light levels, she saw that the reality was less dramatic. Countess Marozny's bedchamber looked much the same as any other at the castle. Of course it would look normal – not like a vampire's lair – Madam Varney came up here every day. Vivi muttered a rhyme to herself to settle her nerves:

> *"Great to see no heads on spikes*
> *But maybe that's not what she likes."*

There was an armoire in the corner by the window that looked like a perfect hiding spot. Vivi crept towards it, glancing at the four-poster bed as she passed. The coverlet was smoothed across. No sleeping countess, as Vivi had suspected.

But then Vivi heard the rustle of sheets and looked again.

The countess *was* in bed. Her slim body made barely a lump or bump under the covers and she was sleeping on her back, quiet and still, the coverlet drawn up to her chin. In the shadowy light, she looked even paler than usual. She might not be sleeping in her coffin but she looked *deathly* pale. Was she even breathing? For the first time, Vivi knew with absolute certainty that Countess Marozny was the thirteenth vampire. Vivi needed to get out of the bedchamber now. She would leave the castle and run into the woods. Forget the threat of wolves and bears! She'd go anywhere just to get away.

Trying not to breathe, or to make any noise at all, Vivi retreated towards the door, keeping her eyes on the countess in case she woke.

In the darkness and confusion, Vivi accidentally kicked the coal scuttle in the fireplace with the back of her heel. It made a dreadful clang.

The countess moaned and Vivi stood still, heart banging, wishing her back to sleep. Then the countess gasped hoarsely in a way that made Vivi shiver. She'd woken the vampire.

Vivi had a choice to make. She could leave and hope the countess hadn't spotted her. Hope that she wouldn't fly after her and attack. Or she could stand her ground and use this opportunity to confront the thirteenth vampire.

Fight or flight.

She chose fight.

It could be her only chance, while the countess was weak and unsuspecting. She tried to stay calm and remember what she'd learned. She knew how to fight a vampire. She touched the stake in her pocket with trembling hands. If she had to use it, she would.

Countess Marozny shuffled to a seated position. She squinted in the darkness and fumbled to light the gas lamp on her nightstand. "Viviana? What are you doing in here? I thought you were unwell. Have you taken a turn for the worse?"

Vivi's heart thumped. "The real question is, what are *you* doing here?"

"I was sleeping," yawned the countess.

"Yes, but why in the middle of the day, when everyone else is awake?"

Sunlight weakened vampires.

Of course. Vivi ran over to the window and tugged at the heavy damask curtains to pull them open. The day was misty as usual, so the effect wasn't quite as dramatic as she'd hoped, but some weak sunlight filtered into the room.

In the daylight, the furniture looked old and tired.

So did Countess Marozny. The shadows under her eyes, even the very bones under her skin, were more visible than ever before. Her hair was loose around her shoulders and her high-necked frilled nightgown looked more beige than white. She was more dishevelled than Vivi had ever seen. Less like a countess and more like a monster.

The countess raised an arm to shield her eyes. "Why are you opening the drapes, Viviana? I don't think the light is very good for me."

Vivi laughed a hollow laugh. "Ha! My ma always said, 'a little light'll put you right!'"

The countess stared in her direction, but her eyes were glassy and unfocused. "Why are you talking like a kitchen maid, Viviana?"

In her excitement and fear, Vivi had forgotten all about her 'lady' act. But none of that mattered any more. She ignored the question and continued in her normal voice. "Let's look at the evidence, shall we?"

"What do you mean?" There was a wobble in the countess's

voice, which Vivi hadn't been expecting. Vivi began to feel bad, but she reminded herself what this creature really was. Not human, at all. Her grip on the sharp stake in her pocket tightened.

"How do you manage to survive when you never eat?"

"Never eat? But I *do* eat. When I wake and before I go to sleep, Madam Varney brings me a meal. I can't face the rich food in the dining room. Madam Varney thinks it will tempt me to eat but I prefer simple fare…"

"Ha! So you say. And the portraits. Why would you keep the portraits of *vampires* on the walls of the gallery?"

"They are my ancestors – the Marozny family."

"Oh, my ladyship, they might be your ancestors, but they're not the Marozny family, are they?"

"I always thought they were…"

"So why then, did you remove the thirteenth portrait, *Helga Marozny*?

"I don't know what you're talking about. Which portrait? I'm so tired… please, let me sleep." The countess brought her hand up to her pillow, so her upper arm was covering her face, and moaned again.

"That's another thing!" cried Vivi. "Why do you sleep all day, and prowl around the castle at night? Vampire behaviour! And what about Dorïce and Margareta? They were supposed to have left, yet I found their luggage, packed and stowed away. Their farewell notes were written by the same hand!"

The countess gasped, her hand flying up to her mouth. Guilt!

"Yes, you lured them here and you killed them! Maybe they realized who you really were and you stopped them from leaving. Well, I'm not going to succumb to the same fate! I will not be a victim of the thirteenth vampire!"

The countess shook her head. "No, no, no. It's not me!" She got out of bed. Her legs and feet were startlingly bony, like a skeleton's.

Vivi backed away towards the door, pulling the stick from her pocket and holding it out like a dagger. Her whole arm was now shaking despite her best efforts to keep it steady. If Countess Marozny got any closer, would Vivi have to stab her? She tried to tell herself the old woman was an undead monster, but it was harder in practice than in theory…

"Kurt! Get help!" she called, but Vivi heard no response. She had no idea if he could hear what was going on.

The countess began to walk towards Vivi, her arms outstretched. "Oh, my child! You are so, so wrong about me. I'm not a vampire. Yet I fear you might be right about the rest … the thirteenth vampire … I have long suspected … and yet…"

Countess Marozny swayed from side to side, stretching out

her hand to balance herself, although there was no furniture within reach. It was only as she began to totter, delicate little steps like a ballerina in her final act, that Vivi realized she'd been wrong. Very wrong. These weren't the actions of a vampire: the countess was ill. Vivi thrust the stake in her pocket and ran towards the countess. She caught her around the waist as she collapsed, the older woman's arms and head hanging down towards the floor like a rag doll's. She weighed next to nothing. This wasn't what was supposed to happen.

"Kurt, Kurt!" Vivi cried, as loudly as she could this time, lowering Countess Marozny as gently as possible down to the floor.

Kurt's pale, scared face appeared around the door. He was gripping his own wooden stake.

"I got it all wrong, Kurt. Terribly, terribly wrong. Get Madam Varney, quickly. The countess is unwell!"

The sight of the proud woman lying on the patterned rug was pitiful. She was breathing, at least, but the breath came in little puffs, which caused her some effort. Vivi took a pillow from the bed and put it underneath the countess's head to make her more comfortable.

Vivi had an awful feeling she knew exactly why the countess was so weak. Hands still shaking, Vivi undid the collar ties at the neck of the countess's nightgown. There, on the lower part of her neck, were two angry red bumps, with puncture wounds in the centre. Vivi gasped. She might once have thought they were spider bites, but now, after all her research, she knew better.

These were bites, but not from a spider.

These were made by sharp fangs.

These were the marks left by a vampire.

CHAPTER TWENTY-THREE
TERRIBLY WRONG

Vivi stared in horror at the bite marks on Countess Marozny's neck. The countess wasn't an evil vampire at all. She'd been the victim of one. The greyish skin, the loss of appetite, the fatigue. It was all consistent with blood loss. How could Vivi have been so wrong?

The countess's claw-like hand clutched at Vivi's upper arm. "Viviana," she said weakly. "I think you're right. About the thirteenth vampire. I think it visits me when I'm sleeping. I began to sleep in the daytime but still it haunts me. I've been so scared…"

"It will all be all right, my lady. Kurt is getting help. We'll look after you now."

"We must look after you, too, Viviana. I think I knew in my heart there were still vampires in these parts. That was why I put you in the north tower and asked you to lock the door. I hoped you'd be safe there. But I see now it was selfish of me to bring you to the castle in the first place. Oh, I hope you will forgive me!"

"Shhh, my lady. Please don't distress yourself!" Vivi felt awful. For one thing, the countess was trying to protect her, even after Vivi had been prowling in her bedchamber with a sharpened stick in her pocket. But also, all the time that Vivi had been wrongly accusing the countess, the thirteenth vampire had continued to prey on its victim. The countess had been suffering and Vivi hadn't realized a thing.

The grip on Vivi's arm loosened and the countess's arm fell heavily back on the floor. Her eyes shut and her head rolled to one side as her breath came in painful-sounding rasps.

Vivi tapped her gently on the cheek.

"My lady! My lady! Stay with me please!"

A voice came from over by the door. "What's been going on here?"

Madam Varney stood in the doorway, hands on her hips.

Despite the anger on the housekeeper's face, Vivi was relieved to see her. "Her ladyship collapsed. She's so ill. I don't know what to do!"

Madam Varney tutted. "Close those drapes, immediately!"

Vivi rushed over to the heavy bedroom curtains and tugged them shut as Madam Varney bustled into the room. "This is what happens when you go poking your nose in. You only had two rules: stay out of this room and keep the curtains closed. Somehow, you seem to have forgotten both of those instructions."

Madam Varney spat the words out. She was angrier than Vivi had ever seen her before. There was no 'Miss DeRose' or 'my dear' now. Vivi could suddenly understand why Kurt was always so worried about making his Ma Varney cross. She obviously cared very deeply about the countess.

Madam Varney put her large capable arms under the countess's shoulders. "You take her legs," she said to Vivi. Vivi did as she was told. They carried her back on to the bed.

Madam Varney pulled the bedsheets and coverlet tightly across, as they had been when Vivi had walked into the bedchamber. She then plumped the pillow and began doing up the ties of the countess's nightgown collar.

"Madam Varney…"

"Yes?" said the housekeeper sharply.

"There was a bite mark on her ladyship's neck…"

Madam Varney spun around. "A bite. And you think it was made by a vampire, I suppose? I've seen the mark. It's an insect bite, that's all."

"I could send Kurt down to the village for a doctor to check?"

"You will do no such thing, young lady. The countess has had these episodes before, and they are almost always brought on by an attack of nerves. Probably by someone entering her bedchamber when she's fast asleep and opening the curtains."

Vivi swallowed guiltily. "What can I do to help?"

"You can leave the poor countess alone. As you should have done all along. And if I hear another word about vampires, or catch you or Kurt up here again, I will not be happy – do you understand?"

Vivi nodded and left the room, tears of shame and worry smarting in her eyes.

Dol

You didn't reply to the last letter. I do hope it reachd you— I got Kurt to take it to Jarv, but I'm worried she has desertd us for some reason. If this letter and the last do eventully get to Valesti, then know I was wrong.

*Hopelessly, terribly wrong. Countess Marozny is **not** the thirteenth vampire. I think shes one of its victims. There is a bite on her neck. She says shes been attackd in her sleep. Madam Varney says theres no way and that it was just some insect but then she wont let herself beleeve theres a vampire. Probly because shes been here all her life and would have nowhere else to go. We need a doctor and I need help, more than Ive ever needed it before. We can't let her die. We're all in danger, too: Kurt, Madam Varney, me. The threat is very reel and its close. Id flee the castle but without Jarv I don't know what to do. I'd try to make it through the woods to the village but there are bears and wolves out there as well as the thirteenth vampire. And I cant leave the countess here with no one to protect her. We're trappd.*

Please come quickly.
I miss you Dol.
Vivi X

CHAPTER TWENTY-FOUR

ABANDONED

"I can't believe I got it so wrong," said Vivi the next morning. She and Kurt sat side by side on the bench in the kitchen garden. It was growing colder than ever. They'd wiped a layer of frost from the bench before sitting down.

"When I found out her name was Helga, it seemed like proof. How was I to know the countess and the vampire shared a first name?"

To her relief, Kurt didn't say 'I told you so', but shrugged, hat bobbing. "You weren't to know."

Vivi frowned. "Now we're in the same situation as we were before, but worse: the real vampire is still out there somewhere, watching Castle Bezna, and the countess is critically ill. If it attacks again, she might die. What are we going to do?"

"Ma Varney says there is no vampire."

"Madam Varney is in denial. Come on, Kurt – you know as well as I do that the thirteenth vampire is out there somewhere. We saw its coffin, remember?"

Kurt didn't reply, but Vivi knew he agreed. How could he not, after everything they'd seen?

They sat in silence.

"Will you take one more letter to Jarv?" Vivi asked, holding the letter out to him.

Kurt rubbed his forehead in dismay. "It didn't do any good last time. Nobody came!"

"I know. But I don't understand why. Maybe you can find out? It didn't take you that long to get there. Please. Maybe you can ask Jarv to get a doctor for the countess, too."

Kurt hesitated then stood up. "Fine." He took the letter.

"Make sure you tell her just how important it is, won't you?"

"I will," said Kurt, stamping his feet to warm them up.

"I'm going to go and see Madam Varney in the kitchen," said

Vivi.

"Don't tell her any more about vampires – she'll get cross."

"I'm not going to mention the 'V' word," said Vivi. "I'm going to ask some normal questions about normal things."

Kurt started slowly towards the terrace and Vivi marched to the back door and through to the kitchen. Madam Varney was at the stove as usual but no music was playing. The housekeeper had been unhappy with Vivi since last night and clearly wasn't in the mood for singing or dancing.

"Madam Varney, are we due a visit from Jarv any time soon?" Vivi asked quietly.

The housekeeper turned, spoon in hand, tomato sauce dripping on the floor tiles. She snorted. "Who knows?" The housekeeper's tone was sharp. "This isn't the first time she's abandoned us. I told you before – we can't count on anyone up here, especially over the winter. She's probably been waylaid at a tavern in one of the bigger towns. Or perhaps she didn't want to get wet and cold."

Vivi thought of Jarv and her hat full of hailstones on the journey to the castle. The coachwoman didn't seem the type to be put off by a spell of bad weather. "What if something's happened to her? What if she's ill or had an accident?" *Or encountered a vampire*, Vivi thought, but didn't say.

Madam Varney let the spoon clatter back in the pan. "Highly unlikely but we can send Kurt to find out if you like."

Vivi paused. It was time to take control. "Kurt's already left. I asked him to. Countess Marozny needs a doctor."

She expected the housekeeper to react angrily to this, but she just blinked and said, "Well then, let's see what Kurt says when he returns, shall we?"

Vivi stayed in the kitchen for the rest of the morning, quietly reading an old recipe book to pass the time. She wanted to ask after the countess, but didn't dare. Madam Varney barely said a word to her, although she did pass her a simple plate of bread and cheese for lunch. Vivi had eaten about half of it when Kurt burst in, wide-eyed and out of breath.

"Well?" asked Vivi, expectantly.

"There was no one there. At Jarv's house. It was completely empty."

Vivi pushed away her plate. "What do you mean no one there?"

Kurt shrugged. "It was all closed up. The windows were shuttered. Didn't look like anyone had been there for ages. I pushed the letter under the door, but who knows when she'll find it."

Madam Varney looked unsurprised at this news. "As I say, she could be gone for days. Weeks even. The longer you stay here, Miss DeRose, the more you'll realize we're on our own at Castle Bezna. And we're used to it. We won't starve. We have stores of food here that will last until spring, or whenever the coachwoman decides to put in an appearance."

Until spring. Even if the food stores did last until then, Vivi doubted they'd survive up in these deserted mountains with a vampire roaming around. Also, the countess was more unwell than Madam Varney seemed to realize. She would be unlikely to make it through the winter without medical help.

That afternoon, Countess Marozny asked Madam Varney to send Vivi up to her bedchamber. Vivi obeyed, a little nervous about what she might find. The countess's face was white and her breathing shallow. Vivi sat at her bedside. "Would you like me to read to you?"

"No," said the countess weakly, putting her hand on Vivi's arm. It was so cold, Vivi had an urge to take it in her own and rub it for warmth, but she didn't. "I need to speak to you about my will," said the countess.

"Your ... will?" Vivi felt a stab of guilt and tears pricked at her eyes. Did the countess know she'd seen it?

"Yes – my last will and testament." The countess held out an envelope to Vivi. "I have it right here. It is important you know that I've made a change. All these years, I have been looking for a suitable heir to the Marozny fortune, and finally, in you, I've found that person."

Tears began to run down Vivi's face. This was more than she'd ever dreamed of, but she didn't want it now. Not like this. All she wanted was the countess to get better. "You can't leave it all to me—" began Vivi, but the countess raised a finger to stop her talking.

"As soon as I recover – if I recover – I will find a person of legal standing to draw this up. In the meantime, Madam Varney has witnessed the changes."

That was even more of a shock – did Madam Varney know that the original will had left her everything? If so, it would be another reason for her to be cross with Vivi. She had to explain. "I don't deserve this, my lady. I've lied about so many things. I even broke into your secret study and read the will. Then, when I thought you were the vampire, I was going to hurt you—"

The countess patted her arm. "Don't you worry, Viviana. I knew about the lies. This is all my fault. I never should have brought you here. I've just been so lonely and you have such capacity for fun and kindness. When I do die, I want you to make sure that Castle Bezna becomes a happy place..."

Vivi began to protest, "No, my lady, you're not going to die!" but the countess's eyelids had already closed and her soft, even breathing told Vivi she was asleep. All Vivi could feel was guilt. She couldn't inherit the Marozny fortune in this way. On top of that, if the countess did pass away, the thirteenth vampire would surely move on to its next victim, which could be Madam Varney, Kurt or Vivi herself.

If the vampire had anything to do with it then there'd be no one left at Castle Bezna to inherit a thing.

CHAPTER TWENTY-FIVE
WAITING IN THE DARKNESS

Another week passed. Without Jarv, no help arrived. There were also no letters, food parcels or essential supplies. The chickens had gone and meals were growing more basic by the day. Bread and soup, mainly. There was now a single course each evening, rather than three, and Vivi ate alone in the dining room, food laid out for her on the table. Madam Varney tended to her in a clipped manner.

The sensible thing to do would be to head back to Valesti. Tell them the rumours were true – the thirteenth vampire was no myth.

The townspeople had tracked down the vampires before, so surely they could do it again. This time they would have to hunt only one vampire rather than twelve.

But how could she get there? Jarv was Vivi's only means of escape. Without the coachwoman, Vivi or Kurt would have to go on foot to Valesti, or even to the village of Bezna. That could take days, and would involve a trek through the forest. And they knew what was lurking in the forest. At best, wolves and bears. At worst, well…

They needed a plan.

Vivi went to find Kurt. He wasn't in any of his usual spots. Eventually she found him in the maze, cutting back the dead hedge, presumably in the hope that it would grow back again in the spring. Wishful thinking, thought Vivi, but she didn't say anything about it. She had more important matters on her mind. "We can't go on like this. We're running out of food, the countess needs medical attention and we all need sleep. But we can't escape without putting ourselves in danger or abandoning Countess Marozny."

"I know." He kept snipping. "We're stuck here. There's nothing we can do."

"There *is* something we can do. We can face the vampire. And before you say anything – forget about Madam Varney. If we don't have her support then we do this on our own."

He kicked the mound of brown clippings. "But how? How can we face the vampire when we don't know where to find her?"

"Well, we have a good idea she'll be sleeping in the coffin in the crypt—"

Kurt shook his head furiously. "No, I'm not going back there."

Vivi was relieved. "I agree. Too dangerous to come face to face with her down there. If we disturbed her, and she attacked, then we'd be trapped. No, I've been thinking about this and I have a better idea. Do you remember when I caught you spying on me, here in the maze?"

Kurt nodded, looking towards the stone bench at the centre.

"Well, we do the same with the vampire. Although not in the maze, of course! We set a trap to lure her to us, then we pounce." Vivi pounced at Kurt and he leapt backwards, hands over his face.

"But ... how?" he asked, when he'd recovered from the shock.

"Think about it. What is it the vampire wants?"

"Human blood," said Kurt, quickly and quietly.

"Then that's what we use as bait. Countess Marozny, to be precise. She's sleeping around the clock now, so she's particularly vulnerable. The thirteenth vampire – Helga – doesn't know that *we* know about her existence. She'll come back for the countess. And we'll be waiting."

"The countess will be our bait? But isn't that risky?"

"Yes, but we can settle her safely somewhere else, while we wait to pounce."

Kurt looked lost. "But where will we move her? *How* will we move her? And how will we pounce? The vampire might pounce on *you*. On us."

"I haven't figured that out yet, but if we put our heads together, we'll come up with a plan. At the end of all this, either the vampire is going to win, or we are. And I for one want to make sure it's us."

Two nights later, they were ready.

The countess was settled in the north tower, in Vivi's bedchamber, which as the countess had said herself, was the safest place of all. Moving her there had been a difficult task. They'd waited until after Madam Varney had been up to visit at six o'clock, then, once the housekeeper had left, they put the plan to the countess. She'd been confused, but willing, and somehow, they'd managed to walk to the north tower, with Kurt propping her on one side and Vivi on the other.

"We're going to catch this vampire. Tonight. You'll be safe soon, Countess Marozny," said Vivi, as she tucked her in. She was asleep as soon as her head touched the pillow.

Back in the south wing, Vivi padded out the countess's bed with cushions, in case Madam Varney peeped in later. She also made sure the window was wide open: the thirteenth vampire's exclusive invite. The curtains remained closed, as always. Vivi and Kurt would wait just outside, with a view to the window, and when the vampire flew in, they would run into the castle. Vivi hoped that when the vampire discovered the countess's bedchamber empty, she'd go looking in the other bedchambers on the south wing. They would then be able to trap her and lock her in. Or face her, if they had to.

Kurt took all the relevant keys from the key cupboard, and they made their way together outside to the upper garden. From just below the terrace, near the steps, they could see the countess's window and balcony. Their candles remained unlit to avoid drawing attention to themselves. Luckily, the moon was full so it wasn't altogether dark. But thick clouds were threatening, creeping across their only light source. After a few moments, the moon was almost obscured, and large, icy raindrops began to fall.

Vivi tried to ignore the chill creeping through her clothes, hoping the rain would pass. It didn't. It got heavier, splashing off the ground and forming puddles in the already rain-soaked lawns. Vivi wished she had her parasol with her. The weather at Castle Bezna was truly awful.

"It's raining," said Kurt, stating the obvious.

"Don't worry – it's only spitting. Let's concentrate on what we've come to do."

"But my hat's getting wet."

"That's exactly what your hat's for – to protect your head."

"It's to protect my head from the sun when I'm gardening," mumbled Kurt.

"But we never see any sun! You'd be better off with a rain hat."

Kurt frowned. "Can't we shelter in the greenhouse?"

"No, because we wouldn't be able to see the countess's window from there!" Vivi matched Kurt's sigh with a loud, exasperated exhalation of her own. "If the rain's bothering you that much, then why don't you go and get my parasol?"

Kurt frowned. "On my own?"

"Well, we can't both go – we'll miss the thirteenth vampire! The last thing I want is for this whole evening to be wasted. It's up to you. Go and fetch the parasol or get wet."

Kurt looked up at the sky, then towards the foreboding shape of Castle Bezna. He stood up. "Where is the parasol?"

"In the umbrella stand, in the hall. Don't go in the back way, in case you see Madam Varney," said Vivi. "It's not yet seven, but when she notices I'm late for dinner, she might come looking for me."

Vivi watched Kurt run up the terrace steps until he was lost in the shadows.

She was alone.

Everything seemed louder than it had when Kurt was with her. The rain hammered on the empty chicken coop. An owl hooted somewhere deep in the forest. No wolves yet – they didn't seem to be out tonight. She began to wish she hadn't sent Kurt away. She hoped he wouldn't take long. If the thirteenth vampire did appear, she'd rather not be alone.

Vivi looked back in the direction of the crypt and then up towards the balcony outside the countess's window. She was unsure exactly what it was she was looking for. A bat? It was so dark now that she wasn't sure she'd spot a little creature like that. Instead, she looked and listened for any sign, on high alert.

For a while there was nothing.

And then...

Horses' hooves and coach wheels splashed through the puddles at the front of the castle.

Her heart leapt. It was the sound she'd been hoping to hear for weeks. Could it finally be Jarv, just as she and Kurt had given up hope? She left her post and ran up the steps and around the side of the castle to check.

In Vivi's time at Castle Bezna, there had only ever been one visitor. Still, she went cautiously, just in case, knowing it could be anyone – she shivered – maybe even Helga herself.

As soon as she reached the front of the castle, she recognized Jarv's coach. One of the headlamps shone askew, its beam of light shining into the forest; the other was directed towards the castle. Vivi hung back in the shadows and the relative shelter of the castle walls until she could see the passenger. Had Jarv brought a whole team of villagers with her?

The headlamps flickered off but Vivi kept her eyes on the coach. After a moment, she made out the vague outlines of two people, their hand-held lanterns bobbing in the darkness. They moved closer, climbing the steps towards Castle Bezna. The first figure was definitely Jarv: short and rounded with a top hat and long coat. And behind her was someone so familiar that Vivi barely trusted her own eyes. Small and slim, and wearing Vivi's own coat, which came nearly to her ankles.

Vivi forgot about hiding or keeping quiet. She leapt out from the shadows and ran down the steps towards her cousin, shouting "Dol!"

CHAPTER TWENTY-SIX

DOL

Dol broke into a run when she recognized Vivi. She ran up to meet her at the gateposts. They threw their arms around each other as best they could with a lantern in the way, fat raindrops soaking their hair and bouncing off their shoulders.

"You came! Oh, you came." Vivi squeezed Dol in such a tight embrace that her cousin eventually wriggled to get free.

"Vivi, I can't breathe!"

Vivi released her, laughing. She noticed Dol had a wreath of garlic bulbs strung around her neck. "What took you so long? Did you bring anyone else with you?"

Dol frowned. "It's just us. I knew Ma would never let me come, so I got Therese to cover for me at the laundry – Ma doesn't know."

"Didn't you show her my letter?"

"Which one?"

"I wrote a letter to you, telling you how I thought the thirteenth vampire was the countess, but it isn't her after all! The thirteenth vampire has been feeding on the countess and is still out there somewhere… I did write another letter explaining and asking for a doctor, but there was no one at Jarv's so I wasn't sure that letter would get to you—"

Dol shook her head. "I didn't get either letter."

Vivi scowled at Jarv, who was still making her way up the steps towards them. So Jarv hadn't been taken by the vampire – she had simply failed to deliver the letters to Dol. No time to worry about that now. Vivi turned back to her cousin. "I knew you would've come straight away if you got my letters. I was hoping you'd bring people with you to help."

"When I didn't hear from you I started to worry something must be wrong. I kept reading your early letters and trying to figure it out. It was like a puzzle and you know how I love puzzles.

I think I know what's going on. As soon as I thought it, I had to come and find you to tell you. Luckily, Jarv came to find *me* and she had similar concerns—" Dol was speaking at three times her normal pace.

Jarv came back and put her hand on Dol's shoulder: an action which slightly annoyed Vivi. Dol was *her* cousin. "I'm sorry to interrupt, girls, but what were you doing out here in the dark when we arrived, Miss DeRose?"

Vivi pursed her lips. She was still cross with Jarv for abandoning them all at the castle just when they needed her. Still, she was finally providing some backup, and for that, Vivi was grateful. She looked about her and lowered her voice. "I was lying in wait. I have a plan to ambush the thirteenth vampire."

Jarv's face was illuminated by the light from her lantern. She wasn't wearing her glasses and looked different without them. Like Dol, she wore a wreath of garlic around her neck. She raised a single eyebrow. "An admirable plan. But don't you think we are rather exposed out here for an ambush? Let's return to the cover of your hiding spot."

Jarv was right – Vivi had already been gone too long. Vivi led them back round to the terrace, Jarv walking by her side while Dol followed behind, gazing up in wonder at the imposing castle. They settled back in the spot where Vivi and Kurt had been, Dol between them. Kurt wasn't back yet, which was odd. How long could it take him to fetch a parasol?

"Put out the lanterns," said Vivi. "We don't want to draw unnecessary attention to ourselves."

"Can't we leave one—" began Dol, but Jarv had already extinguished both.

"The clouds have cleared again," said the coachwoman. "It's surprising how much you can see in moonlight alone."

The girls both looked up at the moon. It was almost completely visible again. The rain had stopped, too. It reminded Vivi of her journey to the castle and she felt a sudden rush of warmth towards the coachwoman. "I don't understand, Jarv, why didn't you deliver my latest letters to Dol?"

Jarv furrowed her brow and asked innocently, "What letters?"

This triggered in Vivi another hot surge of her earlier anger. "You know which letters!" she said, trying to keep her voice quiet. Why would Jarv lie? Unless she had something to hide ... but if that was the case, then why would she have brought Dol up to Castle Bezna now?

"Calm down, Vivi. Jarv is on our side." Dol took the older woman's arm in her own and smiled up at her.

"You think so?" said Vivi, who still felt wary.

"I know so! You don't understand, Vivi. Jarv knows so much more about all this than we do…"

Vivi huffed at Dol's disloyalty. "I actually know quite a lot about it myself. I've read the vampire book in the library from cover to cover. I know my memory's not always the best, but I could tell you how to recognize a vampire—"

"Yes, and who's the author of that book?" Dol smiled, knowingly.

"The author? I don't know. Dr someone-or-other. He was one of the villagers – one of the hunters who tracked down the original twelve."

"Yes, Dr Arvesson. My father," said Jarv, breaking her silence. "He spent his life researching and recording details about the vampires – and put them together in the book you found."

It came back to Vivi then – her first meeting with Jarv in the cobbled square at Valesti.

"I'm Janette Arvesson. Everyone calls me Jarv for short and you may, too."

And, printed on the front of the vampire book: *The Twelve Vampires of Castle Bezna, by Dr Arnel Arvesson.*

Vivi shook her head slowly. She'd been reading that book almost every day but had never noticed. Jarv continued softly with her explanation. "My father did hear the rumours about a thirteenth vampire, but he couldn't – or wouldn't – believe them. I felt differently. I became convinced there was truth behind the rumours. It caused tension between us. After his death, I took it upon myself to find out everything I could."

In the addendum at the back of the book, Dr Arvesson had said he'd been persuaded to consider the rumour of the thirteenth vampire. Persuaded by his daughter, by the sounds of things.

Jarv opened her long coat to reveal an array of sharp wooden stakes, tucked into special inside pockets. "I come equipped," she explained. "I have different stakes for different purposes. Some specially weighted for throwing, others for close range."

"I have one, too," said Dol, bringing her own stubby stake out of the pocket of her coat.

Vivi felt suddenly furious. All her suspicions, all the work she'd done to uncover the truth, and Jarv knew it all along. "Why didn't you tell me any of this? I asked you about vampires and you didn't say a thing!"

"I said nothing because I had no evidence. Only clues and coincidences that amounted to nothing. I gave you every opportunity to turn back but you refused. I couldn't tell you what I thought I knew, because I had the advantage of secrecy. If I lost that, then I'd have to give up altogether."

Vivi understood. It was the same game she'd played with Kurt in the maze. "Still, to allow me up here, knowing there could be another vampire … you put me in danger."

"But you knew there was danger! You'd heard all the rumours, Miss DeRose—"

"You know that's not my name."

"Old habits die hard. Anyway, you'd heard the same rumours I had, yet you still chose to take that risk. I'm guessing that you favoured other factors over your own personal safety, like financial gain."

Vivi's cheeks flushed to hear the truth spelled out in this way, and was grateful for the cover of the darkness. "At first, maybe that was true, but then I grew to care about everyone. Madam Varney, Kurt and the countess too when I knew the truth about her. But you left me all alone at the castle, knowing I could become the vampire's next victim!"

"I had to. But I knew you were strong. You kept telling me how strong you were! And I was always looking out for you. Why do you think I made all those trips up here?"

Dol nodded fervently at this. "She did, Vivi. And she kept reporting back to me on how you were getting on."

Vivi turned to her cousin. "Don't tell me you were in on this, too?"

"No! I didn't know a thing about vampire hunting until this morning!"

"Fine! It's fine, Dol, I understand." Vivi turned back to Jarv. "So if you were looking out for me so attentively, then why did you stop coming? It wasn't just the letters I missed. Our food deliveries disappeared. I was starting to worry we were going to have to get by on what was in the vegetable patch alone. The countess needed a doctor."

Jarv's face was difficult to read. "I stopped coming because I received this message under my door," she said, reaching into the pocket of her coat.

It was a letter. Vivi couldn't read it in the dim light, so she struck one of her matches and lit the candle, just for a moment, before taking the message from Jarv.

To Whom It May Concern:

The occupants of Castle Bezna have all fallen ill with a terrible fever. This malady is highly contagious and airborne. The residents have entered into a period of quarantine and should not be approached.

Please keep away from the castle itself and the grounds until further notice.

Dr Smithson

She read slowly, shaking her head. "But none of this is true! Nobody's been ill. There's been no doctor here, even when we needed one. I don't understand why anyone would say this..."

"To keep me away," said Jarv, her mouth set in a grim line.

"But who could have sent this? We know the countess is on our side. Who else would want to keep you away?"

Vivi continued to stare at the note. There was something else that was strange about it. And then she realized.

"The writing ... it's the same as the notes that were left by the other girls."

She blew out the candle. What did it all mean? As Vivi tried to make some sense of it, Dol said, "Vivi, we think we know what might be happening. I showed Jarv some of your letters and she agrees—" Dol suddenly stopped and pointed at a figure emerging from the walkway. "Who's that?" she whispered.

"Where?" Vivi turned and looked where Dol was pointing.

Kurt! He was back at last. To Dol, she whispered, "It's Kurt, who I wrote about. He's shy at first, you'll see, but he's been a good friend to me. I've been able to share my theories with him."

Then she called out in a quieter-than-normal voice, "Don't worry, Kurt, it's just Jarv and Dol, my wonderful cousin!"

Kurt shuffled over warily, then silently handed the parasol to her. Vivi laughed good-naturedly. "You took so long that the rain's stopped!"

But Kurt wasn't laughing back. Nor was anyone else. They were all still and silent. It was a terrible sort of silence where each one of them glanced at one another as if a secret message was being passed between them. But Vivi didn't understand the message. She looked at Dol quizzically.

Dol spoke in response, her voice barely above a whisper. "Vivi, ask Kurt what happened to your letters."

At first, Vivi didn't know what she meant and found herself joining in with the mysterious glancing, looking from Dol to Jarv to Kurt and back again. Kurt couldn't seem to look at her. He looked at the ground instead. Then, slowly, he pulled a bundle of papers from the pocket of his trousers. He held them out in front of him, eyes down. "I'm so sorry, Vivi!" he said, his voice cracking.

Vivi stared at the papers. She recognized the blobby wax seal and the slant of her own handwriting. Her missing letters to Dol.

Kurt. *Kurt* had pocketed the letters.

"I think he might have been responsible for the fake letter from the doctor, too," said Jarv.

Kurt nodded slowly, eyes cast downwards.

"But *why?*" Vivi was barely able to voice the question.

Kurt opened his mouth to – *what* – explain? Or justify his behaviour? "I... I..." It was hard to tell in the darkness, but Vivi thought she caught a flash of white. Sharp teeth that she didn't remember seeing before.

Images played in her mind. Kurt wearing a large hat to protect him from the sun. Kurt sobbing by the chicken coop, smeared with dirt and blood. His footsteps in the corridor at night-time. The missing name on the thirteenth coffin. The fact she'd never seen him eat.

She glanced at Dol, who nodded, then back at Kurt, who finally met her gaze, his usually brown irises shining red.

"You?" breathed Vivi. "*You're* the thirteenth vampire?"

More terrible silence in the dark.

Vivi's hand tightened on the sharpened stake in her pocket. Would she be able to use this – or any weapon – against *Kurt*?

But he shook his head in answer to her question, tears sliding down his face. "No…" he whispered. "It's not me."

He looked away from her once again, but this time he looked towards the sky, not the ground. Vivi followed his line of sight. A single bat – a large bat – flitted in a tight figure-of-eight pattern above them. It was almost as if it was watching the events below.

Dol put her hand gently on Vivi's arm. "You must know now who the thirteenth vampire is, Vivi."

And Vivi realized that she did.

CHAPTER TWENTY-SEVEN

THE THIRTEENTH VAMPIRE

All four of them looked up at the bat. It swooped down from its hovering position above their heads to the terrace where they stood. Jarv and Dol drew their weapons and Vivi followed suit, throwing the parasol to the ground and whipping out her sharpened stake. They took a couple of steps backwards to the stone balustrade and stood close together with their backs to the garden. Jarv stood to Vivi's left, Dol to her right. Kurt stayed where he was, rooted to the spot. The bat swooped down to the middle of the terrace, where it hovered a few feet off the ground. Bigger than before.

The flapping wings slowed. They no longer looked like wings, but human arms, stretched out horizontally, a black shawl draped around them.

The legs stretched down to meet the stone slabs of the terrace.

This creature was no longer a bat, but a person, or at least the shape of a person. A person Vivi knew well.

"Madam Varney! No, *Helga* Varney," whispered Vivi.

It was Madam Varney, but not as Vivi knew her. Although she was in her usual housekeeper's uniform with apron and shawl, her cap was gone and her hair sprang out around her head. The housekeeper's eyes blazed red and her smile was sharp-toothed. She was taller, slimmer, sharper. Vivi could see hints of the young girl in the painting – the girl Madam Varney had once been. Those eyes in the portrait that had looked so familiar. The connection was obvious now. How could she have missed it? She thought of how the housekeeper had brushed her hair. Of her comments about Vivi's slender neck. Vivi shuddered.

The housekeeper laughed. "Yes, my dear. I'm Helga Varney – twin sister of Griselda. Pleased to be able to formally make your acquaintance. I'm a little offended you thought Kurt might be the thirteenth vampire. You really thought him capable of evading vampire hunters and leading a double-life for years?"

Kurt snivelled, wiping his nose on his sleeve. Vivi said nothing. She had to admit (if only to herself) he didn't look capable of those things, although his eyes were glowing as red as Madam Varney's.

"So you made him like this? A monster like you?" asked Jarv, her voice steady.

"I gave him the gift of eternal life. You'd think it would give him strength, but he remains as weak as ever."

"He's not weak. Just a young boy," said Dol, quietly.

"Kurt's older than you and your cousin, my dear. In his mid-twenties by now, I should think."

"Mid-twenties?" Vivi stared at Kurt's short trousers and crumpled socks. Was it really possible?

"Yes, but age isn't a factor when it comes to inner strength. I thought that Kurt had found his backbone when he began to help you, with the secret passage and the painting. But he was always too scared of me to really rebel, weren't you, Kurt?" He didn't reply and Madam Varney sneered. "You either have it or you don't, and Kurt is wholly lacking. But I see it in you, Viviana. We both have that strength."

Vivi gripped the stake in her hand, splinters digging into her palm. She didn't like the way Madam Varney – or Helga as she knew now – used the word 'we'. "How dare you talk about me as if we're the same?"

Helga smiled indulgently, her fangs poking over her lower lip. "Because we want the same things, my dear. It's why you came to Castle Bezna in the first place! We talked about the future, don't you remember? How we'd love to see the ballrooms full again!"

"But full of ... vampires?"

"Yes! Glorious, night-loving vampires! Griselda would have wanted it. This time, we won't make the mistakes of the past. We won't take foolish risks and let the townspeople discover us – we'll hunt cleverly – further afield. Expand our hunting ground. The countess will soon sadly pass away of her long illness, and you, Viviana DeRose, will inherit the castle legitimately."

"You know that's not my real name!"

"That may be true, but DeRose has a certain ring to it, as you realized. You will become the new countess and people will talk about your inspiring rags-to-riches tale. They will forget that you ever were Vivi Peste and that this place was known as Vampire Towers. I'll remain here as your housekeeper and we will live in peace – for ever."

"But I'm not a vampire!"

"Not yet, but that will change soon. You will be the daughter

I never lived to have. Kurt will be your brother. Your portrait will hang on the wall of the gallery."

"No!"

"I know it is a big change for you, my dear." Helga spoke in the soothing tones she'd always used. "But you'll soon become used to the idea, like our sweet Kurt here did."

Kurt hid his face in shame, his red eyes downcast.

Vivi stared at Helga. "But I thought you loved the countess. That you cared for her. How could you do this to her?"

"Oh no. I didn't love the countess. I needed her. She was my cover – my respectability. My means to an end. But now I no longer require that cover. *You* will provide the respectable face of Castle Bezna. A lonely countess dies and leaves her fortune to a young woman. What could be *more* respectable? And, unlike me or the countess, there are no question marks over where you came from. The whole of Valesti knows you."

"This is ridiculous! Your plan will never work. How do you think you'll be able to keep a castle full of vampires secret? Everyone here has seen you for who you really are!"

Helga laughed. "Nobody in our present company will live to tell tales about Vampire Towers! They will choose to die, or to join us as vampires!"

"I won't be joining you as a vampire," shouted Jarv.

"Nor me," added Dol, in a tiny voice.

"None of us will, Helga," cried Vivi.

"Please don't call me Helga. Can't I persuade you to call me 'Ma Varney'?"

"No. You're a monster."

"Ah, my dear. You are so sure about everything. You remind me of myself at your age. Those other girls before you were such wet blankets, like your cousin here, shaking in her boots."

Dol *was* shaking. They were standing so close together Vivi could feel it. But Dol was strong in so many other ways. "My cousin is not a wet blanket," shouted Vivi.

"Leave it, Vivi!" Dol put a hand on her arm to calm her, but Vivi was shaking herself now, with anger. "You'll regret your words, Helga Varney!"

"See! You have that spark within you. You don't mind who you confront. You don't mind lying and stealing to get what you want."

"That's not true! I'm nothing like you!"

"Oh, but you are. You even have the blood lust. You're thinking right now about attacking me with your home-made stake. The same stake you would have driven into poor Countess Marozny's heart!" She laughed a high laugh. "It would have been convenient for me if you'd done so. All these years, I've been waiting for her to pass away. A nice, slow, natural death that wouldn't cause anyone to ask any questions. But if you had killed her off, it would have been perfect. The countess would have gone, and it would have quashed all those rumours of a thirteenth vampire. And it can still be done! You can do it and then join me as a vampire, my little protégée."

"No."

"Yes. I think I can persuade you. Our family, you see, is about to grow."

There was a collective gasp as Helga Varney lifted a few inches off the ground, as she'd done in bat form. She swept towards them, arms up, black shawl casting an ominous shadow.

Still shaking, Dol gripped Vivi's arm.

Jarv and Vivi both pointed their stakes at Helga, but she was too quick. She flew over their heads, and in one swift movement grabbed Dol by the shoulders, her fingers uncurling from Vivi's arm as she was wrenched up and away.

Dol screamed. Her legs dangled like a doll's as Helga swept her up and far out of reach.

Helga landed on Countess Marozny's stone balcony, holding Dol carelessly under the arms. Dol's legs hung over the balustrade and she was quiet: her eyes squeezed shut. Vivi's dear, sweet cousin, who never hurt anyone. Now Vivi really wanted to hurt Helga. She wanted to stop this vampire and make her pay.

But Vivi was forced to watched helplessly from below as Helga smiled like an actress enjoying her debut performance. Helga ripped the garlic wreath from around Dol's neck and flung it away in disgust, the bulbs falling and bouncing on the stone terrace. Then she smiled. "It's been so long! For years I've had to satisfy myself with the blood of animals and the odd sip of human blood. I've had to show such restraint! Just enough to give me strength but not enough to kill. But not tonight. Tonight, I feast! Care to dine with me, Kurt?"

Kurt looked away, but Vivi could see he was shaking, too.

"No, of course you won't join me. I can't decide if you are a worse vampire or gardener – ha! You'd better stick to chickens – I'll keep the real feast for myself."

Helga swept back Dol's fine hair and bent over her neck, sharp white teeth glowing in the moonlight.

"You monster! Let her go!" screamed Vivi.

"I don't think you really want me to do that," said Helga, pulling one supporting arm away. Dol screamed as she swung precariously. After a couple of seconds, Helga grabbed her back.

"Your cousin will be the first to join my new family." Helga bit into her neck. Dol stopped screaming and her arm hung limply at her side.

"No!" shrieked Vivi. "Don't hurt her. Take me, not Dol."

Helga Varney looked up, a thin trickle of blood running from her mouth. "Don't you understand, my dear? I will take you both. And you will come to realize what a gift I am giving you. You will live for ever and never again have to be parted, as my sister and I so cruelly were. All you have to do is drink my blood, as Kurt here once did, and you will both be vampires."

At the mention of his name, Kurt looked up with renewed energy and purpose. Helga didn't seem to notice this change in him.

There was a change in Jarv, too. She was pointing her stake at the balcony, aiming right at Helga.

Inspired, Vivi took the sharpened stick from her pocket and threw it towards Helga. She was a good aim and it hit the vampire in the chest, but unfortunately fell away without even piercing her clothes.

Helga looked at the stake lying on the balcony. "Ha! You mean to injure me with that? Why, it's the size of a knitting needle. You'd be lucky to skewer a pipistrelle bat, let alone a vampire!"

Vivi had, of course, aimed to injure Helga, but failing that, at least it had distracted Helga from Dol.

Vivi glanced left and right. Jarv was still taking careful aim, but on the other side, something strange was happening to Kurt. He was rising off the floor, as Helga had done. For an awful moment, Vivi thought he meant to join the vampire feast, which would be a worse betrayal, somehow, than Madam Varney's. But then she saw Kurt's eyes, red and blazing, staring at Helga with what looked like pure hatred. She realized then, even if he hadn't been brave enough before, Kurt was now on their side.

Helga didn't seem to have noticed Kurt rising below her. She was glancing back at Dol like she was a tasty dessert.

Then, it all happened at once.

Kurt flew up, as swiftly as if he were the thirteenth vampire, towards the unsuspecting Helga Varney.

At the very same time, Jarv threw her sharpened stake.

Jarv's aim was spot on, but she wasn't expecting anything to come between her missile and her target.

Just as the stake was about to strike, Kurt threw himself at Dol, grabbed her lifeless figure, and rescued her from her assailant.

Vivi noticed something was wrong from the look on Kurt's face. It should have shown fear or exhilaration, but instead his expression was frozen in shock.

"Kurt?" called Vivi.

He twisted in the air. The wooden stake was buried deep in his chest.

Jarv gasped. "Sorry, wrong vampire!"

Madam Varney leaned over the balcony, an astonished look on her face as Kurt half-flew, half-fell away holding Dol in his arms. He dropped her gently just before he hit the ground. She rolled over and her eyes fluttered open. "Thank you, Kurt," she managed, before they closed again.

Jarv rushed to Dol's side and lifted her up and away to safety.

Vivi ran to Kurt and knelt at his side. His eyes were shut and he was breathing heavily. But was it even real breathing if he'd been dead all along? There was so much Vivi didn't understand.

His face looked greyish in the moonlight and his eyelids fluttered.

"I'm sorry, Vivi – I was weak. I wanted to help you but Ma Varney wouldn't let me. I had to tell her everything. She knows all our conversations. I'm so sorry. I wish I could have been strong like you. I never would have harmed you. Please believe me. I didn't want this life."

Tears ran down Vivi's cheeks. "Don't be sorry. You were a good friend to me in the end. None of this was your fault."

"You were a good friend to me too, Vivi. The best. Thank you for teaching me to be brave."

He looked as if he was about to say something else but stopped, lips slightly parted. His face grew pale, paler than ever before, his features indistinct and his skin the texture of a dried-up bar of laundry soap. He was fading away before her eyes.

"Kurt!" cried Vivi, reaching out to hold him, but there was nothing left to put her arms around; he and the stake crumbled away, leaving nothing but a pile of dust. A gust of wind blew suddenly, scattering the dust into the night.

Vivi sobbed, lying slumped over the spot where he'd been.

Helga called from the balcony. "Oh dear, has the poor boy finally met his end?"

Anger coursed through Vivi once again and she got back on her feet.

Helga Varney. All of this was her fault. First Dol, now Kurt. She was hiding out of reach, like a coward. Vivi might not have the power of flight, but she was going to find a way to confront Helga face to face.

Vivi turned to the castle walls. There were gaps in the old brickwork a little way above where the balustrade met the wall.

Above that were two gargoyles, perfectly spaced as handholds. She could climb from here to the balcony. It was an easier climb even than Mister Vrdoljak's plum tree.

Driven by an anger like nothing she'd ever known, Vivi ran over and pulled herself on top of the balustrade. She practically leapt at the wall, somehow gripping the bricks. She was strong. She could do this.

"How lovely! You're coming to see me," taunted Helga. "Make sure you don't fall."

Vivi was sure she wouldn't fall. But although her handholds were good, she hadn't counted on the age and condition of the Castle Bezna walls. As she gripped the first gargoyle, it snapped away from the building, stone crumbling all around.

And Vivi fell with it, hands scrabbling uselessly at the wall.

She landed in a crumpled heap below, on her side with her leg bent beneath her. Pain shot to her ankle and her hands. Her head span.

Dizziness overtook her and she rolled on to her back on the cold stone. She wanted to get up, but she couldn't move.

"Poor, poor, Vivi," cooed Helga from the balcony. "It's time to end this silly game."

Helga leapt from the balcony and hovered in the air, just as she'd done in the form of a bat.

Despite Vivi's fuzzy head, she knew what would happen next: the thirteenth vampire would swoop down, bite and give her the same choice she'd given to Kurt. Die, or become a vampire. There was no way out now. She must make the strong choice: the right choice. She would never be a vampire – Helga would not become her new mother. She just hoped it would all be over quickly. Vivi's head lolled to one side and she could see Jarv, flustered, calling out to her. She understood the words themselves, if not the meaning. "The parasol, Vivi!" Jarv was shouting. "Use the parasol!"

Helga soared down towards her, her black shadow blocking out the moonlight and everything else. The parasol was lying there on the ground next to Vivi, right where she'd dropped it. Why would she need it now, when it wasn't raining and when she was, in all likelihood, about to die? Nothing made sense. But she trusted Jarv and somehow managed to grasp it in her hand. In her hazy state of mind she noticed that the silver tip had come off once again, leaving an exposed wooden point.

Helga was nearly upon her. At the last moment, as Helga Varney flung herself at Vivi, Vivi held the parasol upright, intending to open it like a shield. If only she could remember how.

Helga's teeth were bared, her eyes hypnotic. This was it. The end. But when she was a few inches away from Vivi, Helga's face changed. Her mouth opened wide as if in a scream, but no sound emerged. She closed her mouth, tears in her eyes, and an expression that may have been regret.

For a moment that was where she stayed, frozen above Vivi, arms reaching out like wings, and the sharp pointed end of the parasol sticking right through her.

Confused and struggling, and expecting the weight of Helga Varney to come crashing down upon her, Vivi finally managed to open up the parasol. The crash didn't come. Vivi missed the thirteenth vampire's final seconds. All she saw was dust, raining down around her and blowing away in the wind.

It was over.

Vivi struggled to a sitting position, brushing herself down, her ankle smarting anew with pain. As Jarv rushed over to check on her, Vivi closed the parasol and stared at it in disbelief. "It was a weapon all along!" she cried, amazed she'd been carrying it around with her in ignorance.

"I thought you knew," said Jarv. "That's why I told you to keep it with you."

Vivi almost laughed. "How was I supposed to know? I just thought you were hinting at what the weather conditions were like up here."

And, as if on cue, large drops of rain began to fall once again, washing away all the remaining dust and tears.

CHAPTER TWENTY-EIGHT
LETTING IN THE LIGHT

Vivi sat out on the terrace, not far from the spot where she'd fallen on that fateful night. This time, however, she was settled in a chair, swaddled in blankets and a headscarf, clutching a cup of cocoa. Her leg was stretched out on a footstool in front of her, her broken ankle mending well. On a chair next to her, similarly attired, was Countess Marozny.

It turned out the sun did occasionally shine on Castle Bezna, even during the winter months. The minute it did, Aunt Ina had insisted they all sat outside. "Daylight is good for you," she said. It was suiting the countess who, it turned out, didn't shrivel away at the first sign of light. She was thriving. Now that the vampire was no longer snacking on her, and she'd begun eating properly again, her cheeks developed some colour, and she even put on some weight. She no longer had such a gaunt appearance. Even her sleeping patterns became more normal, although she was always the last to retire to bed at night.

Vivi was reading a novel to the countess. Every now and then, the countess would stop to comment on a passage of writing or a line of verse, or Vivi would check the pronunciation of a word. Otherwise, Vivi read, the countess listened and hours ticked happily by. Dol was out on the terrace, too, scraping lichen out of the gaps between the stone slabs with a weeding fork. The wound on her neck was healing nicely. Anyway, one little vampire bite and a small tumble was not enough to quash her work ethic.

A week had passed since the final end of Helga Varney, the thirteenth vampire. It was also a week since Kurt had gone. Vivi still mourned Kurt's passing, although Jarv maintained it was a good thing. "If it hadn't happened by accident, we'd have had to finish him off anyway. Can't leave any of the creatures alive. You saw what happened the last time."

"How could you say that, Jarv? He saved Dol!"

"Well, he's at peace now," was all Dol had said, diplomatically. She was right, of course. Dol was right about most things. Vivi was still grateful her cousin had taken the risk to come and find her. Dol had been suspicious when Vivi told her everyone at the castle was tired all the time. She'd also noticed how Madam Varney never left the castle and how Vivi didn't seem to know her first name, even from the will. "But mainly it was just a feeling," she said.

After the dramatic events on the terrace, Jarv had left the girls at the castle with the countess and returned to Valesti for reinforcements. But when she returned, it wasn't with hordes of angry villagers. There was no need for that any more. Instead, she brought a much-needed doctor and Vivi's Aunt Ina.

Vivi had been surprised at how pleased she was to see her aunt. They'd embraced more affectionately than ever before, and Ina even said, "Oh Vivi, how I've missed you."

Any warm words were soon replaced with practicality. The next thing she'd said had been, "This place needs a good clean."

For the next few days, Aunt Ina ran her finger over every dust-covered surface, shaking her head and clucking her tongue with disapproval. She flung open the windows and pushed back the drapes to let the fresh air and the light flood in. They washed years of dirt off the windows. Aunt Ina handed a cloth, a mop or some polish to anyone who would accept it. It turned out quite a few people were happy to help: Dol, of course. Jarv, on her daily visits. The laundry was shut for a week to allow the ladies to come up and lend a hand. Aunt Ina even handed Vivi a stack of silverware to polish as she convalesced. And Vivi made quite a good job of it. Aunt Ina was clearly surprised at how hard Vivi could work when she set her mind to something.

The castle began to look quite different.

It gleamed. It hummed with life and merriment. It began to look more like Castle Bezna and less like Vampire Towers.

Vivi stared out at the sun on the treetops, trying to imagine what it would be like in the spring.

Dol stopped scraping the terrace for a moment and stood up, something glittering at the end of the weeding fork. She held it up to show the others. "Look at this gold bracelet I found. Do you recognize it?"

Countess Marozny peered at it from her chair. "I couldn't be sure, but I think that belonged to one of the other girls, before Vivi. Dorïce, perhaps."

"Oh." Dol gazed at the bracelet, which caught the light as it swung at the end of the fork.

"What do you think *really* happened to the other girls, my lady?" asked Vivi, voicing a question which had been on her mind for a long time.

Countess Marozny stared down at her hands. "I suppose they fell victim to Helga Varney. It's clear now the letters were fakes, both written in her hand, so the stories of their adventures were probably invented, too."

Vivi nodded. That was what she'd thought since finding the cases on top of the armoire.

"What shall I do with the bracelet?" asked Dol.

"Do you think you could take it in to your mother? She is welcome to keep it or sell it on as she sees fit. I don't suppose Dorïce will be coming back for it now."

Dol nodded. "Will you two be all right out here on your own?"

Vivi rolled her eyes. "There is nothing wrong with me apart from a broken ankle! We should survive for a few minutes."

Dol disappeared down the steps. "Good. Don't forget to eat your snacks," she said, pointing to the side table between them.

Vivi obediently picked up the plate and held it out to the countess. She took a seed-sprinkled pastry stick between her thumb and forefinger and dipped it into the white sauce in the side bowl.

Vivi made a face. "I should warn you, that has garlic in it."

The countess raised her eyebrows and scooped up a dollop of the sauce. "But I love garlic. I'm sure I've told you that before."

"Yes, but then Kurt said you weren't partial to it, which is why it never appeared on the dinner table here. Only chives."

The countess nibbled delicately at the end of the breadstick. "I suspect Madam Varney said many things about me that were untrue in an effort to deflect attention away from her—"

"And to make me suspect you. All those Castle Bezna rules. No mirrors and everything. It was all for her."

The countess smiled. "Perhaps we should treat this as a new beginning. We can get to know each other properly. The real versions."

Vivi grinned. "Warts and all?"

"Warts and all," agreed the countess, with a chuckle. "I should begin by telling you my given name isn't Helga."

Of course it wasn't. It *had* seemed like a bit of a coincidence. "Another lie from Madam Varney?"

"Indeed."

Vivi took a breadstick of her own and crunched up the whole thing before the countess was even a third of the way through hers. "Well, what is your name? It must begin with an H."

"It does. My given name is Hortense."

"Hortense Marozny," mused Vivi. "Nice name. Can I call you Hortense?"

The countess pursed her lips. "No, you may not."

"How about *Little Miss Lovage*?" Vivi suggested cheekily.

"Most definitely not."

"How about … *Lady* Lovage?" tried Vivi.

The countess laughed. "Perhaps I would allow that."

Vivi smiled. She wouldn't test her patience any more. "You've taught me so much, my lady. I can't believe I'm reading novels to you, and when I first came to Castle Bezna, I couldn't even read that book of poetry."

It was an admission of sorts. Neither of them had ever formally acknowledged Vivi's lie about the reading glasses. The countess didn't even mention it now. Instead, she patted Vivi's arm. "What you may not be aware of, Viviana, is that you've taught me, too."

"I've taught you?" It seemed unlikely.

"Ah yes, you've taught me many important lessons. You see, I spent many years – most of my life in fact – shut away. I have been so concerned with doing the right thing, with putting on the right appearances to the right people. Then you came along…"

"And I wasn't one of the right people?" Vivi laughed loudly.

"Most definitely not. But you brought warmth and kindness and even fun into my life – all things that were lacking before. All those wasted years. And now, in the final stage of my life, I'm beginning to learn how to enjoy myself."

"You're planning to live for a while longer, then?"

"Yes, I'm in fine fettle. I'm afraid you'll have to keep waiting for your inheritance."

"Ah, that's a shame," said Vivi, with a grin.

"I beg your pardon?"

"Well, it's nearly my birthday and I was planning to hold a party here. I thought once the terrace is clean, we could put some tables out here and string up some lanterns. We could even wear fancy dress—"

"I'm not sure about fancy dress. Heavens."

"Ah – but we can have a party? If we're both feeling better by then?"

"Maybe."

"Hmmm, a maybe. Is that a maybe yes, or a maybe no?"

The countess popped the remainder of her breadstick into her mouth, pointing to indicate she couldn't possibly reply. Vivi smiled. She didn't know what the future held. She didn't know if there would be a party, if she would stay at the castle or return to Valesti. She wasn't even sure that Castle Bezna had revealed all its secrets yet. But she did know that she felt happier than she had done in a long, long time. She patted the countess's arm. "You know, if we have a party, I bet my Aunt Ina would make some more of this garlic sauce. And piles of breadsticks."

The countess swallowed her mouthful. "Really? Well, in that case, I suppose it's a maybe yes." She winked and they both laughed so hard that Dol rushed back out to the terrace to see what was going on.

THE END

ACKNOWLEDGEMENTS

Thanks to:

Fiz Osborne, for your ongoing support, advice and friendship and for accompanying me to that special Nosferatu screening.

Sarah Dutton, Emma Young and Chris Modafferi for all your tremendous editorial skills.

Fab designer, Kayt Bochenski.

The Streamers. Louise Morris and Jodi Carmichael, thanks as always for your support, suggestions and humour.

Simon, Clara and Tom Thorp for figuring out the ending with me on the train.

Clara again for helping me come up with all those vampire names.

Paul Hemming for introducing me to vampire graphic novels. Bit scary, though.

Special fangs to Ruth Shallcross for the endless supply of vampire facts, jokes and memes and for helping me name my baddy.

I read (and watched) lots of vampire fiction over the course of writing this book, and I found a lot of inspiration in the pages of *Dracula* by Bram Stoker, *The Pale Lady* by Alexandre Dumas and of course the 19th century 'penny dreadfuls', *Varney the Vampire; or the Feast of Blood* by James Malcolm Rymer and Thomas Peckett Prest (edited by Finn JD John and Natalie L Conaway).

Also from Alice Hemming:

In a faraway kingdom, two girls live separate lives. Growing up in the wilderness of the west, Alette is the daughter of a sorcerer. In the warmth of the east, Audrey is the daughter of a baker. The girls could not be more different ... and yet something draws them together.

The girls are on a collision course that cannot be avoided, as a past they never knew they had leaves them hurtling towards a future they could never have dreamed of.

Their story began once upon a time. But how will it end?

In the usually peaceful kingdom of Essendor, people are going missing. And when Thandie is startled by a strange boy one night, she instantly questions whether he's someone she can trust.

Little does she know that this meeting will force her life wildly off-track, pushing her towards an unexpected danger and a fearsome unicorn who is at the very heart of the terrible disappearances she's heard so much about…

In the faraway kingdom of Elithia, a powerful king holds the throne, with ten Royal Knights under his trusted command. Fearsome warriors and talented fighters, the knights are led by Celene, the most exceptional of them all.

When Celene's brother, Hero, falls ill, she seeks out a sorcerer, Sidra, who practises dark magic. Sidra promises Celene the chance to save her brother's life.

The cost? Her soul.

When Celene refuses, Sidra curses her in his rage, forcing her to take the form of a unicorn. Will Celene remain a unicorn for ever, or will she break the magic that binds her?

When Marie stumbles across a magical unicorn deep in the forest who grants her three wishes, she makes the mistake of telling her father, King Jacob, who takes the wishes for himself. Driven by greed, he enslaves the unicorn by demanding for never-ending wishes.

Years later, the Kingdom of Quessia has fallen into poverty and ruin under the reign of King Jacob. He's hated by all his subjects, but a revolution threatening his throne and life is starting…

Will King Jacob keep the Blazing Unicorn enslaved for ever and retain his throne? Will Marie ever be able to right the wrongs of her past?

The Frozen Unicorn

ALICE HEMMING
An evil unicorn. A frozen heart.

Long ago, a cruel winter plagued the land and people started to mysteriously disappear. A girl called Violet heard all the stories and the rumours that an evil unicorn was behind it all.

Years later, when a terrible winter descends once more. Violet's True Love, Nicolas, goes missing. Realizing that the old stories must be true, Violet embarks on a risky journey to the far north to save him. The journey will push her to her limits, but one thing is for sure: Nicolas is out there and he needs Violet's help.

But how long will he survive in the bitter cold of winter?